LOST AND
GONE
FOREVER

ALSO BY ALEX GRECIAN

The Yard

The Black Country

The Devil's Workshop

The Harvest Man

G. P. PUTNAM'S SONS

NEW YORK

LOST AND GONE FOREVER

A NOVEL OF SCOTLAND YARD'S
MURDER SQUAD

ALEX GRECIAN

G. P. PUTNAM'S SONS
Publishers Since 1838
An imprint of Penguin Random House LLC
375 Hudson Street
New York, New York 10014

ISBN 9780399176104

Printed in the United States of America
1   3   5   7   9   10   8   6   4   2

BOOK DESIGN BY MEIGHAN CAVANAUGH

This is a work of fiction. Names, characters, places, and incidents either are the product
of the author's imagination or are used fictitiously, and any resemblance to actual persons,
living or dead, businesses, companies, events, or locales is entirely coincidental.

For Christy,

as always

BOOK ONE

P eter?" *Anna could hear how frightened she sounded, her voice echoing back to her from the flat face of a curio cabinet that blocked the narrow path. She stood still and listened, but there came no* answering cry.

She called his name again, louder this time, but with the same result. Or, rather, the same lack of result.

Perhaps, *she thought,* if I were to climb to the top of that curio, I would be able to see quite far along the path.

She approached the hulking cabinet and opened the doors at the bottom. There was nothing inside. She slid open a drawer and pulled it out, set it beside her on the grass. She pulled herself up, hanging on tight to the knurled trim along the side, and used the empty slot where the drawer had been as a toehold. Once begun, the climb was easy, shelves positioned at convenient intervals as if it had all been purposefully fashioned for small children to scale. At the top was an elegant pointed façade, and she clung to it and crouched low, willing herself not to look back down at the ground. I am not really so high up, after all, *she thought.* Were I to fall, I might not break my arms and legs. *But this thought was not so comforting as she had felt it would be.*

She looked ahead of her up the path, which wound around a dining set and through a great herd of French desk chairs, disappearing at the juncture of a Chippendale butcher block and a dollhouse cupboard. A small blue bird of some sort hopped from the base of a painted white sideboard, then flapped away to the top of a jumbled mountain of coatracks. Behind her, she could see that the sun was beginning to set, the sky bruised and livid.

She opened her mouth to call Peter again, but did not make a sound. All at once she felt utterly alone and afraid.

A grandfather clock chimed nearby. Startled, Anna lost her grip on the façade and nearly tumbled from her perch. She slid down the back of the curio and landed neatly on her feet on the packed dirt of the path.

Well, *she thought,* I suppose there is nothing for it but to find Peter and drag him back home in time for his supper. Otherwise, we shall both get the switch, and I should never forgive him if that happened.

And so she mustered her resolve and marched away into the ever-darkening wood without glancing back even once at the warm yellow lights of her house.

—Rupert Winthrop, from
The Wandering Wood (1893)

PROLOGUE

He woke in the dark and saw that his cell door was open.

Just a crack, but lamplight shone through and into the room. He lay on his cot and watched that chink of yellow through his shivering eyelashes. But the door didn't open any farther, and the man—*the man Jack*—didn't enter the room. Had Jack forgotten to latch the door after his last visit? Or was he waiting to pounce, somewhere just out of sight in the passage beyond the cell?

He kept his eyes half-shut and watched the door for an hour. The sun came up and the quality of light in the room changed. The crack between the door and the jamb remained the same, but the lamplight behind it faded, washed out by the brighter gleam of the rising sun. At last, he threw his thin grey blanket aside and sat up, swung his legs over the side of the cot, and padded across the room to the bucket in the corner. When he had finished the morning's business, he scooped sand into the bucket and went to the table under the window. He splashed water on his face from the bowl, his back to the open door, ignoring it. He drank from a ladle and looked out through the bars at the narrow stony yard, all he could see of the outside world. Then he went back to the cot and sat down and waited.

His breakfast didn't come, but sometimes it didn't. Sometimes Jack forgot or was busy. A missed meal here or there was hardly the end of the world. So he sat and he waited. He began to worry when midday passed without any sign of food. His stomach grumbled. He checked the positions of the shadows in the yard, but they told him nothing he didn't already know. He had an excellent internal clock. He knew full well when it was time to eat.

When teatime passed with no tea or bread, he stood again and went to the door. He put his hand on the knob and closed his eyes. He concentrated on his breathing, calmed himself. He pulled the door half an inch wider and took his hand off the knob. He stood behind the door and braced himself.

But nothing happened.

Braver now, he touched the doorknob again, wrapped his fist around it, and opened the door wide enough that he could see out into the hallway. He put his head out of the room and pulled it back immediately. But despite his expectations, nothing had hit him or cut him. Nobody had laughed at him or screamed at him. All was quiet.

And so he stepped out of the room for the first time in as long as he could remember. He wasn't at all comfortable being outside his cell. His memory of the things beyond that room was vague and untrustworthy. He swallowed hard and looked back at his cot. It represented all he knew, relative security bound up with stark terror, the twin pillars that supported his existence.

He left it behind and crept down the passage on his bare feet, leaving the lantern where it hung on a peg outside the chamber. When he reached the end of the hallway there was another door, and he seized the knob without flinching. He stifled a gasp when it turned under his hand and the second door swung open, revealing a long wedge of wan afternoon sunlight. He had expected the door to be locked, had expected to have to turn around and retreat to his cell and his cot and his bucket. Had, in fact, almost wished for it.

He stepped out into fresh air. He felt the warmth of the sun-baked stones on the soles of his feet. When his eyes had accustomed themselves to the bright light, he looked around him at the empty street and turned and looked up at the nondescript house that had been his home for so long. He didn't remember ever seeing the front of the house before, and it occurred to him that he might have been born there, might never have been outside it. Perhaps his half-remembered notions of the world beyond his cell were only dreams.

A breeze stirred the hair on his bare arms, and he felt suddenly self-conscious. After hesitating a moment, he turned and went back inside, back down the passage, back into his room, to the cot. He picked up his grey blanket and draped it over his shoulders and left again.

Back outside, he looked up and down the street and smiled. He had a choice to make and he felt proud to have been given the opportunity. Jack was testing him, he was sure of it. He could go left to the end of the road where he saw another street running perpendicular to this one. Or he could go right. Far away to his right he could see the green tops of trees waving to him from somewhere over a steep hill. Perhaps a park or a garden. Trees. He could imagine how their bark would feel under the palm of his hand. He was certain he had touched trees before. He really had been outside his room. He nodded. The trees meant something.

Walter Day turned to his right and limped naked down the street toward the beckoning green.

1

Plumm's Emporium had for years occupied a large building at the south end of Moorgate, not far from where Walter Day spent a year in captivity and not far from Drapers' Gardens, where Day found shelter in the trees. Plumm's was bordered on one side by an accountant's office and on the other by that famous gentlemen's club, Smithfield and Gordon. In the winter of 1890, it had been announced that Smithfield would be moving to posher headquarters in Belgravia, and the renowned entrepreneur John Plumm purchased the club's building. At the same time, he made an offer to the accountant, who was only too glad to relocate. The Emporium then closed its doors for nearly four months. The great blizzard that hit London in March of 1891 slowed construction of the new building and caused much speculation about Plumm's financial stability. There were rumors that corners had been cut and cheaper materials used in order to get the place ready for the announced date. But when it reopened it was three times the size and four stories taller and had adopted its founder's name, John Plumm, though most shoppers continued to refer to it simply as Plumm's.

Beyond the cast-iron and glass storefront, the ground floor of Plumm's held two tea shops, a bank, three full restaurants, a public reading room, and a confectionery. There was an electric lift at the back, something most people had never seen, and this generated a fair amount of foot traffic, people coming in just to ride up and down. The first through third stories were supported by thick iron pillars and held a staggering variety of merchandise: toys and dolls, fabric of every variety, ready-made clothing, shoes and umbrellas and hats, groceries, baked goods and bedding, men's ties and cuff-links, coffee, books and maps and sheet music, jewelry, cutlery and crockery and cookware, rooms for lounging, rooms for smoking, and fitting rooms. At the top of the building was an enormous glass dome that was cleaned daily, along with the forty-three windows on the lower floors, by four men hired specifically for that purpose.

John Plumm himself gave a speech on the day of the opening and then stepped aside, gesturing wide for the gathered throng to enter. Men wearing white gloves held the doors open as hundreds of women (and more than a few men) hurried inside, and more staff waited within holding complimentary brandy and wine balanced on silver trays. These men, along with two hundred other Plumm's employees, were housed on-site in apartments that faced Coleman Street. In this way, as John Plumm explained, there was always some-one in the store, and no customer would ever want for advice or ser-vice.

There was a workshop next to the apartments at the back, where skilled artisans created papier-mâché mannequins and display racks made of wood and brass.

John Plumm was rarely seen on the premises, but his lieutenant, Joseph Hargreave, who managed the daily affairs of the store, con-stantly patrolled the floor, adjusting scarves on the mannequins, resolving customer issues, and replacing the employees' soiled white gloves when needed. Hargreave had an eagle eye for imperfections among his workers and had shown three shopgirls the door before end of business on Plumm's opening day.

But he did not show up for work the second week after Plumm's opened its doors to the public, leading many of his employees to think that perhaps Mr Plumm had taken matters into his own hands and let his overzealous manager go. Joseph Hargreave was never seen alive again and was not missed by anyone except his brother, Richard, who decided to hire a private investigator.

2

On Monday, the evening after he left his cell, Walter Day hid, shivering, behind a stand of trees until Drapers' Gardens had emptied. When he was alone, he pulled up the grass beneath him and dug a shallow trench in the hard soil. He lay down and hugged his legs to his chest, waited until his teeth stopped chattering, and he eventually fell asleep.

Tuesday morning, Walter kept himself hidden at the edge of the gardens until a vendor stepped away from his wagon long enough to scold a band of street urchins who were driving away customers. Walter snatched a loose cotton dress from the vendor's awning where it hung. He pulled it over his head, then, hungry and filthy and ashamed, but no longer naked, he scurried away. He clung to the side of the footpath, away from traffic, and tried to seem inconspicuous in his ladies' dress, his bare feet visible below the hem. He found half a fish pie discarded in the slush at the side of the road and ate it as quickly as he could, cramming the soggy mess into his mouth so fast that he could hardly breathe. He watched the shadows and the passing people while waiting for the man Jack to appear and take him back to his cell. When teatime had come and gone again and Jack still had not materialized, Walter began to cry.

Wednesday, as omnibuses rattled past carrying early-morning commuters, Day crawled out of the box he had slept in and joined the flow of pedestrians. When he came to a busy intersection, he watched a gang of children who rushed forward, one at a time, to assist people as they crossed the wet road, holding up their hands to halt the buses and taxis and private carriages, and collecting small coins in return. Hopeful, Walter caught a young woman's attention and held out his elbow for her. She looked away, her cheeks red with embarrassment, and a man standing behind Walter threatened to send for the police. It began to sleet and the foot traffic thinned. He took shelter beneath an oriel and sat on the ground, pulled his muddy dress down so that it covered his ankles, and waited.

On Thursday he returned to that same corner and watched the children more carefully, studying how they solicited pedestrians, and by afternoon had managed to help an elderly blind man cross the street. He earned a ha'penny in return and spent it on a cup of weak tea at a wagon across from the gardens. He slept in the trench again and used the dress as a blanket.

When he woke Friday morning, he found a small pile of clothing had been left on the ground next to him. A pair of patched and faded trousers, a threadbare shirt, a thick wool coat, and boots with a hole in one toe. Next to the clothing was a walking stick with a round brass handle. He recognized it as his own from some long-ago time, like seeing a cherished toy he had played with as a child. There was little doubt about who had visited him in the night. He looked around, but saw no one, and so he put on the new clothes and buried his dress next to the trench so that it would not be stolen or discarded. More appropriately attired, he was able to help seven people cross the busy intersection that day and, for the first time since leaving his cell, he ate an entire meal. That night he slept well and was not bothered by any rumblings in his stomach.

The children were waiting for him at his corner on Saturday. Walter listened as they explained their position. This was their corner and, although he was much larger than they were, they outnumbered him and would cause him grievous harm if he continued to interfere with their ability to earn a living. He nodded and wished them well and wandered away in search of another intersection. He had no luck, but later that day he was struck on the back of the head by a cigar butt that was tossed from a passing carriage. He picked up the smoldering butt and carried it away with him. Over the course of two hours, he found nearly twenty more, an even mix of cigars and cigarettes. He took them back to his trench in the gardens and unrolled them all, using a piece of bark stripped from a tree to catch the precious bits of tobacco left inside them. It took some time, but eventually he was able to form two new crude-looking cigars from the leftovers. He took off his boots, put the cigars in the toe of the left boot, and slept on top of them so they wouldn't be stolen from him in the night.

On Sunday, he chose the two biggest and smartest of the children at the corner and made arrangements with them. He gave each of them a cigar and they shook hands. He spent the rest of the day combing gutters and alleyways, gathering butts and drying them in the sun. When he returned to the corner, his young business partners had sold the cigars and they each gave him half their earnings: four pennies. Walter ate another meal that night before getting back to work repurposing the used tobacco he had found. By the time he went to sleep, he had five new cigars hidden in his left boot.

3

The vast majority of London had failed to note Walter Day's disappearance and had gone about its business without marking his absence. But, even a year later, there were still people who woke up each morning with the expectation that they might see him again, perhaps that very day.

Among that select group was the former Sergeant Nevil Hammersmith, who because of his headstrong and reckless manner had been let go from Scotland Yard. He had opened his own detective agency, which he now operated in a headstrong and reckless manner. His offices were housed in a compact two-room suite in Camden, and a plaque outside the door read simply HAMMERSMITH. Beneath that, in smaller script, were the words DISCREET ENQUIRIES.

The outer office lacked privacy, but the inner office lacked furniture, aside from a small table and a bedroll in the corner where Hammersmith often napped when sleep overtook him. Every other inch of floor space was occupied by stacks of notes and newspapers, sketches and blurry photographs, witness reports, location descriptions, and a record of every step Hammersmith had taken in the year since his closest friend and colleague had vanished.

One thick file folder was dedicated to the other cities and countries where men matching Walter Day's description had been seen. Hammersmith had traveled to Ireland and France and even as far as New York in his search, but being cooped up aboard a ship for weeks on end had frustrated him and made him wary afterward of any leads that might take him away from London.

Hammersmith knew he was not the detective Walter Day had been and he felt he had to work twice as hard to make up for his lack of skill. For every dead end he encountered in his search for Day, he redoubled his efforts until his determination became an end in itself.

Hammersmith (the agency) had few clients, and they labored under the false impression that Hammersmith (the detective) worked for them. He did not. He worked for Claire Day only, and he cared about little other than finding her husband. He had two employees, both of them young women he had met in the course of a previous investigation.

Eugenia Merrilow sat behind a desk just inside the front door and screened potential clients. If a case was simple enough and if she judged that the agency was close to running out of oil for the lamps and therefore needed money, she would take down pertinent details and promise to pass the information on to Mr Hammersmith. In fact, she gave nearly all their new cases to Hatty Pitt.

Hatty had become a widow when she was seventeen years old. A murderer called the Harvest Man had escaped prison, tied Hatty to her bed, and butchered her husband, John Charles Pitt. She had been unhappy in her marriage and was pleased to have got her freedom back (a selfish thought that never failed to cause a twinge of guilt and sorrow for poor John Charles).

Hatty had no training as a detective, no training in anything else, either. But she had been interested and available when Mr Hammersmith had announced he was opening his own detective agency. When he had taken her on, she'd assumed she would be his secretary or clerk and the thought had been acceptable, but not really very exciting. She had a new lease on life, and she had decided early on that she didn't want to do the same sorts of things her friends were all doing, the same sorts of things she surely would have done if she'd remained married to poor John Charles. ("Poor" was beginning to seem like John Charles's first name.) And so she had persuaded Mr Hammersmith to hire Eugenia Merrilow as well, suggesting that it might take more than two people to manage the task of finding anyone in a city the size of London. It was her way of paying Eugenia back for taking Hatty in when she had first lost John Charles and had nowhere else to go. Eugenia had not asked for a salary (she was wealthy and bored), but wanted interesting work, which meant Mr Hammersmith could afford her. With Eugenia to take up the secretarial duties, Hatty had been free to begin insinuating herself into Mr Hammersmith's investigative work. He had been too distracted to object or even to notice what she was doing. Within a few months she had created a satisfying occupation for herself.

The cases Eugenia gave her were simple enough: follow a wandering husband on the train and note where he disembarked, deliver a note of foreclosure to a small business, hunt down a missing pet, etc. She thought the fact that detective work was not commonly performed by women actually gave her an advantage. No one suspected her of following them, no one viewed her inquiries as suspicious. She was nearly invisible. Eugenia did not accept cases that involved any hint of serious danger, and Hatty consulted with Mr Hammersmith, who seemed always to be under the impression that Hatty was asking hypothetical questions. He would generally give her an hour of his time before she could see his attention wandering back to the case of the missing Inspector Day. She was often frustrated by his single-mindedness, but admired his sense of purpose and his dogged determination.

She also admired his long eyelashes and his long fingers and the way his uncombed hair flopped down into his eyes at inconvenient moments. She suspected Eugenia Merrilow harbored similar feelings, but the two of them had never discussed the matter.

Most days, when Eugenia unlocked the door and brought the post to the desk, Hammersmith would emerge from the inner office rubbing his red-rimmed eyes. He would greet her absently, take his hat from the rack, and leave. Some days he would go to Scotland Yard and pester Inspector Tiffany or Inspector Blacker. They were sympathetic, but never had any new information for him about Day's disappearance. The men of the Murder Squad had finished moving to a new headquarters on the Victoria Embankment, and their search for Day was necessarily interrupted by the minutiae of daily life, by other cases, by other crimes.

Some mornings Hammersmith would visit Claire Day and they would discuss the investigation. Walter Day's wife was now caught up in her own routines and distractions, the demands of four children, a busy household staff, and a new career. It was a poorly guarded secret that Claire had written a popular book of children's rhymes under the pen name Rupert Winthrop. But a series of unfortunate events in the previous year had traumatized her to the extent that she rarely went anywhere in London alone. She still wrote her poems and had begun to think she might like to write a prose story for children. In the evenings after the dishes had been cleared, she would compose a new rhyme and read it to her adopted boys, Robert and Simon (they had been orphaned by the Harvest Man, the same madman who had widowed Hatty Pitt), before tucking them into bed. Then she would work until dawn, or sometimes she would lie in her bed and watch shadows move across her ceiling. She did not sleep much, and her eyes were generally as bloodshot as Hammersmith's. The sales of Claire's poems, and the advance she had received for her next book, had paid for the Hammersmith Agency's office.

The blizzard of that March had kept most people inside, where they didn't get into the sorts of trouble that might require detecting of the private variety. But the sun had begun to come out sporadically and snow had melted and become slush, which was now beginning to disappear as well. People were leaving their homes and, after being pent up for so long, were getting into all manner of mischief, both minor and calamitous.

On the first warm day of spring, fog had lifted off the Thames and invaded the neighborhoods north of the river. Hatty stood in the outer office, watching grey nothingness roll by outside the window, obscuring the fish-and-chips shop across the street. She held a pencil and a small notebook of the sort preferred by her employer. Eugenia sat behind her desk, sorting papers into piles that Hatty suspected were entirely random. Eugenia had provided (and was prominently posed in) the many framed photographs of tableaux vivants that lined the agency's walls. Across the desk from her, draped across the client chair like an empty suit, was a bespectacled older man with a silver fringe of hair and an untidy mustache. He had carefully arranged two long hairs across the gleaming pink expanse of his scalp. Hatty felt pity and a touch of admiration for the futile vanity of her new client.

"I would like to speak directly to Mr Hammersmith," the man

said. "This is a matter of some importance to the family, as you may imagine."

"I'm afraid," Hatty said, "that Mr Hammersmith is busy elsewhere at the moment, but he will review my notes the moment he returns."

"I'll wait for him."

"It may be some time."

"Then I'll find another detective."

"You should certainly feel free to do so, sir, but Mr Hammersmith asked me to tell you how much he appreciates your confidence in him. He wanted so very badly to meet you himself." In fact, Hammersmith had said no such thing. He had probably forgotten all about the meeting and the potential client, who was now drawing himself up in the chair and adjusting his waistcoat.

"Then why isn't he here?"

"He's with the commissioner of police," Eugenia said. "You can't very well say no to the commissioner of police when he sends for you."

Hatty frowned at Eugenia, but Eugenia didn't notice, didn't even look up from her busywork. It was the standard lie they always gave and it made Mr Hammersmith seem very important indeed, but Hatty didn't care for it. As far as she was concerned, the business of the Hammersmith Agency was the uncovering of lies, not the propagation of them. When Eugenia didn't note her disapproval, Hatty gave up and turned her attention back to the client.

"Mr Hammersmith had to go immediately to see about the details of another case." It was not entirely a lie.

"Called on by Sir Edward himself?"

Now the client was impressed and Hatty knew they had him on the hook. She just wished she'd been able to impress the man herself, instead of invoking Sir Edward's reputation in order to secure this new piece of business. She glanced at the first page of her tiny notebook.

"Your name is . . . ?"

"I never gave my name when I made this appointment," the man said. "I didn't want the family's reputation to be jeopardized."

Hatty made an impatient gesture at Eugenia, who glared at her for a moment before rising and retreating to the inner office. Hatty took her chair and set the notebook on the desk in front of her. She couldn't very well stand against the wall and question their new client.

"Surely you don't mind telling me your name now that you're here, sir," Hatty said.

"I'd rather—"

Hatty interrupted him. "Then what is the nature of your trouble?"

"My brother is missing. I wouldn't say he's disappeared so much, only that I don't know where he is."

"Of course. Well, you've come to the right place. We specialize in looking for missing people." True enough, although Hatty didn't mention their lack of success in actually *finding* missing people. "But we can't begin to search for your brother unless we know his name."

"I don't doubt it, but see here, young lady, this is a very delicate situation."

"A business matter hinges on his availability?"

"Something like that." He sat up even straighter now. "In fact, his position has been given to someone else in his absence, and I have every hope that the situation might still be reversed. But how did you know?"

"I told you. We do this sort of thing all the time." Hatty had made an educated guess based on the client's pomposity. She leaned forward over the desk and lowered her voice. "Anything you tell us will be held in the strictest of confidence. Just as it says on the sign outside. We are extremely discreet."

The man cleared his throat and looked around the tiny room as if to assure himself that they were alone. His nostrils needed to be trimmed, and Hatty noticed a dried yellow nugget clinging for life to the wiry grey hairs. She absently rubbed her own nose. It had been broken a year before and had healed with a slight bump halfway down the bridge. She thought it gave her a worldly appearance and she took perverse pride in this exotic imperfection.

She waited, her pencil poised over a blank sheet in the notebook, and finally the man cleared his throat and spoke. "If . . . I mean to say, once you find my brother, I would like all notes and records of your inquiries turned over to me so I may burn them."

"As you wish," Hatty said. First, get the man to talk, then worry about keeping promises.

"Good. Well, then . . . I say, this is awkward."

"How so?"

"I've never had occasion to employ your sort before, you know."

"Ah. My sort."

"It feels a bit . . ." The man left off as if there were too many adjectives to choose from.

"Your brother's name?"

"Yes. Just so. His name." A deep sigh, and the man straightened his shoulders, ready to take the plunge. "His name was—pardon me, his name *is* Joseph Hargreave."

Hatty wrote this down. "And your name?"

"You need my name as well?"

"It would help us when it comes time to make out the bill for services."

"Of course. My name is Richard Hargreave. *Doctor* Richard Hargreave."

"And what's happened to your brother?"

"He left the flat—we share an apartment in the city—three mornings ago very early, straight after breakfast, and was headed for the store, but he never arrived. The first day he was gone I became mildly concerned, because he usually tells me if he has an engagement and needs me to allow for his absence. By that evening I was distraught and have remained so ever since."

"You say he sometimes has engagements? Business affairs?"

"He manages the bulk of our parents' estate, which keeps him just busy enough, I suppose, in addition to his duties at Plumm's. Occasionally he has to meet with a banker or with our solicitor about one thing or another having to do with our investments. I don't trouble myself with all that, but he's quite capable."

She had written the word *Plumm's* in her notebook and underlined it, but she decided to wait a moment before following up. She didn't want the client to lose his train of thought. "And you think he would have told you if he had a meeting of that sort? With an investor? Is it possible he's had to leave town for some reason and it slipped his mind that he hadn't informed you?"

"No, no, no. His money is also my money, after all. He always keeps me up to the minute about everything. He wouldn't have . . . Well, he would have told me, that's all."

Hatty looked up from her notebook. "You're afraid he's met with foul play?"

"I certainly hope not. But the thought has occurred to me, and I don't know what to do about it."

"I'd say you've done it already. You've come to us and put the matter in our hands." She smiled at him, and he managed some sort of a

23

sneer in return. "Now," Hatty said, "I need details. Tell me every-thing you can about his habits, his appearance, his acquaintances, everything you can think of that might be helpful."

"And you'll relay this information to Mr Hammersmith straight-away?"

"Absolutely."

"Very well." Dr Richard Hargreave cleared his throat, adjusted his spectacles on his nose, and began to talk about his brother. The nugget of snot dropped to his lap, and Hatty looked down at the desk and wrote as fast as she could.

4

A two-wheeler pulled up to the mouth of a narrow alley in Saffron Hill. Two people alighted, a man and a woman, both dressed head to foot in black. Their fashions indicated they were not native to England. The man took a bag from the floor of the cab and tipped the driver, who sped away as fast as his horse could move. The couple in black stepped into the alley and walked slowly along, looking all round them at the stalls of stinking fish and yesterday's vegetables. The man held his elbow out to the woman, who slipped her arm in his. A pickpocket circled and came up behind them but the man in black casually swung his bag, without looking, and the pickpocket went down in a heap. They walked on as if they hadn't noticed him.

The alley wandered on, and they followed it through the fog, their boot heels clacking on broken stones, awnings above them dripping on the woman's umbrella, held above them both. They did not speak, nor did they look at each other, but they stopped together when they reached a small home with no garden and a stinking garbage pile against the front bricks. One shutter was painted with the notice: LOGINGS FOR TRAFFELERS.

The man led the way to the front door and, without knocking, opened it for his companion. She nodded to him as she passed over the threshold. Inside, the place was small and damp and reeked of old sweat and gin. A tiny old woman came rushing from some back room to greet them.

"Yer in luck," she said. Her voice was thick, both with liquor and a Cockney dialect. "I've two beds left."

"We'll take a room to ourselves," the man said.

"Oh, you'd be wantin' a posher place 'n this, then. We goes by the mattress here, and you'll be furnishin' yourselves when it comes to linens."

"A room," the man said again. His companion did not speak, nor did she look at the landlady. She stared straight ahead and worried her thumb along the handle of her umbrella.

"That'd come dear, sir," the old woman said. "I can't be givin' out a whole room to just two people, can I?"

Now that the matter had come down to money, the man seemed to relax. He smiled for the first time, and when he did, the landlady shivered.

"We'll give you forty a week for the room. Two weeks in advance. And we'll take our meals elsewhere."

"Forty? A week?" The old woman leaned toward him and shook her head. "I hate to say it, I do, but you can get a better place 'n this for forty a week, sir."

"Yes."

"Well then, I'll take yer money. What name would you like on the register?"

"None. If we wanted a name on the register, we'd stay somewhere that didn't smell of rat piss."

"Gotta put sumpin' down for the inspectors."

"Very well, put down Parker."

"Mr and Mrs, then?"

"If it suits you."

"Gimme an hour or so to clear out a room."

"Clear the mattresses off the beds, too, or the floor if there are no beds."

"We got proper beds here, like."

"Good. Send a boy round for new mattresses. Clean mattresses. We'll pay for those, too."

"New mattresses?"

"And linens. New. Never used. Have them on the beds when we return."

"New mattresses, new linens. That'll cost, sir."

The man smiled again, and the old woman backed away from him. He reached into his pocket and drew out three coins. He took the landlady's hand, turned it over, and laid the coins on her palm. "I trust that will suffice."

The old woman drew in a sharp breath through her nose and nodded. The man nodded in return.

"Never seen a lady wear a man's clothings before." The old lady jerked her thumb in the woman's direction. "Don't she talk?"

"Oh, you wouldn't want her to talk," the man said. "I'm the polite one." He took his companion's arm, and the two of them left the house without another word or a backward look. The man pulled the door quietly shut behind them.

When she was sure they were gone, the old woman clutched her wrist where the man had touched her. It felt icy cold.

5

Nevil Hammersmith stood in the middle of his flat and looked round, expecting to see a thick layer of dust and cobwebs coating the familiar mantel, the table under the window, the single wooden chair, and the hot plate. He had always lived a monastic existence, but had spent the majority of his time lately in the cluttered office, eating fish pies and tea and sleeping on the floor when his eyes grew heavy from poring over the same witness reports and news articles again and again, looking for some previously neglected clue that might lead him to Walter Day. But the flat was neat and tidy. There was a flowerpot on the table, and a green plant stretched upward toward the window above. Hammersmith peered at this new addition to the flat and blinked twice, not sure what to think about it. He leaned slightly forward on his toes, his hands behind his back, as if in unconscious competition with the plant for sunlight.

He heard footsteps on the stairs, and a moment later the door opened and Timothy Pinch entered, bringing with him the mingled scents of chocolate and sugar and lemon rind from the confectionery downstairs. Timothy paused when he saw Hammersmith, then grinned and crossed the room to him.

"Nevil," he said. "Good to see you. It's been weeks, hasn't it?"

Hammersmith nodded. "I stayed here last Tuesday night, I think. Maybe Wednesday."

"Sorry to have missed you. It's been so lonely, I had to get some company for myself." Pinch pointed to the plant. "A maidenhair fern. It's almost as talkative as you are."

Hammersmith grimaced, then tried to turn it into a smile.

"Sorry," Pinch said. "What brings you?"

"I left a file here," Hammersmith said. "At least, I think I did. Can't remember where I put it."

"Ah, yes, I've tidied up a bit here and there. Anything that looked like it might be related to your work I've put in the top drawer of the desk." Pinch pointed to the small rolltop in the corner where the hallway narrowed and led back to the two bedrooms.

Hammersmith nodded his thanks and rummaged through the drawer. The file he wanted was beneath a report on the weather conditions the evening Walter Day had disappeared.

"Perfect," he said.

"Tea?"

"No, thank you," Hammersmith said. "I really ought to get back to the office. Unless you . . ."

"I was going to have some myself."

"Well, then, I suppose I'd be glad of it."

"Good."

Pinch busied himself at the fireplace while Hammersmith waited, feeling like a stranger in his own home, which he decided he probably was. Once a fire was going and a kettle had been put on to boil, Pinch stood and rubbed his hands together. He grinned again and clapped.

"Now," he said, "tell me everything."

"About what?"

"You know. Cases. Investigations. That sort of thing."

"Ah, no, nothing much to report, I'm afraid."

Pinch clicked his tongue and frowned, disappointed. He was two or three years younger than Hammersmith, and two or three inches shorter, but he gave the impression of greater height, as if he only needed to straighten out his gawky frame and unkink his limbs to throw off the shackles of adolescence. Under slick fawn-colored hair, his eyes were the clear blue of an undisturbed pool, and a family of squirrels might have comfortably sheltered in the shadow of his nose. He vibrated with nervous energy. Hammersmith glanced at the complex pattern of chemical burns and stains on Pinch's laboratory coat, which he never seemed to remove, except for dinner.

Hammersmith looked away, back at the intruder houseplant. "And what about you? How go the studies?"

"Fascinating," Pinch said. "Really just fascinating. I can't tell you. Dr Kingsley is ahead of his time. I'm just incredibly lucky to be able to work with him."

In addition to his duties at University College Hospital, Dr Bernard Kingsley was the official forensics examiner for the Metropolitan Police. The busy doctor had been in need of a capable assistant for some time, and Pinch was his most promising student. Pinch squatted before the fire again and launched into a one-sided discussion of the migratory habits of maggots within a festering corpse. Hammersmith nodded and sat at the table, watched as thick tendrils of fog brushed against the windowpanes.

He missed his previous flatmate. Charming, funny, proudly superficial Pringle. He and Colin Pringle had not been much alike, but he had trusted Colin, depended on him. He sniffed the air as if he might still catch a phantom whiff of the hair tonic Colin had worn or the sprig of mint he had chewed. But the act of conjuring Pringle's memory made his absence more acute. Hammersmith blinked, grimaced, focused on Timothy Pinch and his wide, guileless face. Pinch was a friendly sort, but Hammersmith was in no mood to feign friendliness.

Hammersmith understood that he was becoming more reserved lately, that he sought out the company of others with decreasing frequency. He had never been a particularly outgoing person, had always been dedicated almost obsessively to his work, but he was getting worse. It seemed to him that the murder of Colin Pringle had been the first link in an ugly chain that stretched back over a year and a half: the formation of the Murder Squad, the discovery of Jack the Ripper in a cell under the city, Jack's escape from his tormentors and Walter's abduction, Hammersmith's ouster from the police force, the new detective agency.

He wondered what Pringle might have thought of it all.

"I say," Pinch said. "You look pale. Awfully sorry, old man. I forget most people don't have the same affinity for maggots that I do."

"More's the pity."

Pinch grinned at him and brought the kettle to the table, where he poured out two steaming cups of tea and added lemon. Hammersmith stood, and they both sipped while watching the variations of grey move beyond their window.

6

The fog embraced Claire Day, cradled her as she moved along the street, protected her from the gaze of her fellow travelers. She carried an umbrella, but didn't open it. The fog wasn't wet or cold; it didn't oppress. She saw nothing but grey in its many shades and variations, but she knew that there were other people around her somewhere, other streets ahead. Somewhere. Given enough time, she would stumble upon them, and given more time the fog would burn away and everything would be made clear.

Horses clopped along beside her, but Claire stayed on the path, unseen and self-contained. Today was a day for walking, and for once she didn't want companionship. She strolled slowly, watching for the shapes of children and call boxes and tall thin gas lamps when they materialized in front of her.

She sensed movement and stopped, watched the rolling greyness, and waited for someone to appear, but no one did. She took a tentative step, then another, and saw a shape cross the path ahead. Another shape, a man, followed, and another, this one a woman connected to a smaller shape, a child holding her hand. Two men carried a huge box, a dark grey square punched out of its surroundings. Claire moved to the side of the path and stopped, reluctant to try navigating through the ragged parade. There was comfort in being unnoticed, but she didn't want to surprise anyone. After a moment, as the queue of people marched past her and into the unseen street, she felt for the wall of the building behind her and sidled along it until she came to the corner. The quality of the fog changed. The spots and patches of light, of dark, of density and thinness, disappeared, the grey no longer adopting the characteristics of the doors and windows of the buildings around it. Here, there was only a swirling sameness. She stepped into an empty lot, weeds reaching at her through the dirt and fog.

There was no way to know how large the lot was or where the next building might be hiding. She shuffled forward, swinging her umbrella gently back and forth in front of her. Sounds—muffled voices, faraway footsteps, and hooves against cobblestones—drifted at her from somewhere, seeming remote and unimportant. She looked down just in time to stop herself from tripping over a chair.

It was a plain wooden chair set down in the middle of nowhere, and yet perhaps ten feet away from the street. Beyond it was another chair, and another, dark shapes squatting in the mist. She counted twenty of them, placed in haphazard rows, facing nothing. The queue of fogbound drifters had been some sort of impromptu audience for . . . for what? A preacher? A balladeer? One of the many science shows that had sprung up without a headquarters, traveling from post to post in a coach, demonstrating the latest electrical advances to passersby?

She gathered her skirts and sat in the chair closest to her. One leg of the chair was resting on a pebble or perhaps in a hole, and it rocked under her weight. The soft sound of her own breathing echoed back from faraway nearby walls. She listened and heard, too, shuffling footsteps coming from somewhere behind her, or in front of her, or even above her (for all she knew, there was a walkway of some sort up there), and yet she knew that nobody could see her, nobody would find her there unless they literally stumbled over her.

In a way, she thought, she was as lost as Walter was. She had never faltered in her conviction that he was alive. More precisely, she would have known if he were dead. She didn't need evidence that he was out there somewhere in the fog. She only needed to know where. He might even be sitting in another chair in the same empty lot with her, only an arm's length away and yet unreachable.

She imagined she might snap some make-believe reins and the chair under her would take off at a trot, lead her to her husband, the other chairs following behind. Poor Walter astonished but overjoyed to see her arrive at the head of a galloping wooden herd. They would ride away together, gather the boys and the twin girls on chairs of their own, and leave the city behind with all its wretchedness and mystery.

"If you don't mind, miss."

She started at the sound of the voice and jumped up off the chair, holding her umbrella like a weapon.

"Didn't mean to frighten you." She still couldn't see the man who was talking, but his voice was quiet and gentle.

"I suppose I'm a bit nervous," Claire said to the nothingness. "Have you been standing here all along?"

"Thought I'd give you a minute to yerself. Looked like you might need a rest."

"How could you know what I look like? You must have eyes like a bird."

"Aye, that I do. You'll excuse me I hope, but I've gotta get this last chair on the wagon soon or the horses'll leave without me."

"Last chair?" She peered around her and realized that the other squat shapes were gone. She was standing in front of the only chair left in the lot. "I didn't even hear you take the others."

"I'm a quiet sort when I need to be. Like I say, you looked like you needed the rest."

"Thank you for letting me sit for so long." How long had it been? "Do you mind if I ask, why were the chairs here? A meeting of some sort?"

"Puppet show, ma'am. Like for the children. Not many showed today, though. Too gloomy to see the show. Mostly we just done the voices and left the puppets in the box. Let them children imagine what they don't see."

"A puppet show. How lovely."

"Well, thank you. Next time, when it's cleared up some, you bring yer own young ones and they can watch the play for nothin'. You tell the ticket taker Jim said it was all right."

"Very kind of you. I suppose I should get out of your way."

"Not at all." A small man detached himself from the fog and limped past her. One of his legs was short and twisted. He tipped his hat at her, bent and picked up the chair, and was almost instantly gone, faded away. She strained to hear his footsteps, but there was no sound. She turned her head back and forth and felt a small spike of panic in her throat.

"Wait," she said. "Wait, sir. I don't know which direction to walk. Where's the street?"

There was no answer. Claire raised her umbrella so that it was parallel to the ground and took small steps until she felt the umbrella touch a wall. She scraped the point of the umbrella along bricks until it encountered empty air and then thrust forward, almost making her stumble.

"Oi! Watch it." Someone marched past her, and she followed. Now she could once more hear the horses and the cries of vendors and the happy shrieks of children playing in the mist. She smiled and took a deep breath and made her slow way along the path, hoping she was headed in the direction of home.

As soon as she got there, she shut the door to the parlor, sat at her writing desk, and began to compose a new story about furniture that returned to the wood where it had once stood tall as trees. She did not hear the governess knock at the door or see the sun set. Everything disappeared for her except the scratching of her pen on paper, and she wrote well into the night.

7

Day woke and brushed a leaf off his face. The sky was completely dark and it took him a moment to realize that there was someone hovering over him. Day waited, tensing himself and wondering whether the cigars in his boot were still there. Somewhere he heard a fox rustling in the brush.

"I know you're awake, Walter Day."

Day took a quick shallow breath. He recognized the voice. It was him. It was the man Jack. He reached for his walking stick, but Jack put a hand on his arm.

"Why are you lying in a trench in a park, Walter Day? Why are you here in the mud, instead of . . . Well, you confound me. Why haven't you gone home? Why aren't you doing what I told you to do?"

Day swallowed hard. The words made little sense, but the voice filled him with fear. His mouth was dry and his eyes stung and he felt his bladder trying to give out. He closed his eyes—there was nothing to see anyway—and concentrated on maintaining his dignity.

"You should answer me now."

"I don't . . . I don't know what you mean."

"I gave you a task, Walter Day."

"I don't know who that is."

"You don't know your own name?"

"I don't know my name. Am I . . . Did you say my name? Just now, was that my name? Is that who I am?"

"Fascinating. In retrospect, I suppose I should have experimented with someone else before mesmerizing you."

"Mez . . . ?"

"To be truthful, I was growing bored with you and I may have rushed things."

"I don't understand anything."

"I know. What a shame. To think I once admired you. It's my own fault, really. I've gone and broken my favorite toy." Jack sighed, and Day heard him shift, leaning away. He kept his eyes closed. "I see you're wearing the clothes I left for you," Jack said. "Are they warm enough?"

"Yes. Thank you."

"We can't have the great Walter Day wandering about in a woman's dress. It's remarkable you haven't become sick. How awfully hardy you are."

"What name did you say?"

"Remarkable. I suppose I'll have to fall back on my secondary plan now. A shame. It would have been so much more fun if things had worked out with you. But perhaps I'll give you a bit more time."

"Time for what?"

"Go home, Walter Day. Go home to your wife and her adorable children."

"Home? I don't know . . . Where is my home?" Day waited. "Jack?"

There was a long silence, and when Day opened his eyes, the shape had gone.

8

He did not hear from Jack again and, after enough time passed, he stopped having nightmares. He threw out the cotton dress when it became too filthy and too threadbare to keep him warm at night and bought a second shirt, which he washed and wore every other day while his primary shirt dried. He traded his boots, along with eleven recycled cigarettes, for another pair that fit him well. They were also secondhand, but in better repair, and they did not blister his feet and ankles as badly as the old pair had. He left money for the vendor who had unwittingly provided him with a dress in that first difficult week outside his cell. He also purchased a shallow wooden tray that folded over on itself and fastened with a simple clasp. At night, he stored his cigarettes and cigars inside it to keep them dry. During the day, he opened the tray and displayed his wares, taking a corner at the busy junction just north of London Bridge.

He worked there seven days a week, from six o'clock in the morning until just past four in the afternoon, then closed whatever remained unsold inside the tray, along with a small hand-lettered sign that read REASONABLE TOBACCO.

He would walk to Finsbury Circus and around its perimeter, scanning the ground for discarded butts, then up Moorgate to the Artillery Ground, or sometimes back down to Trinity Square and the Tower. He bypassed the end of Moorgate, where a new department store had recently opened. Traffic there was terrible and cigarette ends were hard to find.

Once, on Featherstone near Bunhill Fields, a stranger shouted at him. He turned, and the man yelled, "Walter! Walter, is that you?" and jumped up and down, waving his arms. Day hurried away, and the stranger followed after him for a few minutes, trying to get his attention. Eventually, the stranger shrugged and turned back, and Day slowed his pace. Within minutes he had forgotten about the man, but he unconsciously avoided Featherstone after that.

He retained a slight limp, the result of an old injury that he could no longer recall, but his leg didn't cause him pain until late in the day and he rarely leaned on his cane.

By now he was well known, and the local boys would often scout the streets in advance, hoarding butts that they traded to Day in exchange for a smoke from his leftover stock in the folding tray. He learned the names of the most talented scouts and saved cigarettes back for those boys. Soon he had a network of children searching out tobacco for him, and he would retire early in the afternoon, receiving them in a short queue outside the warehouses of the East India Company on Seething Lane. Each evening he returned to Drapers' Gardens by various circuitous routes, always careful that he wasn't followed.

Within a few weeks of opening his Reasonable Tobacco business, itinerant though it was, he was doing well enough to rent a room above a shop that overlooked the gardens. For sixpence a night he was able to look out his window at the trees and shrubbery he had slept in during the first and most difficult days of his freedom.

He began stockpiling the butts that were brought to him, sorting the used tobacco by color and collecting it all in three jars. He rolled new cigarettes and cigars on Saturdays, never leaving his room except for tea with his landlady, Mrs Paxton.

She was a kindhearted young widow, and she picked out a new wardrobe for him, allowing him to pay for it over time with the small addition of a penny a night on his room. Sundays he would help Mrs Paxton press the blouses and skirts to hang in the window of her downstairs shop. Her wares were strung on a thin wire across the bay window that faced the gardens. Before dawn each day he swept the path to her door and filled the gas lamp above it. She told him that she enjoyed having a man about, but she continued to be troubled by his lack of memory.

One Sunday she was folding a petticoat when she stopped and let it hang from her hands. She looked across the room at him, frowned, and bit her lower lip. "What if you have a family somewhere?"

He shrugged. "If so, there's not a thing I can do about it."

"Why haven't you gone to the police?"

The question troubled him. He wasn't sure why he'd avoided the police. He shook his head and tested the iron that was heating over the fireplace. A drop of water sizzled on its surface, but he left it where it was for a moment. "I think the police would put me in the workhouse," he said. "I couldn't stand it. I prefer to be my own man. I value my freedom." But he knew it was a lie as he said it. Or, rather, it was a half-truth. He did enjoy his freedom, but there was another reason he avoided the police, some compulsion. Even thinking of it brought a deep feeling of doom. He knew he must stay far away from New Scotland Yard and he must not think about the possibility of a family waiting for him somewhere.

But his answer was enough to satisfy Mrs Paxton. She finished folding the petticoat and placed it atop a stack on the window seat. "And what about your name? Do you enjoy not having a name as well?"

He shrugged again and picked up the iron by its blackened wooden handle. "I have a name. But call me whatever you like. I don't care."

"Don't you want to know your full name?"

"Someone told me my full name. It was some time ago and it may even have been a dream. I don't remember it well. I was half-asleep." He thought perhaps he didn't want to remember.

"Maybe if you thought hard about it. Maybe if you say your first name over and over, your last name will occur to you."

"Walter, Walter, Walter . . . No, nothing seems to come after Walter."

"Nothing?" She put a finger to her lips and smiled. "And what if I need to introduce you to someone? Shall I refer to you as Mr Nothing?"

"Why would you introduce me to anyone? Besides, I hardly need a name to press this skirt."

"I could say that you're a cousin of my husband's. I could call you Mr Paxton."

"Did your husband have a cousin?"

"Several, but he was never terribly close with them."

"What was his name? Your husband, I mean."

Another long pause, long enough that he had time to realize how much the memory of her husband might hurt her and to regret giving her reason to return to that memory.

"I'm sorry," she said. "I'd rather not talk about my husband."

"Of course. I apologize." He turned and got to work. After a moment he heard the rustle of fabric and knew that she had returned to her own chore, folding clothes.

It was some time before she spoke again. When she did, he was pressing a white cotton jacket. The work was somewhat delicate, and he did not turn around to look at her.

"His name was Ben. Benjamin Paxton."

"Ben is a good name."

"He was a good man."

"He must have been very good indeed if you chose to marry him. But I'm sorry I made you think of him just now, Mrs Paxton. I didn't intend to upset you."

"I'm not upset. Perhaps a little sad, but that has nothing to do with you."

"I think it might not be a good idea to tell people I'm his cousin. I think for now we can leave my full name a mystery and simply call me Walter. When you need to call me anything at all."

"Walter it is, then," she said. "And you must call me Esther."

"I couldn't," he said.

"I wish you would."

He finally turned and looked at her. Their eyes met, but her face immediately flushed and she took a step farther away from him. He nodded and stared down at the jacket, at the iron in his hand. The thought of calling Mrs Paxton by her given name stirred the same feelings of wrongness in him that the idea of the police did. And yet, he had nothing, he had no reasons for anything he felt, no memories of anything before his cold cell and the sun shining on a narrow courtyard. Now he was free and alive and he could not bear the notion of shutting himself away again, of giving up the things that life had to offer. If he could not remember his old life, how could it be wrong to build a new one?

"Very well," he said. His throat felt very dry. "Very well, Esther."

9

Of course I feel for you. You're a woman trying to get by on suspect employment, and with four small children, with no man to help her and no future prospects so long as she remains in this city. You can't accuse me of not understanding your life when I'm up late every night thinking only of you and the mess you've made of things."

"That's . . ." Claire stopped and calmed herself before speaking again. "Father, you have to know how cruel that sounds."

"I think you should watch your tone of voice when speaking to me," Leland Carlyle said. "I know women these days are encouraged to speak before they think, but you ought to be grateful to me. Lord knows I've been patient with you."

"Yes, thank you," Claire said. She was so angry she could barely see, but she knew that any outward sign of her feelings would only be used against her.

"Before you launch into another of your unwarranted attacks against me, I was only agreeing with you," Carlyle said. "I was telling you I genuinely understand your position. It can't be easy. That man left you with four children. Although, of course, there's no real reason for you to burden yourself with half of them."

"Robert and Simon are my children just as much as Winnie and Henrietta are. And my husband didn't leave me. I never said that." But her father had struck a nerve, and she hoped the doubt she felt didn't show on her face. She didn't want to believe that Walter might have left her on purpose, and she tried not to even think about the possibility, but it was there.

Carlyle snorted and crossed the room. He poured himself a drink from the decanter of brandy that Claire kept filled for the day Walter returned home.

"You've adopted children when you can't even care for your own children." He took a drink. "Claire, perhaps I've loved you too much, indulged you too much. You must have some perspective, some logical sense of responsibility, rather than tripping gaily about on your feelings. Do you want the boys to go to an orphanage? Of course not. I confess I find them charming. I want what's best for them, too. I simply don't agree that you and this situation are what's best for them."

"I love them, I feed them, I clothe them. They have a roof over their heads."

"And they have no father. They are boys without a father."

"That's not their fault. They lost their parents, and then they lost Walter. Would you have me abandon them, too?"

"So you admit Walter's abandoned them? Abandoned you all?"

"That's not what I said. You keep twisting my words."

"I'm doing no such thing. You continue to evade my points. What kind of men will those boys become when they have no father in their lives?"

"When Walter comes home—"

"I'm tired of hearing about Walter Day. Of all the men you might have married, it escapes me why you would choose that one."

"I did choose him. And I choose to stay here until he comes home to me."

"The wiser choice is to come back to Devon with me. Your mother and I will see to your needs, and the needs of your children. Make the better choice, Claire."

"Between you and Walter? I will always choose Walter over you. Always."

Carlyle raised his hand to hit her, but then took a deep breath and lowered it. He closed his eyes and sipped his brandy. When he opened his eyes again, he smiled at her. "He has no intention of coming home. I know that's a harsh truth, but you need to hear it."

"He will. He's been hurt or imprisoned somewhere."

"Would it shock you to know that Walter is alive and well? And that I saw him?"

"Saw him?" Claire's heart swelled and seemed to fill her, to squeeze her lungs. She couldn't breathe and she couldn't see. Her father's words rang like bells in her ears.

"I debated whether to tell you, but now I think it might be best for you to face the truth."

"What do you mean you saw him?"

"I was leaving the club, and he was on the other side of the street, walking along just as daring as you please. Someone called out to him and he darted away."

"What street? Where were you?"

"Oh, I don't remember. As I say, I was near my club, so it must have been somewhere near the bridge."

"London Bridge?"

"Yes, the bridge."

"What was he doing?"

"Walking."

"What were you doing?"

"I was also walking. There was nothing remarkable about any of it except that he turned and ran when he heard his name."

"Walter can't run. His leg injury prevents it. You saw someone who looked like Walter."

"I know my son-in-law when I see him."

"That's the first time you've ever called him that. You've never acknowledged that he's a part of your family, and you only say it now to hurt me."

"Not at all. If I've kept my distance from him, it's only because he makes his life more complicated than it needs to be. And he complicates the lives of everyone else around him. I honestly don't think you can deny that."

Claire sat on the arm of a chair and threw her hands up in frustration. "I need to know so much. Was it really Walter? Did he see you at the same time you saw him? Did you chase him away? I believe, if it really was Walter, you must have said something awful to him to drive him further from us."

"I assure you that's not the case."

"Well, why *didn't* you say anything? Why didn't you call out his name? Or follow him? You say you watched him as he disappeared again. Why wouldn't you try to bring him home?"

"As I say, he didn't see me, and I didn't wish to make a scene in the middle of the street."

"I need to be alone, Father. Please."

Carlyle drained his glass and set it on the table. He put his hand on Claire's shoulder, and when she tried to move away from him, he tightened his grip.

"I understand," he said. "But you deserved to know the truth. Your husband isn't missing. He simply doesn't want to be with you. It's hard to hear, I'm sure, but I think you'll thank me someday for my honesty."

"Please just go."

"Do you need any money?"

"I don't need anything from you."

"Very well. I'll ask your mother to look in on you tomorrow."

He grabbed his hat and went to the door. He turned back, and he looked as if he might say something more, but then changed his mind and left, closing the door quietly behind him. Claire sat for some time, staring at the door as if it might open again and Walter might be standing there. She knew her father had meant to hurt her with his words, to unmoor her and make her more willing to leave London, to return home with him to the estate in Devon. But he had made a mistake because he didn't understand the depth of her love for her husband. Leland Carlyle had given his daughter renewed hope.

10

The boy's name was Ambrose and he was fourteen years old. He was a clever lad and full of energy, and Day had put him in charge of some of the other boys. Ambrose worked many jobs. Every morning he scouted for cigarette and cigar butts in the streets. He coordinated the efforts of the other children involved and helped to make sure nobody covered the same ground twice in a day. In the evening, after their findings had been given to Day and the other boys had gone, Ambrose took his chess set and sat in Trinity Square, playing all comers for money. He did well. The square was close enough to both Tom's Coffee House and the George and Vulture Tavern, where London's most enthusiastic chess lovers regularly met, so Ambrose's table attracted those players who were not members of chess clubs or who couldn't get in on a game at those reputable establishments.

His board was handmade from grooved and fitted boxwood, and he had fashioned the pieces from materials he had found while scavenging. The white king was made from the bowl of a broken ivory pipe, while the black king was an ebony organ key that he had stolen from a church, then sanded into shape and polished.

He played anyone who sat down across from him and only collected if he won. He usually made enough from three or four games to pay for a room in one of the houses across the bridge. When he lost, or when he couldn't get anyone to play against him, he slept in nearby alleyways or on rooftops.

But whether he was in a room or on a roof, he got little sleep. The rooftops were safer, but he tended to move a lot while dreaming and sometimes came perilously close to rolling off the edges of buildings. It was better when there was a skylight. The boxy frame of a skylight gave him something to anchor himself against. And it gave him a thrill to peek down inside businesses and warehouses. He often wondered about the businessmen who met in top-floor offices, wondered at how their lives had been arranged for them so that they never had to sleep out in the cold. He imagined they had all grown up with parents and families and opportunities that Ambrose would never know.

He had been chased away from the roof of the East India Trading Company and so found himself in the alley behind Plumm's. Two washerwomen passed Ambrose without seeing him in the shadows and entered the department store through a back door. Ambrose waited a few minutes, then tried turning the knob, but the door had been locked behind the women. Too bad. Finding an out-of-the-way corner in a storage room would have been ideal. Instead, he found an access ladder that was semi-concealed in a niche at the back of the building and climbed up. It was a new building, without the customary coat of grimy black soot that covered the bricks of more established stores in the neighborhood. Ambrose was able to hug close to the wall, out of sight of the alley below.

He pulled himself over the edge of the roof and stepped out, testing the boards and shingles beneath him before putting his whole weight on them. From his new vantage point above the fog he could see far in every direction, all the way past Drapers' Gardens to the Thames in the south. He took a deep breath of the cool, clean air and smiled up at the stars. He tiptoed to the enormous domed skylight and peered down into a room below. It didn't occur to him that he might be violating anyone's privacy. Finding things was a big part of his job.

In the room, oblivious to the boy on the roof, eight men sat around a scarred table and talked business. A ninth man, a large fellow wearing white gloves and tails, circulated a box of cigars, and each of the other men took a smoke. The man with the gloves punctured the tips of their cigars and made another circuit of the table, lighting them. The businessmen sent tendrils of smoke upward toward Ambrose, but their gazes did not follow the smoke. They talked together about the day's business, about personnel and shelf space and displays. The man with the gloves took the box of cigars away and set it on a side table that already held four other boxes of cigars and cigarettes and pipe tobacco. There were larger boxes and crates stacked all round the room, marked with symbols that Ambrose could barely make out: alcohol, guns, ammunition, lamp oil, all the most valuable or dangerous goods that the store had to offer, kept on the top floor where they couldn't be easily pilfered.

If he could only find a way into that room, he could take away big handfuls of tobacco, boxes of it, all of it new, none of it found on the street and dried out and reused. It would cost Ambrose nothing, and it would be a boon to his employer.

Reasonable Tobacco, indeed.

He watched as the men smoked and talked for the better part of an hour, and his mind turned over ways to lower himself into the room and get back out. It seemed impossible. Perhaps it would be better to follow the women through the back of the store one night and hide until the place was empty. But he didn't think he could do that. The alley was too narrow for him to go unnoticed. Perhaps he could pay the women to look the other way or leave the door unlocked.

His musings were interrupted when one of the men pushed back his chair, stubbed out his cigar, and stretched. The others followed suit and, in small groups of two or three, the men left the room and closed the door behind them. Ambrose hurried across the roof and watched the fog moving slowly along the street below. In due course, he heard the men exit the building and go their separate ways, creating eddies in the mist and hollering "good night" back and forth.

Ambrose went back to the skylight and looked down into the darkened room, empty but for those crates of volatile merchandise. He felt along the outside of the wooden casing for a lock or a catch and, when he didn't find one, tried pulling upward on it. He heard something creak and felt the frame give. There was the sound of splintering wood and the big pane of glass cracked, a fine silvery thread zigzagging away from Ambrose toward the far edge of the roof. At that moment, below him, the door opened and the man with the white gloves entered the room. Ambrose froze, still clutching the skylight's frame, afraid to let go for fear it would make further noise or, worse, come apart and crash inward. The man with the gloves held the door open for the two washerwomen, who entered behind him. One of them held a rag and a bucket; the other carried a mop. Ambrose could hear their voices as the three people talked, but they were too far away and the cracked glass muffled the sound. Below, the man closed the door and turned a lock. Neither of the women looked up as he removed his gloves, folded them, and put them in his pocket. From another pocket he took a folding razor and opened it. As Ambrose watched, the man stepped up behind one of the women, grabbed a handful of her hair, and snapped her head back. In a flash, he had pulled the razor across her throat, releasing a spray of blood that glistened black in the wan light. Ambrose gasped. The other woman started to turn around, but the man let go of the first woman and stepped over her body as she dropped to the floor. He moved gracefully, like a dancer, and grabbed the second woman's arm before she had a chance to move. Ambrose forgot himself and pounded on the skylight. The silvery crack in the glass widened, but didn't separate. The man below him slashed the razor downward, in one practiced move, opening up the second woman from her throat to her pelvis, and her insides splashed out at his feet.

Then the man looked up and saw Ambrose. He was still holding the arm of the second woman, who had gone limp and lifeless. In his other hand he held the razor. His right shirtsleeve was drenched in dark blood. Ambrose held very still. *He can't see me,* he thought. *It's dark and the glass will obscure my shape against the sky,* he thought.

But the man smiled at Ambrose and saluted him with the dripping razor, and Ambrose could no longer hold himself still. He reeled backward, pushing away from the skylight, and almost fell off the roof. He ran trembling to the access ladder and made his way down to the alley floor so quickly that his feet only touched every third or fourth rung. He ran as fast as he could to the mouth of the alley and didn't stop, but pelted breathlessly down the street.

Behind him, he imagined he could hear the door open and quiet footfalls as the man stepped gracefully out into the grey mist.

Surely, Ambrose thought, *surely he didn't get a look at me. Surely he could never find me again.* But somehow he knew that the man had seen him and would find him, no matter how fast or how far Ambrose ran.

THE DRAPER'S SHOP was closed for the night, the doors locked, the shutters bolted over the display windows that faced the park. Day woke up from a dream about a whispering shadow and leapt out of bed. Someone was pounding on the door. He lit a candle and threw a dressing gown (made especially for him by Esther Paxton) over his nightshirt before taking the back steps to the ground floor. The pounding continued, growing louder as he moved closer. Through the small window in the back door he saw a boy's face against the pitch black of the trees, an ivory cameo on black velvet. He put down his walking stick and unlocked the door, pulled it open, and Ambrose stumbled in.

Day led him to the parlor and left him there to catch his breath. He padded back upstairs and used his hot plate to heat two cups of gunpowder tea, which he brought back down the stairs. Ambrose had already got a cozy fire going and took one of the cups from Day.

"What, no ale?"

"Sorry," Day said.

"It'll do," Ambrose said.

"Are you quite all right?"

"I'm good, yeah," Ambrose said.

"It looked like you were being chased."

"Just in a hurry. Ran over-here. I don't sleep so good anyway and thought I'd take a chance you were about."

"I was sleeping."

"Sorry then."

"But nobody's trying to harm you?"

"I dunno if he even saw me. No, that's not true. He saw me, all right."

"Who? Who saw you?"

Ambrose stared at the fire and sipped his tea. He opened his mouth as if about to talk, then shuddered and took another sip. Day let him be, and after a few minutes the boy straightened his shoulders and spoke quietly, watching the flames. "He kilt them two women. The man with the gloves did it after them others was gone for the night."

"You saw this happen?"

Ambrose nodded.

"A man wearing gloves. But he didn't see you? Are you sure?"

Ambrose shook his head. "No. 'M not sure."

"Did he chase you?"

"No, guv, he looked right at me, he did. Like he was lookin' right into me and knew everything about me."

"This man. Describe him for me."

"Can't. He was in shadows the whole time. Like he stayed in the shadows without even tryin'. Like they followed him round, like they was his dog and stayed at his heel."

"Dark, wavy hair?"

"Yes."

"Tall?"

"Couldn't tell. I was lookin' down on him."

"How did he kill the women?"

"Wiff a razor, like. Calm and collected as he could be, like he was guttin' a fish is all. They didn't hardly stand a chance. They was dead before they even knowed it was happenin'. He didn't have no reason for it; they was just doin' they jobs."

Day set his tea down on the table between them. He sat back and frowned at the boy. He thought he knew who Ambrose was talking about, who the man with the gloves must be. "Where is he? I mean, where did you see him?"

"At the new store. I think he works there."

"Plumm's?"

"That's the one. Ever been in there?"

Day swallowed another mouthful of his green tea. "No."

"Neither me," Ambrose said. "But it's got a window in the roof. A big one, round and beautiful."

"And you've been spying on the goings-on there?"

"Not spying, no. Not me. But I like to sleep up high when I can. Keeps the tearaways offa me. So I was up there on top of the place, like, and just so happened to look down in, and there's gennul-mens of leisure, don't you know? And they got a smoking room in there."

"An office on the top floor?"

"Right."

"Is he there now?"

"I dunno. Maybe. He mighta chased me."

Day stood and went to the door. He pulled the curtain aside on the tiny window and looked out into the night. There was nothing to see. Only the dark shapes of trees and bushes. He drew the lock across, then went around the ground floor and checked the shutters on all the windows.

"You'll stay here," he said. "I can't very well turn you out at this time of night. You can sleep here on the sofa."

"That's kind of you, guv."

"But you must be gone by the time Mrs Paxton arrives in the

morning. I don't think she'd care to find a . . . Well, I don't think she would appreciate my taking the liberty of lending out her sofa. I'll fetch you a blanket from upstairs." Day started toward the staircase, then stopped and turned back. "And, Ambrose . . ."

"Yes, guv?"

"Don't steal anything."

"What, like a ribbon or somethin'? What would I do that for?"

"Just don't."

Ambrose grinned. "Don't worry none, Mr Tobacco. Your lady's ribbons is safe from me."

11

Mr and Mrs Parker had a table at the back of the coffee-house, where the lights were dim. It was early, and foot traffic was minimal. The high judge entered and removed his coat and hat, handing them over to the gentleman at the door before passing under a low arch and scanning the room. His business brought him to London on a regular basis, but he never seemed to have time to enjoy all that Mayfair had to offer. He thought he might stroll down to Piccadilly after tea to buy souvenirs for his family. He spotted the Parkers at their table, recognizable from the description they had sent him, and gave Mr Parker a discreet nod. Parker waved him over and an abrupt feeling of dread washed over him, dispelling pleasant thoughts of long walks and frivolous purchases.

The couple stood as he approached, and the judge saw that the woman was wearing trousers. He shook his head, but decided to say nothing to her about it. Perhaps it was the custom in whatever place they called home. If they wished to travel inconspicuously about the city, though, she would need to update her wardrobe sooner rather than later.

Before he had even taken a chair, the high judge began talking. "I shouldn't be seen with you," he said. "You know I can't. This place is quite out in the open, isn't it?" He glanced around him at the nearly empty room, its tables laid out with latticework napkins and bone china.

"The hour is unusual, and you English are good in the area of staying out of each other's business," Mrs Parker said. Her grammar was stilted and her accent was unplaceable. The high judge flicked his gaze to Mr Parker, but the man didn't seem the least put out that his wife had spoken for them both. There was something unsettling in the woman's expression. Her eyes were flat and dull and regarded him the way he thought he might regard an insect or a bit of soot on his collar.

He smiled at her, but when she didn't smile back, he gave up and turned his attention to the man instead. "Be that as it may," the high judge said, "a less public place might have been better."

"No," Mr Parker said. His voice was low and soft, and the judge leaned forward to hear him. The accent made it difficult to pick out his words. "A less public place makes people wonder."

"I don't know about—" the judge said. But Mr Parker cut him off.

"This is where we are now," Parker said. And that seemed to end the matter. The judge would talk there, or nowhere. His prospective employees would simply return to their home country, where he knew their services were in great demand. He wondered where they had originally come from and whether they felt any native sympathies for anything.

"I understand." The judge sighed. A woman wearing an immaculate apron approached. "I don't care for coffee," the judge said. "Do you also serve tea?"

They did, and he ordered Imperial with strawberry cakes and

brown bread for the table. He shot a glance at the Parkers, and Mrs Parker nodded back. She was satisfied with his choices. When the woman had left, the judge leaned forward and whispered. "I have news."

"Don't whisper," Mr Parker said. "It draws attention. Pretend you are speaking of something mundane . . . What? Anything English is mundane enough, I suppose."

The judge sat back, mildly offended. The insult was hardly merited. He took a moment, wondered if he shouldn't stand and leave and forget the entire affair. But he had set this in motion, had wired a coded message to these vulgar people, and they had traveled all this way. And what did it matter if they were vulgar? Of course they were. One had only to look at what they did for a living. They killed people, without compunction or shame, and with no thought for the justice behind any of it. They were hired to do a job, they were nothing more than tools, and tools did not have manners. He pulled down on the bottom of his waistcoat, straightening it, and cleared his throat.

"No need for that sort of thing," he said. He felt he was displaying admirable restraint.

Mr Parker nodded. "Apologies," he said. "We are tired from the traveling and are not looking forward to our, how do you say it here? Our accommodations tonight."

Mrs Parker smiled, and the high judge felt something cold and wet run up the length of his spine.

"I could arrange . . ." he began, but Mr Parker held up a hand to stop him.

"No," Mr Parker said. "Thank you, but we make our own way. You do not need to know where we are staying. No one needs to know that."

"I see. Trust no one, is that it?"

"I think I would say it more as 'be careful whom you trust.'"

"Just so." The judge was warming to the whole thing. He was sitting across the table from hired assassins and he controlled them. At least for the moment. "I have urgent news. It may change everything."

"Tell us."

"Walter Day is alive," he said. He didn't whisper, but he kept his voice low. "I saw him in the street."

The Parkers exchanged a glance. Mrs Parker shrugged, and Mr Parker spoke. "We don't know who that is."

"He's a detective with Scotland Yard."

"And you wish us to make him go away?"

The judge took a second to realize what the killer meant. He shook his head. "No. It's only that Walter Day complicates the matter."

"In what way?"

"It's . . . Well, it's a bit much to explain."

"Then don't."

"No, I . . . No, it's just that Day is tied up with everything else, and it's hard to see why."

"He's alive, we visit him," Mrs Parker said. "Then he is no longer alive. Very simple. Although to deal with a policeman in this way will be costing more money than we agreed upon."

"No, not Walter," the judge said. "And he's not . . ." He could hear a note of panic creeping into his voice, but was relieved to see the woman with the apron approaching with a big silver tray. He hadn't prepared well enough for the meeting. He was used to working with people who shared his same point of view. He was used to being a leader, being listened to and obeyed, but here he was being forced into a subservient position. He sat back and let the woman set out the tea and cakes and bread, along with butter and cream and lemon, small chocolate biscuits that he hadn't asked for but must be a specialty of the house, jam and honey. She smiled at them and walked away. Neither of the Parkers made a move toward their cups or the food, so the judge helped himself before speaking again. "Walter Day is no longer a policeman, and he is not, not precisely at this moment, the objective."

"What is the objective?" Mrs Parker poured some tea and then swirled in a dollop of cream. The judge was gratified to see that she knew what to do with a cup of tea. Perhaps that same expertise extended to killing people.

"The objective . . ." And here the judge could not help himself. He leaned forward and whispered. "The objective is Jack the Ripper." He leaned back and sipped his tea. It was very hot. He waited for a reaction from the Parkers, but was disappointed. They concentrated on their own cups and did not appear to take any special notice of what he had said. He took a bite of chocolate biscuit and raised his eyebrows. "Jack the Ripper," he said again.

Mr and Mrs Parker exchanged a look. Mrs Parker picked up a bit of bread and smeared it with jam. She took a delicate bite. Mr Parker watched her, then turned to the judge. "The Ripper is already dead. Or gone. One or the other."

"He is neither dead nor gone. He's alive and he's still causing mischief. It's only that the sort of mischief he causes has changed of late."

"So you know where this person is, then, this Jack person?"

"No," the judge said. He had felt a bit of fire banking in his belly, and now it sparked out and died.

"Of course not. The biggest mystery ever in your city, maybe in your entire country, and you expect us to solve it for you now? Like this?" He snapped his fingers and two elderly men several tables away looked over at them.

The high judge turned his head so the men wouldn't recognize him if they saw him later and waited until they went back to their own conversation before he spoke. "If I knew who he was, I wouldn't need you."

"And why do you need us?"

"To kill him, of course. To kill Jack."

Mr Parker looked again at Mrs Parker. As one they pushed back from the table and stood. Mrs Parker reached down for another slice of bread.

"You can't leave," the judge said.

"You've wasted our time," Mr Parker said. "You will get a statement of charges from us shortly. Our traveling expenses. I suggest you pay it with all quickness."

"Wait," the judge said. He stuck out his hand, as if warding off an approaching carriage. "One minute. Hear me out."

"Why?"

"I'm paying you for your time, aren't I? We are, I mean, the Karstphanomen are. I speak for them. Look here, you might just as well finish your tea." He could hear a note of desperation entering his voice and he fought to control it. He hoped the next time he opened his mouth that wheedling tone would be gone. "You've come all this way; why wouldn't you at least finish your tea?"

After a moment Mrs Parker sat, and Mr Parker followed suit. Neither of them looked at the judge, but he took their continued presence as an invitation to speak. "We caught him," he said. "Two years ago. We're the ones. The police couldn't do it, the press couldn't do it. We did it. The Karstphanomen." He smiled at them, proud, but they ignored him.

"Another spot of tea, love?"

Mr Parker nodded, and Mrs Parker poured for him. He sipped without acknowledging her or the judge.

"Well, you see," the judge continued, "we did it. But we couldn't very well just . . . We couldn't just end him. He'd done so much, done so much to them poor women." He stopped and caught himself. His grammar was slipping. It wasn't like him at all. He hadn't even touched a drop.

"So you let him go again? For the sport?" Mrs Parker licked a spot of cream off her upper lip.

"No," the judge said. He felt very warm. "No, we kept him. And we showed him what he'd done. We did the same things to him, over and over, that he'd done to the women, in hopes that we could make amends for some of it, maybe for all the things men have ever done to women."

"Not possible," Mrs Parker said. "Not even a thing to think about."

"But we meant well."

"The road to hell is paved in that sort of rubbish," Mr Parker said. "Isn't that what they say? Rubbish thinking?"

"Very well to say now," the judge said. "But he got himself free, Jack did. And Walter Day helped."

"Walter Day is the fellow you say is alive now."

"Right. We thought he was dead. We thought Jack had got Walter."

"You say this Day fellow avoided you?"

"He did."

"Then what is there to fear from him?"

"What if Jack told him something?"

"What if he did?"

"Walter Day will be found. There are many people looking for him. My own daughter is . . . But if Jack told him who we are, and if Walter tells the police who we are . . . well, things are likely to get a bit hot in London."

"So I repeat myself: You want us to remove Walter Day."

The judge sat back in his chair. The back was high and padded, and he heard a gasp of air as his weight hit it. "No," he said. "No, at all costs you must not harm Walter Day. But you must eliminate any and all things that Walter Day might disclose. If there is no Jack, there is nothing for the police to investigate, do you understand? If Jack is dead, the trail ends with him, and I can deal privately with anything that Walter knows."

"You know this Day person well?"

"Well enough."

"Perhaps Jack has fled. Perhaps he's no longer in London."

"He's here. He's killing us. He's killing the members of the . . . He's killing the ones who tortured him. He's out for revenge, and there are damn few of us left now."

"Ah." Mr Parker leaned back, a bite of cake held halfway to his mouth. "Now I begin to see." He turned to Mrs Parker, and she pursed her lips. She nodded, and he turned his gaze back to the high judge. "You are afraid of this Jack because he is going to kill you and you wish him to be dead before he does so. Why did you not say as much at the very beginning?"

"It's a complicated situation."

"In our experience, most situations can be made to be less complicated. It is our specialty."

"You don't understand," the judge said.

"Then tell us."

He did. He left out everything that he thought the Parkers might use against him, but he told them about finding Jack asleep, sprawled across the body of poor Mary Jane Kelly, about taking Jack and clapping him in irons and leaving Mary there on the bed, her guts spilled out across the mattress. He told them about the year they'd spent, he and the others, cutting Jack, cutting him in every place that he had cut his victims, but keeping him alive so they could cut him again. And again. And he told them about Inspector Walter Day, who had stumbled across their dirty secret, the secret they kept deep underground in abandoned tunnels, how Saucy Jack had somehow changed places with Walter Day, tortured the detective, damaged him physically and mentally, then spirited him away.

When he had finished, Mr and Mrs Parker waited, as if there might be more to tell. They polished off the cakes and the tea, and Mr Parker excused himself. He stood and walked away. When he had gone, Mrs Parker fixed the judge with a contemptuous stare and smacked her lips. "So," she said, "that was a long story, but it only means this: You thought Walter Day was dead, but now he is not, and his being alive is a problem for you."

"We thought we could stop Jack. Find him and kill him," the judge said. (Why was she speaking to him in this manner when her husband wasn't even there? The man ought not involve his wife in business matters. But there was no use trying to make sense of foreign customs. People from other countries were often like animals.) "He keeps killing us, Jack does. There are bloody few of us left."

"So you say, but we still don't understand why you want this Jack dead and not Walter. Finding and killing Walter Day is the simpler task."

"It's too much to go into."

"There must be something personal, some other reason you—"

"Don't you dare." The judge slammed his fist against the table. "I've been patient with you, I've allowed you to speak to me as if . . . as if we were somehow equals, but don't you dare question me or my motives." He shook his finger at her. "You just watch your tone with me. Do you know who I am?"

To his surprise, Mrs Parker smiled again. And the longer she smiled, the bigger her smile became. The judge looked around for Mr Parker and was glad to see the man returning to the table. He stood and grabbed Mr Parker's chair for him. His hands were trembling.

Mr Parker looked at them both and settled a hand on Mrs Parker's arm. He shook his head and waited a moment before addressing her. "What has happened? Our host looks likely to piss himself."

"I've been good," Mrs Parker said. "I haven't hurt him. We have been discussing the work we are to do."

"Ah," Mr Parker said. "Very well then."

"And the . . . I'm sorry, what do you call yourself? Within your silly gentlemen's club?"

"It's not a . . ." The judge paused and wiped his face with a napkin. "It's not a club. It's a society. And I am the high judge because I am responsible for the final decisions as regards the ultimate fates of our subjects." He raised his cup and sipped, trying to regain his composure.

"The judge, then," Mrs Parker said. "The judge of the Karstphanomen. Isn't that what you call yourselves? He has decided to pay us double our usual amount."

"But that's not . . ." The judge aspirated a mouthful of his tea and went through a brief coughing fit. The Parkers watched calmly. No one around them seemed to notice or care. The elderly men had already left, and the waitstaff was nowhere to be seen. When he could breathe again, the judge continued. "I never," he said. It was the best he could do. His throat burned now.

"You have brought the fee we asked for?"

"It's here." The judge pushed an envelope across the table, and Mr Parker made it disappear. "It's all right there. The entire amount you said."

"Good," Mr Parker said.

"But this is sufficient for only one half of the job you require," Mrs Parker said. "This is the amount you will pay us to find Jack the Ripper. And when we do, you must pay us the same amount again to kill him."

"What?"

"We don't care to solve international mysteries. It is not what we do. We do a single job, a job most people, for whatever reason, do not care to do for themselves. You ask us to find this person who is unfindable and then also to put an end to his doings, is that not right?"

"I thought you would—"

"There is no point in thinking about what we do," Mrs Parker said. "You have asked us to do two things, so you should pay us two times. Is that not fair? You will pay us and we will do it and then you will sleep like the babies all night long, is it not so?"

"Mr Parker, surely you won't allow your wife to speak to me—"

"If you haven't noticed, Mr Carlyle, I don't allow or disallow my wife anything. She tends to speak her own mind. Is that the phrase? And you are a lucky man if all she does is speak."

They knew his name. His real name. Perhaps they knew more. Where he lived? The membership of the Karstphanomen? He took a deep, shuddering breath and thought of Claire and the babies. Then he nodded.

"Good," Mr Parker said. "Then it's settled. Thank you very much for the tea and cakes. We'll get on with our business now."

Leland Carlyle, the high judge of the Karstphanomen, sat quietly as the killers left the coffeehouse. Carlyle averted his eyes as Mrs Parker walked away. Her trousers left little to the imagination. On their way out, Mr Parker gave the woman in the apron a coin. He smiled and nodded at her just as if he were a human being.

12

There was a small stack of books on the mantel, and Ambrose pointed to them. "That what you use for cigarette paper? Roll tobacco up in the pages and people get clever when they smoke the words?"

Day chuckled. "No, I don't think I could do that." He picked up the top book, blew a film of dust off the cover. "I like books. Do you know how to read, Ambrose?"

Ambrose shook his head. "I mean, I know a bit from the ragged school, but only barely enough. Books'r hard, and we didn't need to know readin' to make a living."

"You should try again. You're a clever lad, and reading's easy once you've got the hang of it. You could go far with a little education. Do more with your life."

"Like you? Sellin' old leavings on the street?"

Day turned the book over and opened it to a random page.

"I'm sorry," Ambrose said. "Didn't mean nothin' by what I said. What's that book about?"

"I've read it before," Day said. "It's by Lear."

"What's that mean?"

"The author. Edward Lear. It's a book of his poems. My . . . I knew a woman once who liked them. She wrote poetry, too."

"Can't figure the meaning in poems. Thanks, but no thanks."

"Suit yourself," Day said. "But these poems are funny. Do you know the alphabet?"

"Some. I know the shapes."

"Here's a nonsense alphabet. You might like that."

"I appreciate the thought, guv, but I'm only smart about some things."

Day sat on the sofa beside Ambrose. "Here," he said, "do you know this letter?"

"Oh, I seen this before." Ambrose pointed at a small illustration of a cat. "That letter means *cat*, and it means *cigar*, too. But it should mean *moon*, 'cause that's what it looks like, right?"

"'C was a cat who ran after a rat; but his courage did fail when she seized on his tail. Crafty old cat!'"

"That is a bit funny. That's a way to go about teaching a thing. Make it so it's not boring. Lemme see." Ambrose took the book from Day and leafed through it. "That don't look right, that picture."

"Why not?"

"I mean, that letter looks all wrong to spell the word *shrubbery*. Ain't what I remember."

"Because that letter is a *Y*, and the illustration there is of a yew. A yew tree. 'Y was a yew, which flourished and grew by a quiet abode near the side of a road. Dark little yew!'"

"Dark little you?"

"Exactly right."

13

We can't turn him away," Hatty said. "We can't afford to."

"What does . . ." But Hammersmith suddenly decided it wasn't worth arguing with her. He closed his mouth and waved his hand at her, hoping she'd leave his office and go bother Eugenia instead.

She didn't. "We have one client and we haven't made progress in a year on that case, and he was your friend and I'm sorry, I'm truly sorry to put it so bluntly, but we need more clients and we need more work and I'm sure we need more money coming in." She paused for breath, but before Hammersmith could say anything, she started again. "*I* need more work. I'm as good as any man at all this; I just need the chance to actually do something."

Hammersmith waited to be sure she was finished. After a moment of strained silence, he nodded. "He was my friend. He *is* my friend. This agency, such as it is, exists for only one reason, and that's to find Walter Day and return him to his family."

"For all we know he's dead." Hatty's eyes widened, and she swallowed hard. "Oh, no, I'm sorry. I didn't mean to say that. Sometimes I just talk and things come out that I didn't ever intend."

"No, you're right. He may be dead." Hammersmith looked away at the stacks of papers that dominated his office. "He may be." He looked back up at her. "But we have no evidence that he is dead, and so we must assume that he's alive and needs our help. And if he's dead, if he's really gone, then we need to find that out and settle the issue for Claire. She has four children, and the uncertainty is hard on her." *It's hard on all of us,* he thought.

"May I begin again in some way that isn't so rude?"

"No, I understand your frustration and I appreciate your honesty. Just as I appreciate your help here. But I can't handle more clients. I have to think about Walter right now. Anything else would be . . ." He broke off again and waggled his fingers in the air, this time dismissing all the hypothetical cases he couldn't deal with. "Go back to his home and look again for more clues."

"I've been there a hundred times. Or at least a dozen. And I've been to the pub he used to frequent, and I've been to Scotland Yard so much that they don't even talk to me anymore there. There's nothing I can do, and you don't have time to work on the Hargreave case. So let me keep at it, let me do the investigation."

"This is more involved than the usual sort of thing you do," Hammersmith said.

"Yes, it is," she said. "But it's nothing I can't handle, I promise."

"And if I need you here?"

"If you need me, I'll drop everything, I'll let the other case go and be right here to do anything you ask."

He could already see that he'd lost. She was now framing the debate in such a way that it was a foregone conclusion. And he couldn't muster the energy to steer things back the way he wanted them to go. She was probably right. If they hadn't found Walter in a year of looking . . . Well, Walter was probably dead. Or it was even possible he didn't want to be found. Before he'd gone missing, Day had seemed overwhelmed by the prospect of fatherhood, and his career prospects hadn't been good. Some men in that situation might leave their families and start again somewhere else.

Hammersmith shook his head, dispelling the unworthy thought, but Hatty misunderstood the gesture.

"Fine," she said. "I'll go back to 184 Regent's Park Road and I'll look for clues that aren't there and were never there. And then I'll do it all over again tomorrow."

"No," Hammersmith said, "it's not you. I was reacting to a thought I didn't like."

"Thinking what?"

"Something else. Something shameful and unfair. Walter Day was a good man, and he'll be found. But there's no point in combing over his house again. There's nothing there."

"Does that mean . . . ?"

"Tell me about your case. What is it?"

"A missing man."

"We seem to be specializing."

"It's all very mysterious. He works for the new store—you know, the one that opened up where Plumm's used to be, only it's still Plumm's, I suppose, only much larger and with more things to buy."

Hammersmith shook his head. He had no use for stores.

"Well, in any event, it's there," Hatty said. "And this man, Joseph Hargreave, works for the place. Only he didn't come to work one day and he hasn't been seen since."

"Happens all the time."

"I suppose it must, but this time someone came to us about it. His brother is mad with worry and wants you to investigate, only he doesn't know that it's me doing the investigating, not you."

"We should tell him."

"Oh, no, you mustn't. If he knows, he'll hire someone else and won't pay us."

"Hatty, you've never really investigated anything before."

"But I have. I've done it all along, only you didn't hear me properly when I talked to you about those cases and you didn't know what I was doing, Mr Hammersmith. But I've never hidden the truth, not precisely. And I'm really quite capable. You'll see."

"A client ought to be able to expect a certain level of—"

"How old are you, Mr Hammersmith?"

"I have no idea." (He really didn't have any idea.)

"Well, you look quite young to me. And how many years did you work as a detective for the Yard?"

"Well, none, I suppose. But I—"

"You were a sergeant, and I know all about that, but you weren't a sergeant for a terribly long time, were you?"

"I don't know. A few months, perhaps?"

"And before that you were a constable. How long was that?"

"Two years, perhaps?"

"So before opening this agency, you had no detective experience and virtually no experience beyond that of a common bobby."

"There's no such thing as a common bobby. It's a very hard job, and those men put their lives at risk for the safety of their fellow Londoners."

She went on as though he hadn't spoken. "But people like this Dr Hargreave, all our clients, believe you're up to the task, and why?"

"Because—"

"Because you're a man." She stopped, and her shoulders sagged. She suddenly looked tired. Hammersmith wondered where she lived and whether she had anyone to take care of her.

"I'm sure it's not only that," he said. She opened her mouth, but he put up a hand to stop her. "You've had your say. Now let me talk. Yes, I'm a man, and there are certain responsibilities that go along with that. But I'm not the sort who thinks women aren't as smart as men. That's ridiculous. Only I don't like to see you put yourself in any sort of danger, that's all."

"Asking questions here and there won't cause any danger."

"That's precisely what does cause danger. Be quiet and let me think."

He looked again at the Walter Day case files, none of which contained anything useful. He wondered what might become of him if Hatty Pitt left. He would be alone in this office every day, obsessing further and deeper over an unsolvable mystery, caring less and less about everything else in the world. The fog would drift in through the doors and the windows and would envelop him. And he would disappear as surely as Walter had, only his body would still inhabit this office and he would still shuffle about as if he were actually contributing something to society. With no one to interact with him, to contradict him and challenge him, he might very well go mad.

"All right. Take the case." He held up a finger to cut off her excited response. "But every day, at the end of the day, you and I will discuss this case of yours, along with any other case you decide to take into your own hands, and I will be involved in all ways I deem appropriate. You will take no action that is not approved by me. Is that agreeable enough?"

"Yes."

"Good." He scowled at her. "Well, go on, then."

She turned and went, but stopped in the doorway and looked back. "Thank you," she said.

"You're welcome."

"And I promise I won't be in any danger."

"That's not a thing you can promise. Just say you will try to keep yourself out of danger."

"I will."

"Then it's settled."

"You're very kind to care about my well-being."

He blinked at her, unsure of what to say.

"But," she said, "you would be much more attractive if you'd cut your hair back away from your eyes."

She left, and Hammersmith stared, confused, at the door. What did his hair have to do with anything?

14

Esther Paxton pressed Walter's suit, and she picked out the finest merchandise from her shop window for herself. She would be careful with the dress and put it back in the window when they returned from Plumm's.

It had taken a great deal of persuasion on Walter's part to get her to visit the department store, but he had finally won her over by suggesting it might be a good thing for her to be seen there. She would be an ambassador of sorts, welcoming Plumm's in its new glory back to her neighborhood. Far from seeming weak or frightened by the competition, she would be perceived as a confident merchant making a goodwill appearance.

Privately, Day was worried about Esther's financial future. It occurred to him that she might be better off relocating to some smaller shop farther away from the massive competition.

And the midnight visit from Ambrose had left him shaken. Was it possible that Jack was at Plumm's? Did he work there or had he broken in? If it even was Jack. Perhaps Day was inclined to see Jack's hand in everything. But he remained nervous about taking Esther there, and his concern was only ameliorated by the fact that it was broad daylight. Or the closest thing London had seen to broad daylight in the past month.

As the weather grew warmer and the slush evaporated from the streets, fog continued to swirl in, rolling down the roads and pooling in low-lying areas. Esther took Walter's elbow, and he escorted her up Throgmorton Street, listening for oncoming traffic and steering her around puddles in the path ahead. Plumm's seemed to rush at them, pushing its bulk through the fog, and they paused to admire its immensity. In the lower windows, a family of mannequins was picnicking by a stream made of shimmering blue fabric. A gentleman offered a lady a parasol under the light of a gas globe that was meant to evoke the moon. A stuffed horse trotted through a fabulous wood constructed of coatracks and armoires. Above them, in the windows of the next floor up, an Egyptian queen glared down from a throne that was decorated with costume jewelry. Cat-headed mannequin servants ranged outward from the throne, each holding some different item from Plumm's many specialty departments.

"So much glass," Esther said, her voice muffled by the fog and so soft that Day barely heard her.

"The windows?"

"Imagine," she said. "Imagine the expense. Why would anyone be so ostentatious?"

"It attracts people," Walter said.

"But what sort of people? My clients are more tasteful than this." She looked up at him and squeezed his arm. "Aren't they?"

"Vastly," he said. "Shall we?"

She squeezed his arm again (he felt uncomfortable with the intimacy, but couldn't bring himself to tell her so), and he led her across the street. A man with white gloves held the door for them and they entered. Inside, the spectacle of so much sheet glass was dwarfed by even more glass set into the wooden frames of counter after counter, by hanging displays and live models and walkways that led away in every direction through a labyrinth of wares. Esther gasped and turned to leave, but Walter held her there.

"It's no wonder," she said. "Of course my clients would rather shop here."

"Not all of them. Not everyone is so easily won over by this sort of shallow display. Your clients know the difference. They understand the value of quality and of tradition."

"Not all of them. Not enough of them."

"Don't be silly. This is a fad. This sort of thing will never survive. It can't. It'll collapse under its own weight."

She smiled up at him, but he could tell she wasn't convinced. They walked on, past a tea shop and past racks of ready-made dresses, past the shelves full of shoes and the cabinets full of crockery.

"Perhaps this wasn't such a good idea," Walter said.

"No, you were right. I needed to see this. I ought to know what the future looks like."

"You could incorporate some of this into your own business."

"How? Look at this."

They were on the gallery now, high above the sales floor. The framework of an enormous cube was perched atop a pole. Wires ran from beneath it in a thickly braided cord, and workmen scurried about, constructing a globe that was apparently meant to fit inside the cube. Day guessed the sides of the box would be glassed in to represent the store itself and the wires might make the globe revolve. "Plumm's Brings the World to You" or some such puffery.

Walter grimaced. "Just emphasize what makes you different, Esther."

"What do you mean?"

"Look at it all. It's impressive, I grant you, but it's impersonal and, really, it's a bit much, isn't it? They might fit me for a suit, but they don't know my name."

"I don't know your name, either."

"I mean to say that you know your clients, you understand them. That's a commodity."

"Do you think they understand that?"

"They might. If you do."

"You mean if I make them understand."

"You have to believe it first."

She nodded, and he let the subject drop. But it seemed to him that she perked up a bit. At one point she took his arm and guided him quickly away down another aisle, and he shot her a questioning glance.

"A client. I didn't want her to see me."

"She should see you. She'd be ashamed."

"And?"

"And she should feel guilty."

"No, if she feels guilty and ashamed, she'll never come back to me."

He smiled. "Ah. Human nature. That ugly beast."

They continued, touring the various departments, though Esther paid more attention to the fabric selections than anything else. After two or three hours, Walter suggested they have tea at one of the many shops throughout the store. They settled on the smallest tea shop on the first-floor landing, and they took a table near the window so they could look out through the grey at the street below.

"I don't really think this is so bad," Walter said. "I think this place does something completely different from what you do, and you could easily capitalize on that difference."

"I agree," she said. Day saw that the sparkle was back in Esther's eye. "It's completely different, as you say. I think I could change a thing or two, bring in some new fabrics, some new patterns, and my clients will be satisfied. They want modern things, but they don't necessarily want substantial changes."

But Walter had stopped listening. Across the room a man had entered the shop and he stood there now, watching them with a puzzled expression. Esther had her back to the man and didn't see, but Day felt chills up and down his spine. The man caught the arm of a staff member and whispered something in her ear. He handed the shopgirl a slip of paper that was folded in half, nodded to Walter, and left. A moment later, the girl brought the slip of paper to Day's table.

"Are you Walter Day?"

"I don't . . ."

"Walter Day?" Esther leaned forward over the table. "Is that your name?"

"I'm not . . ."

"If that's you, I'm supposed to give you this," the girl said.

Walter reached out his hand and took the note from her. It felt very heavy. He unfolded the paper and read.

MET ME HERE TOMORROW. NOONE. BRING THE
WOMAN IF YOUVE GROAN TIRD OF HER.

"What does it say?" Esther reached for the note, but Day pulled it away.

"Nothing," he said. "Just something about a special price they have on clocks."

"Clocks?"

"Something like that. Timepieces of some sort. We should leave."

Esther looked round the room, but it was empty of anything menacing, only a handful of customers and white-gloved staff going about their business. "What's going on? Is Walter Day your name?"

"It's not. I don't know. Can we leave now?"

"If you want to."

"I do."

They abandoned their tea and their seedcakes. Walter dropped a few coins on the table and they left. Day watched the crowds in Plumm's, but the man was nowhere to be seen. He propelled Esther down the stairs and out by the front door. An attendant saluted them and invited them to come again, but Day didn't hear him. Pushing Esther ahead of him, he rushed out into the fog and didn't slow his pace until they had turned the corner and were on their way back to Drapers' Gardens.

Esther stopped walking and, when she had caught her breath, scowled at him. "Walter, will you please tell me what's going on? Who was it in there, and how do you know those people?"

"Not people. One person. If you can call him a person."

"Who? What's his name?"

"I don't know his real name," Day said, "but he calls himself Jack."

He shrugged off her further questions and lapsed into a brown study until they had returned to the shop. Once there, he hurried up the stairs and locked his door and refused to answer when Esther knocked later in the day.

I should never have gone out in anyone's company, Day thought. *I should never have allowed myself to be seen with someone.*

He curled up in the corner of his room with his back to the wall and watched the shadows move across the ceiling until night came and the room was plunged into darkness. Even then sleep didn't come for a long time. He kept his eyes open and listened for foot-steps on the stairs until the sun came up again.

He knew he would have to return to Plumm's at noon. Otherwise Jack would find him and would hurt him. Worse, Jack would hurt Esther. Day felt trapped and alone, with nobody to turn to and no recourse. His life would never be his own as long as Jack was free in the city.

15

Hammersmith paused in the open door of a large room. He recognized many elements of the Murder Squad as he had known it: the sprawl and bustle, the men huddled in twos or threes, their heads down, murmuring to one another, occasional words like *dismembered* and *mutilated* echoing off the high ceiling and differentiating the atmosphere from that of a gentlemen's club. But there was more of it, more of everything. In the year that had passed since Hammersmith had last worked with these men, the squad had doubled in size. Their desks filled a room that would once have seemed cavernous. Hammersmith recognized Michael Blacker, Tom Wiggins, and one or two other of the inspectors, their jackets hung along the wall below their hats, their shirtsleeves rolled up and their braces let down. But there were many new faces, too.

Sergeant Kett was working behind the desk at the door and he waved. He got up and came around and shook Hammersmith's hand, but he wasn't smiling. Above his bristling red mustache his expression was somber and his clear blue eyes were watery.

"What brings you today, Nevil?"

Kett was the center of the entire Murder Squad, coordinating the movements of his constables and facilitating all communications between the detectives. Hammersmith was certain that without Kett, the Yard would long since have fallen into disarray. When Hammersmith was a constable, Kett had taken special interest in him, had paired him with Day in hopes that they would complement each other's strengths. Hammersmith had always thought of the burly sergeant as a mentor.

"I'm still not used to the new building," Hammersmith said. "It's . . . Well, it's imposing."

"It's already too small," Kett said.

"And the Murder Squad? How is everyone?"

"We've expanded. Twenty detectives now."

"Twenty?" Hammersmith sighed. "At least I still see a man or two I know. I thought it might be worth checking in again to see if there's been progress. Any clues or . . . well, anything at all."

"Don't you think we would've sent for you?"

"I know everybody's busy. It's possible there's been some small thing and nobody's had time to send for me."

Kett sighed and put a hand on Hammersmith's shoulder. "Aye. Everybody's busy. Listen, son, it's time."

"Time?"

"Time to move on, put this thing behind you. I admire the way you've stuck to it, but Walter Day is lost. He's gone, maybe gone for good. And no amount of runnin' round on your part's gonna get him found again." Hammersmith shook his head, but Kett squeezed his shoulder. "Nevil, he's gone. He's gone."

"If it's all the same to you, I'd like to talk to Tiffany, or maybe Blacker. Maybe they've found something they haven't passed along to you."

"You know better than that. Anyway, I can't let you in. Tiffany's got three new cases today all by himself, not to mention what everybody else has to deal with. You'll stir things up and keep 'em from workin'."

Hammersmith looked away, out at the room of busy men. Blacker looked up and nodded to him, but he didn't stop what he was doing, didn't come over for a chat.

"Right," Hammersmith said. "Very well. I'll go."

"One of these days we'll hoist a pint and tell stories about Inspector Day. We'll do it soon."

"Sure we will."

"We will," Kett said. But his attention had already wandered. Hammersmith saw the sergeant's gaze returning to the work waiting for him at his desk. He shook Kett's hand again and turned back to the door.

Outside, he glanced up at the invisible sky. "Walter, where are you?" Hammersmith was completely isolated. He might be the last man on Earth, standing there in front of the Yard, surrounded by layers of nothingness. "Walter, I'm losing you, man. Do something to get their attention or I won't be able to help you. Reach out if you can."

As if in answer, a stranger unfolded from the blanket of grey and passed by within inches of Hammersmith. "Talkin' to yourself? You'll go mad doin' that, you know." The man chuckled and then was gone, swallowed back up by the fog.

Hammersmith stuck his hands deep in his pockets and walked away in the opposite direction. "Wasn't talking to myself," he said. "Not my fault if nobody was listening."

16

Day woke from a dream within a dream. Someone was chasing him, but he was underwater, moving slowly, pushing himself forward. When he had awoken the first time, he was still underwater, but now he was on his cot in his cell. The beams of sunlight that stabbed through his barred window, through the green water, were bars themselves, solid yellow, hot and sharp. He swam around them, straining to get to the window, but the sun kept cutting him, burning him, the water cooling his skin so that he would try again. The second time he woke, he lay there for a long time, his skin still tingling, listening to the quiet. At last he rose and crossed the room and looked outside. There was no sun to cut him or burn him, and the air was diffuse, grey and comforting, a mist that hugged the ground, hiding all the evil and fear that Day knew was there.

He brushed his teeth and splashed water on his face from the basin beside his bed. Within ten minutes, he was dressed and on the path in front of Esther's shop, closing the door behind him. Drapers' Gardens was larger in the fog, bounded on all sides by nothing except his imagination. He could hear horses clop-clopping along Throgmorton Street and he turned in that direction.

"Where are you going?"

Day wheeled, his cane raised and ready, and saw Ambrose standing in the shadows of the shrubbery, blinking sleep from his eyes.

Day lowered his cane. "Did you sleep here in the gardens last night?"

"I meant to be gone already," Ambrose said. "I usually wake up with the sun, but there ain't no sun, is there?" He looked up at the sky, inviting Day to see for himself. "I thought it might be safer for you if I was nearby."

Day smiled and nodded. The boy was still frightened. Day realized he should have found a place for him to sleep out of harm's way. He knew all too well how cold and hard a trench beneath the trees could be. But he had been distracted by other worries.

"So where are you going?"

"Just taking a walk, I suppose," Day said. In fact, he wanted to think a bit before his noon date with Jack, turn the situation over in his mind and try to find some advantage for himself.

"Gimme two minutes." The boy darted into the shrubbery, and Day stood, watching the fog roll at him and away, pushing the air ahead of it, kneading the gardens like so much bread dough. He snapped to attention when Ambrose spilled out onto the path, combing his hair down with his fingers. "Weren't even two minutes, were it?"

"Fast."

"That's me."

They walked in amiable silence, each wrapped in his own grey thoughts. There was almost no traffic yet, and they passed no other people. Then Plumm's rose out of the fog ahead of them. It seemed to vibrate there, humming with kinetic current. Day paused on the path, and Ambrose stopped beside him. They watched the building for a long while, and Day thought he might not be surprised if it uprooted itself and lurched toward them.

Ambrose grabbed his wrist. "Someone's coming."

Day listened. Through the fog came the sound of a man's footsteps, approaching from the direction of the gardens. He knew in an instant who it was. Without a word, Day took Ambrose by the arm and hurried him across the street toward the department store. A white-gloved man exited the front of the store and glanced at them. Day nodded politely but steered the boy diagonally away. The black maw of an alleyway presented itself, and Day ushered Ambrose into it. Behind them, the sound of steady footsteps clocked off the flagstones. When he glanced back over his shoulder, Day saw nothing but swirling grey.

"What's happening, guv?"

"Shh."

He couldn't see anything in the alley. Strange things crunched under his boots, and something furry brushed against his ankle. Ambrose tried to jerk away from him, but Day tightened his grip on the boy's arm and kept him marching forward. A minute later, they came to a wall and Day turned the corner to his left, feeling along the bricks. At last they reached the end and there was nowhere else to go.

"Dead end," Ambrose said. "You think that bloke's still comin' along? You hear him?"

Day could not hear him, but he could sense him circling in the dark. Jack was drawing near, he was somewhere just round the corner, coming closer to them with every panting breath they took. Day felt along the wall and found a knob and tried to turn it. A locked door. He raised his walking stick and rapped on the door with the brass end, but there was no answer, no sound from within the building.

"Quick, Ambrose, feel around the ground here and find something thin and flat, something metal, if possible. A collar stay or hairpin will do."

"What for?"

"Just find me something now."

He heard the boy scrabbling around on the stones, sifting through the filth that accumulated on every square inch of London's streets and alleys. Day felt along the door next to the lock for a keyhole and ran his index finger over it, seeing the shape of it in his head. When he reached back, Ambrose dropped four wet objects in his palm.

"Any of those do, guv?"

"Yes, Ambrose. Perfect." One of the objects seemed to be a flat strip of thin metal, perhaps a rib from a lady's corset. (Day tried not to think about how a corset had come to be torn to pieces at the back of a dead-end alley in Cornhill.) Another was a bit of bent wire. He dropped the other two objects at his feet and went to work on the keyhole, inserting the flat rib and working the bit of wire in next to it, listening all the while for those footsteps behind them. He maneuvered the wire until he heard a click and he smiled, licked his lower lip, and reached for the knob. In a matter of seconds he had ushered Ambrose inside and closed the door behind them. He turned the lock and breathed a sigh of relief.

"Where'd you learn to do that?"

"I don't remember where I learned it," Day said.

"Well, I'm glad you remember the doing of it. You ought to use that little trick of yours to do better than old tobacco leavings. You could clean out a place before nobody knowed you was ever there in the first place."

"But that would be wrong, Ambrose. We must survive, but we must also observe the law at all times."

"All times?"

"Well, perhaps the law might be bent when your life depends on it."

"I'd say. Like now."

Ambrose produced a small box of matches from his pocket, and they rummaged around until they found a lantern hanging from a hook on the opposite wall of the room. Once lit, the lantern revealed that they were in a small storeroom with large double doors. "To bring in big things like furniture," Ambrose said. These interior doors weren't locked, and so the two of them went through and into the vastness of Plumm's main floor. Day immediately ducked down behind a counter and pulled Ambrose down beside him. People were bustling about all round them, preparing the store for opening, laying out fabrics and jewelry, and lighting gas globes. Day waited, but nobody approached their counter; nobody had seen them enter through the storeroom.

"Can't go back that way," Ambrose said, and Day put a finger up to his lips, warning the boy to keep quiet. Ambrose lowered his voice to a whisper. "How're we gettin' outta here, guv?"

"Carefully," Day said. It seemed to him that the safest course of action was to wait where they were until Plumm's opened for the day's business and then leave when there were shoppers about. But there was always the possibility that Jack had a key to the outside door and could pop up behind them through the storeroom.

Was Jack even there? Had Day imagined the familiar cadence of his step? No, Ambrose had heard it, too, and he'd been terrified.

Day reached out and patted the boy's shoulder. It seemed ineffectual, but Ambrose smiled up at him. Whether he was comforted by the gesture or humoring Day, the smile was welcome. Day smiled back.

"Look," he said, "we can't stay here or we'll be discovered. I think the only thing to do is go back into that room and wait." He pointed at the storeroom, and Ambrose nodded.

Together, they crawled along behind the counter and dashed back into the room. They were visible again for perhaps half a minute, but there was no hue and cry. Nobody came to investigate the trespassers, the man and the boy who were hiding from a monster in the fog. And so they sat there in the dark and watched the door and listened for the expected crowd of morning shoppers, when they might slip out unobserved and make their escape.

17

Claire had made a careful inventory of every wooden item in her house: furniture, toys, knickknacks, utensils. She had a list on the table next to her on the sunporch and she referred to it as she wrote. She had used the word *armoire* five times now. She stood and brushed her hair behind her ear and walked into the kitchen. There was the sideboard and the butcher block counter. There were chairs and giant spoons. She walked on down the hall to the sitting room where there was a gliding rocker and an end table and there were several paintings in wooden frames.

She had used them all.

Claire wondered if she wasn't making an enormous mistake. She hadn't told anyone yet, but she was running out of money. Her book of rhymes had sold well, but she didn't feel like writing more rhymes for publication. Her publisher had refused to give her an advance on anything but more poems, and she simply didn't feel she had enough of them in her to make a book. Her babies were getting older and they'd want real stories. She wanted to write about the things that interested them: dolls and toys and playing outside on a clear blue day.

It amazed her that a stray thought had become a full-fledged story in a matter of a day or two and now it was coming along nicely. In her new book, a forest had been razed and the wooden things had all returned to their birthplace, the place where they had been simple trees and known nothing but the green and the rain and the lemon rays of the sun.

The sun that hadn't touched London in months.

The fog that covered the city seemed also to have covered Claire's mind. She worried that she wouldn't be able to keep Nevil's office open and his staff employed, wouldn't be able to keep him from becoming a dustman and abandoning the search for her husband.

She knew she could still take money from her father, but she would rather die. She shook her head and scolded herself for indulging her miserable thoughts. Perhaps it would help to get out of the house.

The governess wandered into the room, saw Claire's dour expression, and turned to leave, but Claire grabbed her arm.

"Dress the children to go out, won't you?"

"An outing, mum? Today?"

"Yes. It's . . . Well, we ought to enjoy the last of the cool weather while we can, don't you think?"

"The cool weather, mum?"

"Yes, it's still a bit cool out, isn't it?"

"If you say."

"I do."

"Of course. Shall I tell them where we're off to?"

"I thought we might step out to the new store. Look at the wares, the furniture and such."

"Furniture? The store?"

"Yes."

"Graham's?"

"No, I was thinking Plumm's."

"Ah. Because Graham's doesn't have furniture."

"No, it doesn't."

"Only groceries."

"Yes."

"But why there? Why Plumm's?"

"Oh, why not? Will you get them ready or won't you?"

"Of course, mum." The woman, Tabitha, scurried off, and Claire sank back against the wall. Everything was a chore. And Walter wouldn't have helped her one bit, really. He would have run off at the first sign of trouble with the governess. But he would have made her laugh about it later. He would have given her a hug and whispered something pleasant in her ear. He would have been sweet. He would have been kind. He would have put the whole rest of the world in perspective somehow.

She tried to think of what Walter might say to her now. She wasn't exactly a match girl, he would have told her. Money was tight, corners had to be trimmed, pennies pinched, but her children had a fine home and food to eat. It wasn't as bad as all that. Was it?

She pushed herself off the wall. Plumm's would have lots of the kinds of things she wanted to see. All sorts of wooden items for sale, and she would be inspired just seeing them all. She would finish her new book and then maybe she would write more rhymes after all. It occurred to her that she ought to invite Fiona Kingsley to come along with them.

What they all needed was a splendid outing to lift the doldrums.

18

The case of the missing Hargreave brother was much bigger and more important than the usual sort of inquiry Hatty Pitt undertook, and she saw it as an opportunity to prove herself in Mr Hammersmith's eyes. She'd wasted no time in getting to work on it and had made a list of the places she thought Joseph Hargreave might be hiding. He lived his life as many London gentlemen of decent means did. He had an apartment in the city that he shared with his brother where he spent the bulk of the week. He and his brother also owned a cottage in Brighton, where they whiled away the weekend hours. Hatty thought she might be able to gain access to both places. Hargreave had his club, of course, and Hatty had no chance of getting in there, so she had drawn a question mark next to that item on her list of locations. Lastly, he had his place of employment: Plumm's. That would be the easiest place to get into, and so she had underlined it on her list, but decided to save it for later in the week when she would be more tired and might need something relatively simple to do.

She did not worry about the fact that she didn't know what she was doing. Nobody, after all, knew what they were doing when they started a new job. They learned. And Hatty was a quick study.

A man gave her his seat on the train to Brighton and she fell asleep, and so felt groggy and bad-tempered when she arrived. She followed a family on holiday off the train, and a solemn woman handed Hatty a pamphlet about the new clock tower. Hatty took it and smiled at her, but the woman didn't smile back. The sky was a dusty blue color, and she could taste salt on the air. No fog to be seen in any direction. The breeze was a bit chilly, but Hatty wasn't the sort to complain. She avoided the taxi rank outside the station and oriented herself before setting out, shading her eyes with one hand (the sun wasn't visible anywhere in the sky, but it was still brighter than anything she'd been accustomed to of late), while in her other hand she clutched a torn piece of notepaper on which she had written Hargreave's address.

She walked south down Queens Road and stopped to admire the clock tower, referring to the pamphlet the woman had given her. The tower was tall and all of polished stone, with decorative arches and little statues guarding little nooks at all the corners. Hatty thought it looked nearly as solid as the woman with the pamphlets. A pair of troubadours sang "Mr and Mrs Brown" while strolling round the square. "Dear Mistress Brown, your clock is fast, I know as well as you . . ." The man played violin, and the woman held out a hat. Hatty dropped a ha'penny in, pretending to herself she was on a seaside holiday.

After the clock tower the road changed to West Street, and she turned left onto Duke and followed that along to the end of Prince Albert Street, where she found the small detached cottage. The home shared by Joseph and Dr Richard Hargreave was in need of a coat of paint and a new roof. The garden needed tending, and the black wrought-iron fence along the street was missing several rails. But through a break between the houses behind it, she could see Kings Road and, beyond that, the endless grey haze of the sea.

A woman came out of the house next door, at the end of a queue of terraced homes, and stood framed in the open doorway. She was perhaps ten years older than Hatty, but her face was lined and she wore the shadows under her eyes like badges.

"They don't want any," the woman said.

"I'm sorry?"

"Those brothers don't want any of whatever it is you're selling. You needn't waste your time."

"Oh, I'm not selling anything," Hatty said. "They're not at home, are they?"

"What do you think, I watch this entire street? I wouldn't have the slightest idea if they're home."

Puzzled, Hatty hesitated with one hand on the gate. She thought she might be able to ask the woman a question or two about the Hargreaves, but she wasn't sure where to begin or how to break through the woman's hostile front. She tried on her best and brightest smile and shone it on the woman. "May I ask your name?"

"I am Mrs Ruskin. Ruth Ruskin. And that's all you'll get from me. I'm not any more interested than my neighbors are in buying from you."

"Again, Mrs Ruskin, I'm not selling anything. I don't suppose your husband's at home?" Perhaps, Hatty thought, Mr Ruskin would be easier to talk to.

"My husband has not been with us for some time now." Ruth Ruskin's frosty exterior cracked, and before she could break entirely, she turned and fled back into her house, slamming the door behind her.

"What an odd woman," Hatty said. "I hope everyone here's not like her." She shrugged and let herself through the gate and marched up the path to the door of the Hargreaves' cottage. She knocked and waited and, when nobody came to the door after a minute or two, she knocked again, keeping one eye on the house next door in case Ruth Ruskin decided to come back out and cause trouble.

She didn't have much of a plan worked out. She thought she might question the servants and perhaps they'd let her have a look round inside. At the very least, she'd be able to verify that Joseph Hargreave was not, in fact, simply away on holiday, which seemed to be a sensible first step in the investigation. She was surprised when Dr Richard Hargreave opened the door wearing a dressing gown and slippers. His hair was disheveled, tufts of silver sticking up in every direction, and he hadn't shaved. He had a book in his hand, a finger holding his place halfway through. Hatty tilted her head to read the title. *Venus in Furs.*

"What are you doing here?" His breath reeked of gin.

"Well," Hatty said, "what are *you* doing here?"

"I live here."

"I thought you'd be in the city, at work."

"I took some well-deserved time away from my practice," Hargreave said. "I find I have too much on my mind at the moment." He turned and walked away, leaving the door open. "Might as well come in, you made it this far."

Hatty stepped over the threshold and looked around. It was a small cottage with no hallways, each room leading to another, and she guessed she was in some sort of sitting room doing double duty as a study. She held a finger up to her nose to help mask the odor in the room and hoped Hargreave wouldn't notice or take offense. The windows were shuttered, and the single lamp at the back of the room didn't illuminate much, a sharp contrast to the delicious sunlight outside. Green wallpaper was peeling away at the corners, and a lazy cobweb drifted in Hargreave's wake as he showed her in. There were three deeply cushioned chairs in the room and a table that was heaped with dirty dishes. Newspapers littered the floor beside one of the chairs. Hargreave bent and tore a piece from one of them, used it as a bookmark. He set *Venus in Furs* on the arm of the chair and looked around, as if seeing the place for the first time.

"Let the staff go a week ago now," he said. "I think they were stealing from us."

"I see."

"I suppose I'll have to find someone to come in and clean, though, won't I?"

"That might not be a bad idea."

"Well, have a seat, if you like." He waved a limp hand in the direction of the other two chairs. Hatty examined the nearest one and flicked a few crumbs away before sitting down. "Got no tea and no coffee, but if you want gin I have that. Maybe some rye. And there's milk, I think, but I wouldn't touch that if I were you. Smelled a bit off yesterday, and I doubt it's got better overnight."

"I'm fine," Hatty said. "Thank you."

"So, you thought maybe Joseph had gone on holiday and forgotten to tell me," Hargreave said. "Is that it? Forgot to tell Mr Plumm, too, hadn't he? Just shimmered off to the sea and not a care in the world, eh?"

"I thought . . ." Hatty said. She cleared her throat and started again. "Mr Hammersmith suggested I come have a look round here."

"Ah. So Hammersmith's handling the likely stuff and leaving the odd tidbits for you."

"Something like that."

"Has he got any clues yet? No, I suppose not, or you wouldn't be nosing round here, where you're not needed, would you?"

Hatty smiled. "You say you've spoken to Mr Plumm?"

"Told him I'd be forced to take legal action if he sacked Joseph. My brother's not been gone so very long, has he? No reason to replace him just yet. Let the detective do his work, I say. And he says back to me that the store's got work of their own needs to be done and no worker to do it, has they? And I say, 'Well then, you'll be hearing from my solicitor unless you're willing to give the matter more time to sort itself.' And Plumm says, 'Very well.' Just like that. 'Very well, Dr Hargreave, I've got solicitors of my own, don't you know?' And before I have a chance to say anything else, the door's hitting me on the backside and I'm out in the street without so much as a fare-thee-well. Is that right? Does that sound right to you?"

"It sounds rather uncaring," Hatty said. "I'm sorry."

Hargreave took a small shuddering breath and smacked his lips and looked down at the book on the arm of his chair. He frowned and turned it over so that Hatty could no longer see the title. "I might eat," he said. "Would you care for anything? I think I've got half a pudding, maybe the butt of a roast. Almost certainly there's a cheese, if it hasn't turned."

Hatty hesitated. She was hungry, but suspicious of anything that might be found in Hargreave's pantry. Still, she wanted to take a look round the place, and a detective's work wasn't always meant to be easy, was it? "Yes, please," she said.

"Well, come along, then, and let us see what there is to see." He led the way through a door at the back of the room, which Hatty discovered led to a dining room. The table was heaped with financial papers. Through another door and she found herself in a grubby kitchen. Food-encrusted crockery filled the basin and every surface in the room was covered with butcher's paper, shriveled ends of sausages, puddles of beer and gin and clotted cream, half an apple, brown and withered, a bowl with something that had formed a skin, a knife embedded upright in a hard barm cake. A cloud of insects, tiny pinpricks in the air, hovered over some sort of gelatinous substance on the wall. Hatty's heart sank.

"This isn't all my own mess," Hargreave said. He seemed embarrassed, which Hatty took as a good sign. It was the sort of room that called for embarrassment. "As I say, we let the servants go, and Joseph and I forgot to clean up after ourselves last weekend. Besides, there's dishes here I know we didn't use. They must have snuck back in here while we were in the city and helped themselves to our provisions." He drew himself up in a pose of indignity. "They bloody well deserved the sack, didn't they?"

"Do you have a broom?"

While Hargreave looked for a broom, an activity that involved standing in the middle of his kitchen and turning slowly round and round while peering at the skirting board, Hatty found an apron hanging on a hook inside the pantry door and put it on. She decided to tackle the goo on the wall first and rinsed a rag in a pitcher of water that was only slightly yellow. She discovered that the goo had cleaned the wallpaper beneath it, so that once she had wiped it all away there was a bright spot on the wall, but she wasn't committed enough to the task to keep going. The bright spot would have to remain isolated there until Hargreave spilled more of whatever the goo was and dealt with it himself.

Hatty was reasonably certain that housekeeping and cooking weren't in the average detective's job description, but she wasn't the average detective. Besides, she was still hungry and she wasn't about to eat anything that came out of Hargreave's kitchen until the place was properly cleaned.

After the muck was washed off the wall, she tackled the dishes, wiping them down with more rags and leaving the pots and pans to soak in more yellowish water. She gathered the garbage in a pile on the counter and caught Hargreave's attention.

"Where's your rubbish?"

"My rubbish?"

"I need to toss all this or you'll have more bugs and other vermin even nastier."

"Oh, the bin is . . . um, I think right outside the door there. At least, I think it is." He pointed at an outside door next to the pantry, and Hatty unlocked it, stepped out, and took a deep breath of clean sea air. Sure enough, there was a big bin, swarming with flies, resting against the back wall of the cottage. She would have to cart the leftover food out to it, rather than bringing it in.

She stepped inside and realized how bad Hargreave's home smelled. She decided she must have grown used to the odor, but the cool breeze outside beckoned her, and she decided she'd much rather find a vendor and buy a meat pie on the way home than try to cook something edible in that particular kitchen. She would get the old food out of the house and then be done with it all. Richard Hargreave hadn't hired her to clean his house, he had hired her to find his missing brother.

She scowled at him as she walked back past, but he didn't seem to notice. Nor did he help her gather the garbage and take it out. So she didn't bother to try to salvage the dirty knife or the bowl. She tossed them along with the rest of it.

The bowl was heavy, though, and it sank quickly to the bottom of the bin, causing layers of refuse to topple in on top of it, upsetting whatever delicate ecosystem had begun to form. Something grey and pink and strange caught Hatty's eye as it was uncovered in the process. She held her breath and leaned in for a closer view, then ran back inside the kitchen for a rag. She took it to the bin and reached down inside, wrapped it around the pinkish grey thing, careful not to touch anything with her fingers, and fished it out.

Dragged into the light it wasn't nearly as odd-looking, but still she stared at it, trying to understand what it might be. It seemed harmless, if disgusting: wilted and tough, but not like any cut of meat she had seen before. She brought it closer to her face and licked her lower lip while she thought, then thought about the fact that she was licking her lip and suddenly recognized the thing wrapped in the rag. She dropped it in the dirt.

She leaned against the house and waited until she was calm again. Back inside, she stalked through the kitchen, leaving the back door open, and sat down at the dining room table. She found a pencil and used the back of one of the financial documents to take notes. (She was going to have to remember to carry round one of those little notebooks Mr Hammersmith always used.) When Hargreave followed her into the room, she indicated that he should sit across from her.

"Are you going to finish cleaning in there?"

"No," Hatty said.

"Well, it needs cleaning."

"Then hire someone whose job it is to clean. Or do it yourself. Meanwhile, I'd like some information from you."

"What sort of information? I've told you everything I know."

"I want you to remember exactly when you let the household staff go and when you and your brother were last here."

"I can try to remember, but I'm not sure—"

"Just do your best, sir. Anything you can tell me might be of help."

"Well—"

"And when we're done here, I'm going to have to head back to London to share this information with Mr Hammersmith, but I want you to fetch the thing on the ground beside the rubbish bin, if you would be so kind, and keep it safe here until the Brighton police arrive."

"The police are coming?"

"They will be as soon as I alert them."

"Alert them? Alert them to what?"

"I believe you had a human tongue in your bin. It's entirely possible there are other bits of your brother in there, too. Now, let's focus on that timetable."

Of course, Hatty had no evidence that the tongue had ever belonged in Joseph Hargreave's head, but it gave her great satisfaction to shock Richard Hargreave and it made her feel very much like she imagined a detective ought to feel. The best part was that Hargreave became immediately cooperative and gave her no more arguments.

19

Day woke and sat up. His hair was damp, his collar limp with sweat, and his mouth tasted stale. For a moment he thought he was back in his cell, but then he felt a wave of relief as he recalled his experiences of the past weeks. The relief was tinged with a sense of dread. He would be meeting Jack again today, and Jack might take him back to that cell.

But Day no longer wanted to return to his little cot with its rough grey blanket, or to his tiny window that looked out on stones and snow.

He struggled to his feet in the cramped space and cracked open the door to the storeroom. People bustled this way and that, but nobody looked his way. He glanced back at Ambrose. The boy was sprawled in what seemed to Day to be a very uncomfortable position, his neck bent awkwardly, his mouth wide open. But his chest was rising and falling steadily. Day left him there in the dark, where he was safe for the time being, and stepped out, shutting the door behind him.

He was on the main floor of the department store, all shining wood and glass and a black spiral staircase that ran up through the center of the room to the gallery, where he and Esther had sipped their tea and eaten their seedcakes and looked down on the other shoppers. The whole place smelled of perfumes and talcum, mixed with wood polish and body odor.

Day drew his watch (another gift from Esther) from his pocket and was astonished to see that it was already half past eleven. He had slept for three hours on the floor of the storeroom. Did he still have time to get back to the draper's shop and change his collar, comb his hair, splash a little water on his face? There was certainly no time to nose around the store, as he'd wanted to, to try to find some advantage over Jack before their meeting, but he at least wanted to look presentable, to seem confident. Jack sniffed out weakness in other men and exploited it. And he knew all of Day's weaknesses, had already exploited every one of them.

On thinking about it, Day decided a fresh collar probably wouldn't change anything. All he could do was brace himself and face whatever was coming his way, whatever Jack had planned for him.

As if on cue, Day looked up and saw the man himself at the gallery rail. Jack smiled and waved at him, gestured for him to come up.

No time anymore to do anything except climb those steps. His decisions were all made for him. He put his watch away and trudged to the spiral stairs and went up. His leg suddenly hurt, and he had to use his cane to push himself off each step. Along the way he passed several shoppers, all of whom gave him nervous glances and sidled as far to the other side of the steps as they could. He thought he must reek of doom.

Jack was waiting for him at the top and took his arm.

"You're early," Jack said. "How lovely." He led him to a little table with a lacy cloth draped over it and he pulled out a chair for him.

. . .

"It's incredible."

Fiona Kingsley had been available to accompany the Day clan on their outing to Plumm's. She had brought a sketch pad and a small case of pencils, paints, brushes, and charcoals. Everything there seemed false to her, designed to evoke some feeling or response, but she still felt a little thrill as she looked round at it all.

There was a giant globe in a box above her being glassed in by men who reminded her of busy ants.

"It is very big," Claire said. "And there're so many things. How can they sell all these things?"

"Who would buy some of them?" Fiona was looking at a brooch shaped like a butterfly, with mother-of-pearl inlays and antennae made of thin wire with beads on the ends.

"You could illustrate some of it," Claire said.

"I think they'd expect me to buy something if I tried to draw it. But I'll do a quick sketch of some wooden things to help the book if we find anything new or different. Do you think we ought to try the furniture department or the— Oh, Claire, we should look in the books department and see if they have yours."

"Do you think they do?"

"Why wouldn't they?"

"Surrounded by all of this? That would be . . ."

"It would be incredible."

"That is the word."

"Miss Tinsley!"

Fiona jumped and turned. A small round fellow was hurrying toward them. Fiona blinked and tried to remember where she had seen him before, but he was on them before she could place him.

"You remember me," the man said. He was perhaps fifty years old, and his face was red all over and beaming with pleasure. She could not help herself and broke out into a huge smile despite herself.

"It's me," the little man said. "Alastair Goodpenny. You do re-member me?" He stopped short and his face changed; his smile dis-appeared and his forehead creased with wrinkles.

She did remember him. She had consulted with him the previous year on a case her father and Hammersmith had been involved in. He was the proprietor of a kiosk in the Marylebone bazaar and had advised her on a pair of cufflinks that had been owned by a murderer.

"Her name is Miss Kingsley, not Tinsley," one of the boys said. She thought it was Robert, but she didn't turn round to see.

"There's no need to shout," Goodpenny said. "I can hear you. Miss Tinsley and I have known each other longer than you've been alive." He softened then and bent down, and Fiona turned to see which of the boys he was talking to. It was Simon. "What's your name, little boy?"

"My name is Simon."

"How unusual. Jemima is commonly a girl's name. From the Bible, isn't it?"

"Simon. My name is Simon."

"Just so. And you should be proud. Though you might also want to strengthen your upper body. With that name you'll be forced to defend yourself often enough, I should think." Goodpenny straight-ened back up and beamed at Fiona. "How are you, Miss Tinsley? How is that boy you were so fond of? Mr Angerschmid?"

"Thank you, Mr Goodpenny. I believe Nevil is fine, although I don't see much of him these days."

"Oh, what a shame. He seemed in need of a woman's attention, don't you think?"

Fiona blushed. "Have you met my friend? Mr Goodpenny, this is Mrs Day."

Claire offered her hand, and Goodpenny leaned over it, his manner courtly and endearing. "My great pleasure, Mrs Dew."

"The pleasure is mine," Claire said. She gave Fiona a knowing smile that Mr Goodpenny failed to notice.

"What are you doing here, Mr Goodpenny? Are you shopping?"

"No, no, Miss Tinsley. I'm employed here now. They need good people who know how to judge a piece of silver and who understand what a man needs in the way of accessories. You're not after such a thing today, are you?"

"No, thank you. We're here to look for things made of wood."

"Of course I would. You have only to tell me what you need."

Fiona glanced round at Claire, who looked puzzled, and whispered, "He can't hear a thing." Claire hid a smile behind her hand.

"Shall I give you the grand tour? We've only been open a short while, and I'm still learning the place myself." Mr Goodpenny seemed proud and happy, and Fiona felt glad for him.

"We'd be delighted," she said.

"Well, let's see if we can find the thing you're after," Mr Goodpenny said. "I wouldn't be surprised if Plumm's carries it."

They had no idea what he had in mind, but he led the way down a narrow path between two counters and Fiona followed. Claire and the boys and the nanny with her double pram all came along.

AMBROSE CRAWLED OUT of the storeroom and crept along behind the counter. He had awoken as the latch clicked shut, and his boss was walking away from the room by the time Ambrose rubbed the sleep from his eyes and peeked out the door. He'd been abandoned there.

He knew he'd be thrown out of the store as soon as anyone of authority saw him. He didn't look like he had money or a reason to be there. The only way he could think to explore Plumm's and catch up to the guv was to pretend he was running deliveries for someone posh. He stood up and straightened his threadbare jacket and tried to look like he imagined a delivery boy might look. He marched past a grouping of chairs and tables and sofas, then along in front of the cabinets of jewelry and scarves without paying attention to any of the fineries on display. *These things,* he thought, *don't impress me. I see finer things all day long at my employer's home.* He kept this silent mantra going, in hopes that if he thought a thing, however false it might be, it would manifest itself in his face and his bearing. His real employer barely had a home at all and didn't seem to care about much of anything except tobacco leavings, but thinking about that was of no use in this situation. He passed several shopgirls and not one of them stopped him, so he imagined he was carrying off the internal disguise well. His manner was almost regal.

But he couldn't keep himself from looking upward, past the huge installation that was being constructed. Somewhere up there was a skylight, on beyond the vaulted ceiling and the shops and offices. Somewhere up there Ambrose had watched two women being murdered.

And the man who had murdered them was right there, standing in plain sight above him!

Ambrose actually gasped when he saw him and ducked down behind a display of silk trousers. The murderer was taking the guv's hand, escorting the boss of Reasonable Tobacco to a little table as if they were going to have tea together right there in front of God and everybody.

Like they was friends.

Was his employer going to turn him over to the killer? Had Ambrose been lured to the store on purpose so they could do away with the only witness to the murders? But no, if the guv planned to betray Ambrose, surely he wouldn't have left him sleeping in a closet with the door practically open. He would have locked Ambrose in until he could make his arrangements. At least, that's how Ambrose thought *he* would have done it if he were that sort of person.

So it wasn't a trap for him. But it might be a trap for his employer. He'd told the guv all about it, and now the killer was saying something to him up there, telling the guv something, and the guv didn't look none too happy about it, either. The killer was threatening him.

And then Ambrose understood: His employer was protecting him by hiding Ambrose and diverting the killer's attention.

Ambrose wasn't the bravest boy on the streets, but he was loyal. He'd never let anyone down, so far as he knew. He had to do something and he had to do it fast.

"Excuse me, young man, but you're blocking the aisle."

Ambrose turned and saw a nasty old nanny pushing a pram that held two babies. Behind her were two more children, boys who were maybe a little younger than Ambrose himself. There was a slender girl with her nose in a sketch pad and a fat little clerk who was jabbering about something. And behind them all was the most beautiful woman Ambrose had ever seen, with golden hair that shone brilliantly under Plumm's yellow lights.

"Well, get a move on, why dontcha?" The nanny raised her hand as though she meant to swat at Ambrose from three feet away and with a pram between them.

The beautiful woman frowned at her governess. "Tabitha, be nice." Then she smiled at Ambrose and said, "This place is amazing, isn't it? I've never seen a store so large."

Ambrose managed to nod at the beautiful woman, stunned that she had spoken directly to him. She was the nicest posh lady he had ever seen.

Before he could find his voice and answer her, the nanny said, "Yes, Mrs Day." And all eight of them swept past Ambrose and into the furniture department behind him.

TABITHA WAS SIMPLY NOT going to work out. Claire scowled at the nanny's back and tried to figure out how to let her go when she had no one to take up the slack. Tabitha was the third governess the babies had been through in the past year. And none of them had worked out. The first had left them because there always seemed to be a killer of some sort prowling about the house. (Claire couldn't blame her.) The second had hit one of the boys. And now Tabitha was acting willfully awful.

Imagine! Talking to a poor delivery boy as if he were street scum.

She rolled her eyes and noticed something familiar at the outside edge of her vision. Her attention was drawn by two workmen having a row over something they were building, a huge globe, perhaps fifty feet around, in a glassed-in box. She ignored them and focused on one of the men taking tea at the gallery above.

The big gas lamps behind them shone down through a mass of dark hair, and it only took her a moment to place the man. She had once met Jack the Ripper. He had even come into her bedroom. And the man sitting above her, having tea like any other ordinary person, was that same man. She was certain of it.

"Missus?"

Claire came to herself and shook her head.

Tabitha touched her arm. "What is it, ma'am?"

"Can't you leave me alone for a single moment and let me think?"

"Yes, ma'am."

"Watch after the children. Isn't that your job? Isn't that the whole of your job?"

"Yes, ma'am." The nanny hung her head and hurried after the boys, who had taken the pram and were pushing their way into the books department. Mr Goodpenny and Fiona had disappeared together around a bank of tall wardrobes with double doors. Claire could hear the cheerful little gentleman going on about the quality of the wood finish.

Claire made a mental note to apologize to poor Tabitha. She looked up again at the tea shop near the railing. And Jack was still there. He was sipping from a cup and he was . . . He was looking down at her. He saw her. His features were sketched out in grey upon grey, like the mist outside, but she could see a smile crease his face. He was smiling at her. He set down his cup and raised his hand, touched his forehead in a salute.

Claire looked away and closed her eyes. She heard a train racing through the department store and she nearly jumped before realizing it was her own heavy breath. Her heart was racing, her lungs were laboring. She opened her eyes and looked up again. The devil was sitting across from someone, and Claire finally turned her gaze on him. His back was to her, but she had known him most of her life and she knew him now. She knew him like she knew the freckle on the back of her ring finger, knew him like she knew the strawberry birthmark on the small of Winnie's back.

Walter Day did not turn around and look at her, but she knew him. Oh, she knew him! And he was alive. And he was taking tea at Plumm's with Jack the Ripper.

Claire Day felt the room rush at her from all directions, and she fell unconscious at the feet of a mannequin.

AMBROSE HAD MOVED ON, humiliated by the angry governess, but he turned back when he heard a loud thump. Her companions were gathering round her, so it took Ambrose a minute to realize that the beautiful woman had fallen. Several people had already noticed, and a commotion was in its beginning stages. Shopgirls were coming from every corner of the store now, and an officious-looking manager-type with a waxed mustache popped his head up over a partition across the main floor, craning his neck to see what was going on. Ambrose hurried and got to the beautiful woman right away. He bent over her, pushing the nasty nanny away. He heard the nanny squawk, but he didn't care. He was in love. He patted the beautiful woman's cheeks. Gently. And her eyelids fluttered.

"Danger," she said.

"Yes, missus?"

She raised one tremulous arm and pointed above them. She pointed at the gallery, at the killer, who was smiling down at them. She knew about the killer the same as Ambrose did. They had something in common. The guv, sitting up there with his back to them, started to rise at the sound from below, but the killer pushed the guv back down, physically turned his head so that he wouldn't see what was below him. Ambrose wanted to call out, wanted to shout at the guv, tell him to get away. But the beautiful woman grabbed his arm.

"Walter," she said.

"Ambrose, mum," he said. "My name's Ambrose."

"He's up there," she said. "Save him." She tried to point again, but failed and fell unconscious once more.

It didn't matter. He understood. This beautiful woman had seen Ambrose's employer and she loved him as Ambrose did. She somehow understood the danger the guv was in. And Ambrose knew that he had to save his employer if he wanted this woman, this angel, to ever look at him again. If she had fallen for the guv, then Ambrose might have to give her up, but he still wanted to win her favor.

He let the awful governess take his place at the beautiful woman's side and he rose and hurried away. He picked up his pace and elbowed his way through the other shoppers that had gathered round, through the gaggles of shopgirls and the officious managers like green-headed mallards, went to the spiral staircase, and took the steps two at a time to the top.

20

We have to move on," Jack said.

"Wait," Day said. "I didn't come here to be manipulated by you."

"Yes, you did." Jack took Day's arm and almost bodily lifted him from his chair. Day looked to his left and right, embarrassed, wondering if anyone saw, but no one reacted. At this time of the late morning, people were not quite ready for their lunch and had long ago finished their breakfasts. There were only two other occupied tables, and the old ladies at both of them were rising now, approaching the railing, curious about some sort of row that had broken out below them.

He glanced over the railing and saw that a blond woman had collapsed. He opened his mouth to call her name, but then closed it and looked away. He didn't know her. She was a stranger to him.

"Tut tut," Jack said. "It won't do if you and I are seen together at the moment you're discovered." He leaned in closer. "We'll have to get this done another way. Work first, play later." And he ushered Day up and away, past a phalanx of workmen in canvas trousers who were wrestling with sheets of glass bigger than they were, along the queue of tables, to the back of the floor, where there was a long hallway lined with heavy oak doors.

"What do you mean? What do you mean when you say 'discovered'?" But Day allowed himself to be led. If Jack was concentrating on him, he wasn't killing anyone else, he wasn't exploring the other floors and finding the urchin in the storeroom. He wasn't hurting the unconscious woman with blond hair. If Day could keep Jack distracted, then Jack would continue to be Day's own private monster.

"Never you mind. Come in here." Jack opened a door and led Day into a quiet office, really nothing but a small room with a desk and two chairs. A typewriter and a telephone sat atop the desk, next to a blotter arranged with a pen, a letter opener, a small stack of plain envelopes, and an inkwell.

Jack was breathing hard and he moved round to the other side of the desk. He sat with a grunt and winced. "I shouldn't have exerted myself quite so much," he said. "Listen, do you trust me?"

"No, of course I don't trust you," Day said. "You're horrible and you'll most likely kill me once I stop providing you with amusement."

Jack leaned forward in his chair. Day could smell his breath, all copper and rot. Jack moved from the waist, his shoulders straight up and down, as if he were one of those wind-up automatons that swiveled back and forth, performing some simple task over and over. In this case the task was murder. Back and forth, again and again, until Jack's rusted gears wound down.

"I could never kill you, Walter Day," Jack said. *(That name again.)* "You're my mirror image, the flip side of my spinning coin."

"You're not the other side of my coin," Day said.

"No, I'm the edge of it. And I circle round and round and never stop, so don't think that I will." Had he read Day's thoughts about the declining automaton? Day almost believed that he had, that he could. Nothing seemed impossible where Jack was concerned.

"Whose office is this?"

"You know, I don't remember his name," Jack said. "I call him Kitten because he makes a lovely soft animal noise when I hurt him. Like a pleading cat. I'd have you in sometime so you could hear it for yourself, but I don't know how much longer poor Kitten can hold out."

Day shuddered.

"I went to your house," Jack said. "Except it's not your house anymore, is it? And I'm not talking about that new place your wife's moved to. That was never your home. You've never even seen it. No, I went to the house with the blue door, the one where we had so many adventures. I knew you weren't there, but I've missed you lately and I wanted to bask in the air that you'd walked through so many times."

"I don't know the place you're talking about."

"If you ever go back, you'll have a surprise waiting for you. I left something there."

"Left something?"

"It wasn't easy, either. Cost me more than a little."

"What do you want?"

"Ah, yes, to business, then." Jack picked up the letter opener from the desk. He poked the tip of his finger with the dull blade and frowned. "Not as useful as one might wish," he said under his breath, as if he were talking to himself, not to Day. "Anyway, let's be done with all this silliness. I'm a patient man, I really am, but you've drawn it all out to the point that it's no longer much fun, I'm afraid."

"I've drawn what out? You talk in riddles, in maths I don't understand. If you want to take me back there, back to that cell, you can try, but I won't go quietly and I'm no longer afraid of you."

"Ah. That draper woman, the one with the little shop in the gardens, she's influenced you, hasn't she? Turned you against me."

"You leave her out of this."

"That's just it, you see," Jack said. "I didn't include her in the first place. You did. I let you go free and you should have gone home, should have returned to your employment, but you didn't. And you didn't return to me, either. I would have taken you back in, cared for you as I always have. But instead of coming back to me, or doing anything at all useful, you took up with this slattern—"

"Don't say that," Day said. He felt his face getting warm. "Don't you dare say that about her."

"Oh, it wasn't meant to be an insult. She's quite my type. Yes, my type indeed. You've good taste in female flesh, Walter Day." He closed his eyes and seemed to gather himself, his shoulders hunching and his fists clenching, unclenching. Then he opened his eyes and smiled. "But regardless of how you'd describe her, you brought her into this, and so I should leave it to you to get her out of it."

"Get her out of what? I don't know what you mean."

Jack sighed and waved his hand at a cabinet on the opposite wall. "I wonder if you wouldn't help me out and fetch some gauze from the top drawer there."

Day opened a door in the top of the cabinet and Jack snapped at him. "The drawer, I said. It's in the drawer. You never listen to me!"

Startled, Day slammed the door shut and slid open the drawer, found a roll of gauze, and tossed it over the desk to Jack.

"Thank you. The scissors, too, if you'd be so kind."

Day found a pair of surgical scissors and laid them on the desk, slid them across. He wondered if Jack planned to use them on him, to stab him to death.

"Now sit," Jack said. "Let's pretend we're adults discussing something of importance."

Day stepped forward as if in a dream, everything moving in half-time, his limbs heavy, and he was reminded of his underwater dream. Jack was like some unceasing, irresistible tide. Day sat and laid his cane across his lap.

Jack smiled. He pulled off his jacket, leaning forward to tug on the sleeves, then unbuttoned his waistcoat and removed it. The front of his white shirt was soaked in blood. He untucked it and pulled it up, revealing a nasty gash under his ribs on the right side of his torso. "I'm afraid they may have nicked my liver," Jack said. He smiled again and winked at Day, then unspooled some of the gauze and began wrapping it round himself.

"What happened?"

"Those Karstphanomen are getting tricky. They laid an ambush for me. But don't worry, I took care of them."

"You killed them?"

"Four of them. They're waiting for you. Oh, but I've ruined the surprise."

"I don't think I care for any more surprises."

"Walter Day, I must admit something. There is something about you, some stolid . . . justiceness. Is that a word? You look exactly like justice. You need only a scale and a blindfold. And perhaps a surgical alteration or two. You are Lustitia, the symbol of fair play. Lust. Lustitia. We want what we see and we take it, the basis for all our modern ideas of justice. Might makes right? It was always so, and I may be misappropriating the words of our cousin in the colonies. But it doesn't matter."

"I don't understand anything you say," Day said.

"Of course, your intelligence is not what attracted me to you. It's, as I say, your solidity. You are a marble slab of sheer goodness."

"Please just . . . Will you tell me . . . What about Esther?"

"Yes. Esther. She is disposable, I'm afraid."

"No!" Day stood quickly and the chair fell back, smacking against the floor.

Jack scowled at him and held a finger to his lips. He tucked the loose end of his bandage under itself, then rose and went to the door and looked out, up and down the hall, shut it softly, and returned. "Pick up your chair, Walter Day. And lower your walking stick. What do you plan to do? You can't hurt me and you don't want to. Let's not pretend to be other than what we are. And let's not bring passion into this. Lust and passion are not the same things at all."

Day shook his head, but picked up the chair. He sat down and waited, but he kept his fist gripped tight on his cane. He might get one chance to swing, and he didn't want to waste it.

Jack crossed behind him and went to the cabinet. He found a clean white shirt and took his seat across from Day. "You have much to learn, and we've only begun our journey." He pulled the shirt on, and Day noticed again how strangely he moved. Jack was clearly in a great deal of pain. "I think perhaps you didn't have a strong father figure in your life. Was Arthur Day too busy valeting to teach you about the world? Or have I asked you that before? I get confused."

"You keep bringing other people into our discussion." Day fixed Jack with what he hoped was a steely glare. "Leave Arthur . . . you leave my father out of it. Leave Esther and everyone else I know out of it. It's you and me."

"It has ever been thus. But you miss the larger point. I genuinely don't care about anyone else, but you do, and that makes you vulnerable. So I am going to have to harm Esther Paxton to get my point across to you. I ask you, is that fair to her? Is that justice, Walter Day?" Day started to rise again from his chair, but Jack waved him back. "Be calm."

"I told you. This doesn't involve her." Day could barely speak.

"It didn't, but now it does. And that's your fault." Jack looked down at the blotter. "I'm still so . . . All you had to do was go home, live your life, and go back to work. Why didn't you do that?"

"Is it too late?"

Jack raised his fist and brought it down in an arc that would have ended with the blotter, but he pulled his arm up at the last minute and opened his hand and laid it atop the other and took a deep, shuddering breath. Then he smiled again, but it was not a real smile at all; it was nothing Day had ever seen on another human being's face. "I unlocked your door. I left your clothes where you would find them at the end of the hall—"

"I never saw them. I was out in the cold, naked, with nothing. You left me with nothing."

"I gave you everything, even money. Certainly enough to hire a cab to take you anywhere you might have wished. It was all right there, great detective, and you walked past it."

"I never saw any of that," Day said. "I never saw it."

"I asked so little of you. Only the smallest favor in return for months of my hospitality."

"Why? Why did you let me go?"

Jack's eyes narrowed. "I think you've deliberately forgotten. And you've somehow made yourself unable to see things around you. Even today, you didn't seem to recognize your own . . . Well, Walter Day, you are turning backflips to avoid going home."

"I'll go home now."

"And where is that? Where is your home? Tell me."

Day said nothing.

"You see? You are determined to forget," Jack said. "Perhaps your forgetting begets a deeper strength than I knew you had. Your ability to trick yourself and to build a new life indicates a bottomless capacity for rightness within you. As I say, one coin, two men, you, me. I learn from you, you learn from me, and we both benefit, don't we? But enough. Here." Jack turned the telephone around, swiveling it on its post so that the receiver hung nearer to Day. "Ask for Scotland Yard."

"Scotland Yard?"

"Ask for the commissioner, and when he accepts the call, tell him where you are. Ask him to send someone for you. Have him send that ass Tiffany. Or Blacker, or even Wiggins. It doesn't matter. If you value Esther Paxton's life, do it."

Day picked up the telephone receiver and held it to his ear. When the switchboard responded, he was able to choke out the words Jack had told him to say.

"Tell them who you are," Jack said.

They waited in silence in that anonymous office, Day and Jack, and the space seemed to Day to grow smaller and more uncomfortable as each minute passed. He could hear the operator and other voices in the background like distant birds, other women connecting other calls, and he wondered what those people had to say to each other, what might be important to them, whether there were other lives depending on other calls. When Sir Edward Bradford's voice finally came on the line, Day couldn't remember what he was supposed to say.

"Hello," he said.

"Walter? Is this Walter Day on the line?"

"Please," Day said, "help me."

Sir Edward continued to talk, but Day could no longer hear him. He looked up and into Jack's eyes, and the room seemed to spin round him. He dropped the receiver and fell sideways off his chair, dragging the telephone with him. As darkness crept in from the edges of his vision, he heard Jack say (kindly, as if talking about a particularly troublesome but much-loved child), "Oh, Walter Day. What am I to do with you?"

21

When Claire Day opened her eyes again, Robert and Simon were kneeling beside her on the floor. Simon was holding her hand, and Robert bore a worried expression that Claire would have done anything to erase. Behind them, Fiona was shielding the pram, keeping the babies from seeing what had happened, and Mr Goodpenny was turning in circles, hollering for help. She felt ashamed that she was the cause of so much concern and embarrassed that she had fainted. After everything she had been through in the past two years, she felt she ought to be made of sterner stuff than that.

She smiled at Robert, but he didn't smile back. That wasn't a surprise. Robert and Simon had seen their parents murdered and had barely escaped the same fate. Claire had tried to give them some semblance of a normal life, but the boys rarely let her out of their sight. They were convinced she would die, too, or disappear the same way Walter had, leaving them alone again.

"I'm all right, Robert," she said. "Everything's fine."

He nodded, but put his small hand on her forehead. Two shopgirls and a floor manager were hovering nearby, clearly not sure how to deal with the situation. Claire nodded at them, trying to convey that she was fine, no harm done, everyone could go about their business in the usual way.

She looked up at the gallery. The table where Walter had been sitting was empty now. Had she really seen him there? Or had she been searching crowds for her husband for so long that her mind was now playing tricks on her?

"I'm not ill," she said. She held out her hand, and the floor manager stepped forward to help her up, but Robert waved him away. He and Simon pulled at her arms with all their might. If she let go of Robert's arm, she thought he would fly backward into a display case.

She smiled again, this time at the floor manager.

"Please, ma'am, are you sure you're entirely well?" he said.

"It's this place. It's so huge and lovely. I'm afraid I was overwhelmed."

The manager finally smiled back at her, relieved and flattered. "It is a bit much, isn't it? Please, we have an automatic lift at the back, just this way; won't you have a cup of tea? It's courtesy of Plumm's. You can relax and catch your breath and look around while resting your feet." He glanced down at Robert and Simon, who were now clinging to her skirts as if they intended to prop her up in the event of another fall. "And cakes for these brave little boys," the manager said.

"Thank you," Claire said. "Perhaps I should sit down. Please give me a minute to catch my breath, won't you?"

The manager clapped his hands once and turned to show them to the lift. The customers, disappointed that the drama had ended so bloodlessly, resumed shopping, and the staff returned to their duties.

It seemed impossible that the man on the gallery had been her husband. If she claimed to have seen Walter, she would be raising the boys' hopes, and what if it was a case of mistaken identity?

And if she wasn't wrong, if she really had seen Walter? Why hadn't he seen her? He hadn't even looked. He wasn't a cruel or insensitive man, and she couldn't believe, couldn't allow herself to even think, that he didn't love her anymore, that he had decided to leave and never look back.

"Robert," Claire said, "and Simon, would you boys check on the little girls for me? I don't want them to be worried."

Robert clearly didn't want to leave her side, but he allowed Simon to lead him a few feet away to where the governess was walking slowly along behind the manager, cooing at the babies. Claire moved closer to Fiona.

Fiona whispered, "Are you quite sure you're all right?"

"I am," Claire said. "But tell me . . . Did you happen to look up there, at the tea shop right there, a bit ago? A minute ago, when I fainted?"

"No, I was sketching the furniture for ideas to help with your book. Is it the book? The pressure of it, I mean. Is that why you passed out?"

"No. At least, I don't think so. It's . . . Well, you're going to think me mad."

"I won't."

"Oh, please don't, Fiona. You're the only one I can tell, and if you give me that look, that pitying look that says you're only humoring me, then I think I shall scream."

"I wouldn't do that. Not ever. Not even if you really were mad."

Claire smiled and shook her head. "I saw him."

"Saw who? You mean Mr Day? You saw him here?" Fiona gasped

and stood on tiptoe, turning her head this way and that. "Where is he?"

"Stop that. We don't want to attract any attention to ourselves. He was at the tea shop up there."

"But where is he now?"

"So you do believe me?"

"Of course I do."

"He was right there, sitting at a table there."

"And you didn't call out to him?"

"He wasn't alone," Claire said.

"Not . . ."

"Not what?"

"Not another woman."

"No, of course not."

"Then who?"

"I'll tell you later. It's too complicated to tell you here."

"But do you think he's still here? In the store?"

"I hope so. Surely we would have seen him leave, unless there's a back way."

"We have to tell Nevil," Fiona said. "I mean Mr Hammersmith. We have to find him and get him here right away, before it's too late and Mr Day disappears again."

"Oh," Claire said. "Oh, of course. Nevil will help us."

She hadn't even thought. She wasn't alone. She had so many people around her who loved her and who loved her husband. And if Fiona believed her, then Nevil Hammersmith would believe her, too. He would search the place from top to bottom as soon as he arrived. Nevil would search the entire neighborhood if need be. She had to talk to him right away. She could send a runner to his office later in the day, but she knew he had gone to Scotland Yard today to check once more on any progress that might have been made. If he was still there . . .

She raised her voice. "Excuse me."

The manager turned around and raised his eyebrows at her.

"I wonder if you might have a telephone somewhere here."

22

Jack hung up the receiver and set the telephone upright on the desk. He checked Day's pulse, which was strong and regular. People were such fragile things, full of delicate organs and unbalanced humors.

"Well," Jack said, "I can't simply leave you here, can I?" He squatted and got his hands under Day's arms, lifted him into the chair, then stepped back and pressed his hand to his abdomen. The gauze wrapped around his torso was already spotted with fresh blood. He gave the unconscious man a black look. "This would have been so much easier if you only did what was expected of you, if you only acted like any other ordinary human being."

But of course, if Walter Day had been any other ordinary human being, Jack might have killed him months ago. Walter Day seemed ordinary enough, but there was something about him, some special quality, that drew Jack to him. Jack wished he understood what it was so he could cut it out of the detective and move on.

He shook Day and, when there was no response, slapped him across the face. Still, Day didn't wake up.

"Walter Day, I can't decide whether you're the strongest person I've met or the weakest," Jack said. "I've never seen anyone so thoroughly hide away inside his own head."

The office door opened and Jack looked up, surprised to see a child standing there, a boy perhaps thirteen or fourteen years old. The boy's face was full of fear and anger, and Jack smiled. He heard the distant rumble of the electric lift.

"Please," Jack said, "come in. I've been expecting you. Close the door, would you?"

THE FLOOR MANAGER knocked on the door and, when there was no response, he jiggled the knob. He shrugged at Claire. "The new fellow has a lot of work to catch up on. We've had some minor staffing problems recently. Not to worry, all smoothed over. I suppose Mr Oberon doesn't want to be disturbed just now. But come, there's a second phone in Mr Plumm's office. He's out at the moment, and I'm sure he wouldn't mind."

He led the way down the passage toward a door at the end, but Claire hesitated. She touched the doorknob and quietly twisted it, thinking perhaps it might magically open for her where it hadn't for the manager. But it was indeed locked, and after scowling at it for a moment, she turned and followed along in the manager's wake. She rubbed her fingers against the fabric of her dress. The doorknob had given her a slight shock when she'd touched it.

THE MURDERER TOOK his hand off Ambrose's mouth and held a finger to his lips.

"There's a good lad." His voice was barely more than a whisper, rasping against Ambrose's skin. "Be quiet now. There will be big trouble for us all if my friend is found here."

Ambrose nodded. He was trembling, and his nose was running.

"You seem frightened," the murderer said. "Don't be. As long as we're quiet, we won't have any trouble. Do I know you, boy?"

Ambrose shook his head.

"Well, I could swear . . . But if not . . ." He frowned down at Day. "My friend's had a bit too much to drink, I'm afraid."

"Guv?" It was the best Ambrose could manage under the circumstances, but there was no response from the motionless man in the chair.

The murderer looked back and forth between Ambrose and the guv. "Oh, you know him! For how long?"

"A few . . . A week or three."

"What has he told you about me?"

"Nothin', sir, I swear it. I don't know nothin'."

"He's never mentioned me? Never mentioned old Jack?"

"No, sir."

"I'm wounded." There was indeed a patch of blood creeping up Jack's belly. He was literally wounded, and Ambrose wondered if the guv had done it. The man calling himself Jack stared at Ambrose until he could feel the hairs on his neck creeping. "I have seen you somewhere," the murderer said.

"What did you mean you was expectin' me? What you said before."

"Providence always provides. I can't move our mutual friend by myself. I need help, and so you've happened by in the nick of time."

"I need to . . ." Ambrose's voice trailed off, and he turned toward the door.

"Don't leave, little boy."

"But I—"

"I said don't leave. Now be quiet until they've passed back by again. After that, we'll talk." The murderer sat on the edge of the desk and smiled at Ambrose. Ambrose felt very cold.

"Is he dead?"

"No. Not in the least."

"You gonna kill him?"

"Now why would you ask me that?"

"I don't know." Ambrose realized he was panting, as if he'd run a long distance.

"Be quiet now," Jack said. "They're coming back through."

Ambrose nodded and swallowed. He could hear footsteps and a lady talking outside the office door, but he couldn't make out what she was saying. Whoever she was, the murderer didn't want her to find him here. Ambrose knew that Jack was going to kill him and would probably kill the guv, too, and his only chance was to speak up, to scream and holler and make the people outside in the hallway break down the door. If there were enough people round them, the murderer wouldn't dare do anything. They could catch him. Ambrose would tell them about the two dead women, and they would put Jack in prison, and there would be no more worries. He opened his mouth, but before he could utter a sound, Jack's hot, dusty hand was suddenly clapped over his lips again. He hadn't heard Jack move up behind him. The voices in the passage were fading as the woman and her entourage reached the lift and the door closed behind them.

The murderer's lips touched Ambrose's ear. "Now we can talk."

The hand disappeared from Ambrose's mouth, and Jack was already sitting again on the corner of the desk when Ambrose lifted his head.

"What's your name, boy?"

"Ambrose."

"Good. Did I already say you can call me Jack if you want to? Some people do."

"Is it your name?"

"Sometimes. But I have many names and I have no preferences among any of them. Now." Jack clapped the palms of his hands against his thighs and looked round the office as if he'd only now arrived there. "I've had a chance to think our situation over and I've decided there's no polite way to proceed. Don't you agree?"

"No, sir. We can be polite."

"My advice to you, Ambrose, is to embrace the moment. Of course, you must be polite if you can, but there are times when a small amount of rudeness is unavoidable. And there are times when outright savagery is required."

"Savagery?"

"Indeed. And if we shrink from the occasion, then we miss our chance to enjoy the savagery for itself. For the marvelous change of pace that it is."

"What are you going to do?"

"It's not what I'm going to do, Ambrose, it's what you're going to do. You seem to feel some regard for our friend here." He waved a loose, languid hand at Day's slumbering form. "And so you will run a small errand for me and come right back here."

Ambrose shook his head, but couldn't speak.

"Yes," Jack said. "If you do not, or if you tell anyone about me or bring anyone back to this office, I will kill our friend while you watch. And I will kill anyone else you've brought here. And then I will kill you. Only I will kill you very slowly. Very slowly indeed. And I will enjoy it so much more than you will. Do you understand?"

Ambrose shook his head again, then gasped and nodded.

"Good. Do you believe I will do what I say?"

Another nod.

"Wonderful. We're getting on splendidly, aren't we?"

Ambrose cleared his throat and licked his lips with a dry tongue. "What is it that you want me to do?"

23

Mr and Mrs Parker had waited outside the coffeehouse and followed Leland Carlyle when he emerged because, as Mrs Parker had rightly pointed out, "The best way to find our man is to track his man." Jack the Ripper was claiming the lives of the Karstphanomen. They had no clue to his identity, but they did know the identity of the high judge of the Karstphanomen, and it stood to reason that Jack would, sooner or later, get round to murdering Leland Carlyle. So they followed him and waited for someone to make an attempt on his life.

Carlyle and his wife had taken Hardwick House for the summer months. It was situated on Brook Street near Grosvenor Square, and after leaving the coffeehouse, Carlyle returned there. Mr and Mrs Parker waited outside, across the road in the mews, for hours, but the high judge did not reappear.

"I'm terribly bored," Mrs Parker said.

"You're speaking English."

"When in England . . . It's good practicing. But I'm bored."

"Yes," Mr Parker said. "This job of work is less straightforward than I would prefer."

"It's all tangled up in itself."

"Anything involving Jack the Ripper is bound to be. We're tasked with discovering the whereabouts of a fellow who escaped the police and a whole club of gents that've been trying to find him for a year now."

"And killing him. That's the fun part, of course."

"Of course. That's always the fun part."

"It's just, there aren't usually so many dull parts before the killing."

"But it's worth it, wouldn't you say? We'll be the ones to finally put an end to this whole Ripper business."

"You know he plans to have us killed in turn. Carlyle does."

"You think so, too?"

"I do. We'll do his dirty business for him, and then he'll do away with us and put it all behind him."

"Well," Mr Parker said, "I don't plan to let him do that."

"I didn't think you did. But forewarned is forearmed."

"I am always armed."

Mrs Parker laughed, a light tinkling sound that always reminded Mr Parker of chimes in a gentle breeze. Part of what he enjoyed about the act of murder was the way it made Mrs Parker laugh. It reminded him of her childhood in the country, of watching her ride horses and playing with her in the wood behind the estate, where she had tortured small creatures for fun.

"Let's go and come back tomorrow," Mrs Parker said.

Mr Parker could rarely deny Mrs Parker anything, but now he frowned. A deep crease appeared between his eyes. "He may not be coming out tonight, but it's still possible Jack the Ripper might make an appearance while we're gone, and then we'll have lost the only means we have for finding him."

"He won't come tonight," Mrs Parker said.

"And you know this because?"

"Because he's no doubt off doing something more fun than watching a boring old house. Something gooey, like slitting open a serving wench and turning her on a spit over a crackling fire. Watching the fat roll down the skin of her thighs and sizzle on the coals." Her eyes were closed, and she licked her top lip.

He watched the tip of her pink tongue. "And if he's not? If he's waiting for us to leave so he can kill our client before we do?"

"Then I will most sincerely apologize to you," she said.

"Don't you want to find our target quickly?"

"We're not going to find him tonight."

He felt he had pushed her as hard as he could. Any more and she might become dangerous. "Very well," he said. "What would you prefer?"

"That place," she said. "That place he told us about."

"He," in this context, could mean only one person: an old man they had killed in his bedroom in Alsace. His death had taken several days to play out, and Mr Parker's daughter had spent the entirety of that time at his side. Mr Parker had slept on and off, but Mrs Parker had never slept; she had listened to the old man's ravings as his body had fed on itself and his fluids had soaked into the mattress beneath him.

"That place is in France, my dear," Mr Parker said. "He was talking about Paris, I think."

"And where are we now?"

"London."

"And they are different?"

"They are some miles apart from each other."

"Can we go to Paris tonight?"

"Not if we want to fulfill this contract." She was tugging her earlobe and tapping her finger against her throat and, watching her, Mr Parker began to feel nervous himself. Without realizing he was doing it, he began to rub the two-inch scar on his left temple. One of many reminders he carried of Mrs Parker's temper. "Very well," he said. "We need to stay in London if we're to make any money this trip, but perhaps we can take the rest of the evening off and find something fun to do here."

Mrs Parker instantly relaxed and lowered her hand from her throat. Mr Parker smiled at her. She really was quite lovely when she wasn't screaming or hurting him.

"Nobody old this time," she said. "I want to find someone young and healthy. It's so much more satisfying when they start out strong."

"Yes, my darling," Mr Parker said. He reasoned that they might find a suitable distraction for her in Hyde Park and gestured for her to walk ahead of him down Brook Street. There was no way he would have her at his back. Never again.

24

Esther Paxton was worried. She had taken down the wire from across her front window and folded and put away the display clothes. She had shuttered the windows, but she'd left the globe above the door lit. She had not seen Walter all day. Normally he would have returned before she closed up the shop. He would have walked her home, and perhaps they would have shared a light supper along the way. Then he would go back and lock up the shop and get busy rolling cigarettes and cigars for the following day's business. He was unfailing in his routine. But today he had been gone before she arrived and there was still no sign of him.

Of course, he was free to leave, to find another place to live, though Esther would miss the extra income. But surely he would have told her, would have given her proper notice, would have been more considerate than to simply disappear. There were unresolved issues between them, at least she felt there were, and Walter would not have left her alone without warning.

She had just resolved to stroll about the neighborhood and look for him when there was a knock at the door. She peeked out the small inset window and saw a tall man with dark wavy hair smiling back at her. He was quite handsome, but there was something unusual about his smile, like it had been painted on, like he was a mannequin made up to look human. She banished the thought and silently chided herself for being so ridiculous. She was just worried about Walter, that was all.

"I'm afraid I'm closed for today," she said, loudly enough to be heard through the door. "Please come back in the morning."

"Oh," the stranger said, "but I have a message from Walter Day for you."

"Walter Day?" (Was that Walter's full name?) "A message?"

"It's a note from him. He's sorry to be so late this evening, but wondered if you'd wait for him. There's more, but he wanted me to give it to you myself."

"Please slide it under the door." That mannequin smile still bothered her. She was watching the man through the window, and his mouth barely moved as he spoke. He was like a puppet being worked by invisible strings and rods.

"There's also a small box here," from the unmoving grin. "I'm afraid it won't all fit."

"Oh, very well," Esther said. She threw the bolt and opened the door.

The man stepped across the threshold and removed his hat. He was carrying Walter's cane, with the bright brass knob at the top. He bowed to her, too low and too formal, making a show of it. "Thank you, madam."

"Where is it? The box?"

"Oh, that." The man turned and shut the door behind him. "I'm afraid I lied about the box. But I do have a message for you from

Walter Day. Or rather, it's about Walter Day. He didn't send it personally."

"Who are you?"

"Didn't I introduce myself? Please, call me Jack."

He raised Walter's walking stick high above his head and brought it down in a glimmering arc.

25

Leland Carlyle woke in the wee hours with a dreadful realization that felt physical, like some enormous toad sitting on his chest, crushing him, sucking the breath out of him. The girl at the coffeehouse, the one with the apron, she had heard everything. Carlyle couldn't remember what he'd said, what the Parkers had said. He had been careful, hadn't hinted at any impropriety while the girl had been within earshot, but now he felt convinced that she had listened in. Why wouldn't she? Carlyle was clearly a gentleman of means, and girls like that were always trying to better themselves. She would have listened to their conversation. She might, even now, be planning to blackmail him, might be writing a note to his wife or to the authorities. He should have known, should have been more careful.

He snorted and rubbed his eyes. They were tearing up, and he felt a lump in his throat. It was so hard to be strong, to remain resolute in all situations, all day every day. Sometimes a man struggled to bear up under it all. Especially when there were so many people around him who would take advantage if he showed weakness, who were waiting for an opportunity to turn things around, to work against him.

He had been strong once, much stronger than he was now, but a year of being hunted like a damn fox had begun to wear him down. He jumped at every shadow now, distrusted every new person he met. It was impossible to be too careful when Jack was lurking somewhere nearby.

If the girl had heard anything—had she? He felt certain, but he'd also felt certain he was being careful—if she had heard him use specific names or heard him mention the killing specifically, then she was a danger to him and to the entire Karstphanomen. The thought of disappointing those worthy men was somehow worse than his fear of Jack.

He turned over onto his side and stared at the wall, glad Mrs Carlyle slept in another room. Perhaps the girl hadn't heard him order a murder. And perhaps, if she had heard, she would applaud him for hiring the murder of Jack the Ripper. Surely nobody wanted that madman running around free.

But if she had heard, and no matter what she thought of it, she could implicate Leland Carlyle, she could ruin him.

He would have to do something about her.

Perhaps he could add her to the task he'd given the Parkers. One more body would be nothing to them. They could dispatch her easily. But, of course, in doing so they would have a certain power over him. They would know that he was frightened of a girl. And what would they charge him for it? Whatever the amount, it would be difficult to hide any more money from his accountant. No, he couldn't ask them to take care of any more than they already were.

He would have to do it himself.

And, satisfied that he had arrived at the proper conclusion, Leland Carlyle turned onto his back again and fell instantly asleep. Within moments he was snoring.

26

At the back of the Whistle and Flute, in a corner where there were no lamps and the light from the street failed to reach, was a large round table with four chairs. Blackleg was not always to be found sitting at this table, but when he was gone nobody else sat there. It was his table. And anyone who had the second chair, across from him, should be bearing good news if he wished to be seen anywhere again.

Hammersmith entered the pub and waited for his eyes to adjust. *How strange,* he thought, *that the gas lamps outside are so much brighter than the light inside.* The table in the corner was occupied. The chair opposite Blackleg was empty. The burly criminal was reading a newspaper, and there were two glasses of beer in front of him. Sometimes Hammersmith had seen men pull chairs over from neighboring tables and play games of Happy Families with the powerful criminal, but this was not one of those times. Hammersmith snaked his way around the other tables, which were set about in no discernible pattern, and pulled out the empty chair. Blackleg folded his newspaper and slid one of the two glasses across to Hammersmith.

"You're on time," Blackleg said.

"I always am."

"I took the liberty of ordering for you."

"Thanks." Hammersmith raised the glass and drained half of the murky liquid, then wiped his lips on his sleeve. He noticed a suspicious yellow stain on his cuff and frowned at it. He couldn't remember eating or drinking anything yellow recently.

"This about your missing mate again?" Blackleg gestured for another two glasses, and a woman across the room nodded to show she'd seen him.

"It is," Hammersmith said.

"I been lookin'. Like I told you I would. And had my girls lookin'. Everybody else, too."

"You know what he looked like?"

Blackleg smiled. He knew whatever he wanted to know. He had started as a common criminal, crossing picket lines at the docks, but had worked his way to the center of certain crime rings in London. He controlled all the illegal activities that his warped moral code told him were necessary to society, which meant in practical terms that he avoided anything that might harm children. And unnecessary murders.

What he considered "unnecessary" seemed to change from moment to moment.

"And there's no sign of him in any of your . . ." Hammersmith broke off, not sure how to phrase the rest of the question.

"Naw, none of my people have seen anything," Blackleg said.

Hammersmith took another pull from the glass and stared off at the back wall of the pub, which was streaked liberally with rust and mildew.

"Don't take it bad," Blackleg said. "One good thing is there's no sign of any bodies or nuthin', either."

Hammersmith turned his gaze on the criminal and scowled.

"What I mean," Blackleg said, "is I done questioned everybody I know might've done your friend bodily harm, might've had it in for a peeler and taken matters in their own hands, so to speak. Nobody knows nuthin'."

"Nothing they're telling you."

Blackleg sat back and smiled. The woman appeared and set down two more glasses, foam sloshing over her hands and across the table-top. She flicked her fingers at the wall and hurried away.

"They'd tell me," Blackleg said. "The one thing, the *one* thing, is they don't lie to me. Most other problems I can help with or forgive, but lying destroys trust, and without trust . . . well, what do we have?" He spread his hands wide, then clapped them together and lifted his glass.

"So there's no body," Hammersmith said. "No body after a year of looking. Then someone hid his body very well, don't you think?"

"No. No, I don't just mean there ain't a corpse. I mean nobody kilt him."

"I mean no offense, but isn't it possible someone else harmed him, someone you don't know or doesn't work for you?"

"No, it's not possible without my knowing. A body's a big thing, it is, if it's a grown man. You can chop it up, you can melt it with certain things, but then you've got pieces or chemicals, you've got evidence. That's the sort of evidence you lot, you police, look for. But that's the evidence the rest of us hide from you, and I know about hidin' better than you or anybody you know. Nuthin' stays hidden from me if I want it found."

Hammersmith frowned and sipped his beer.

Blackleg leaned forward and clasped his hands atop his folded newspaper. "Sumpin's odd about all this, I'll grant you that," he said. "But what I'm givin' you here's good news. If he's dead, he died in another city, maybe a different country entire. But he didn't die here. Not in my city."

Hammersmith nodded. He had inquired in other cities, other countries, spent time in Paris, in America and Canada. All of those places were dead ends.

"We been lookin' for Jack, too, you know," Blackleg said. "Made it hard for him to operate, hard to get about easy. If he's still in the city, he's had to go to ground somewheres. Like a rat in a hole. Ol' Blackleg's been a busy man lately."

"It sounds like it."

"Just so long's you know I'm doin' what I can. We'll find one or the other, and we'll do it soon. And if I don't, you will. Then Jack'll lead us to your mate or he'll lead us to Jack. And then we can go on about our business like old times."

"I hope you're right." Hammersmith finished his second beer and set the glass down, took a deep breath, and stood. "Thank you."

"You owe me now," Blackleg said. "And you know I won't ask nothin' bad, like, but you'd best be ready to pay if I do ask it."

Hammersmith felt his scalp tingle, but he nodded. "I know." He had gone to the Devil for a favor and had been well aware of the price when he did it. There had been nothing else he could do.

"You're a good man, Nevil." Hammersmith wasn't sure how to take the compliment coming, as it did, from the worst criminal in London. "If anybody can find this bloke, it's you. Keep at it."

Of course he would keep at it. What else was he going to do? He'd opened an agency for the express purpose of keeping at it. He had employees now who depended on him to keep at it. And, of course, his closest friend was out there somewhere, probably in terrible trouble, and counting on Nevil Hammersmith to keep at it.

He left the pub and stepped outside. The air was cool and wet, and he coughed, a deep booming sound that cleared his lungs and surprised him. He stepped off the curb and sat down and rested his arms on his knees. He stared out into the dark street. It stretched in both directions away from him, disappearing into the fog.

Which way to go? Was there anywhere he hadn't already looked for Walter Day?

Hammersmith put his head down on his arms and closed his eyes. If only he had Day there to help him look for Day. He was only one half of a team, after all. It shouldn't all be on his shoulders.

"Oi! Are you Mr Hammersmith?" Hammersmith looked up to see a boy on a bicycle approaching him. The boy stopped against the curb and stood there with one foot on the ground and his head tilted, breathing hard and blinking at him. "I said, are you Hammersmith, sir? Do you know him?"

"Um. Yes, I'm Hammersmith. But what—"

"Oh, thank God, sir. I been all over since this afternoon. Practically all night. To your flat, to Scotland Yard, to your office. Everywhere. Your lady at the agency opened up and said you might be here, and thank God again, 'cause you are and now I can go have a rest. My legs are done and gone."

"What is it? Do you have a message for me?"

"Right." The boy patted his jacket pockets and found a folded piece of notepaper. He handed it over.

"Who sent this?" Hammersmith took the note and stood, angling the paper so it caught the dim gaslight from a globe above him.

"'Nother lady name of Day, sir."

"Claire." Hammersmith opened the note and dropped it. He bent and picked it up, wiped it on his trousers, and read it again.

"Sir? Is it good news?"

Hammersmith looked up at the boy, who was holding out his hand for a coin. He smiled. "It's the best news," Hammersmith said. "Walter's alive!"

BOOK TWO

S omewhere between an array of water closet cabinets and a jumble of upside-down daybeds, Anna had got herself turned around and stepped off the path. Confident that she knew the way back, she had circled around an enormous bath and shower combination, had turned left at a washstand, and had stumbled over a pull toy shaped like a frog. She had sat for a moment, waiting for her skinned knee to stop hurting quite so terribly much, and when she stood up again she realized that she did not at all know the way back. Nor did she know the way forward. The path was completely obscured in both directions by wooden things of every type and sort.

"Well," she sniffed. "This is a fine situation you've got yourself into, Anna."

She almost answered herself but did not want to appear mad, and so she set her shoulders and chose a direction that seemed promising and marched off, expecting at any moment to rediscover the path.

When the sun set somewhere behind an enormous stack of church doors, Anna stopped.

"At least it isn't terribly cold," she said. "But I wonder if anything lives in this wood and whether it is friendly. That is, if there's anything here at all."

"I have wondered the very same thing," said a voice behind her.

She turned and saw a perfectly formed little girl made of wood, holding a wooden cross that was nearly as big as she was. She was no more than two feet tall and she balanced the cross on one end in the dirt. Long tangled strings stretched from the four corners of the cross to the girl's wooden arms and legs, which were each jointed at the middle with stout wooden hinges. Her head was a smooth polished ball attached to her body by a broomstick, and her quizzical little face and glossy hair were painted on.

"Why, your dress is painted on as well, isn't it?" Anna asked.

The girl looked down at herself and then looked back up at Anna, but her expression did not change. "Of course it's painted," she replied. "I'm a puppet."

"Are you really?" Anna said. "It's only that I've never seen a puppet speak all by itself."

"And I have never seen a puppet without any strings."

"But I'm not a puppet. My name is Anna, which is a very proper name for a girl. And my dress is made of cotton, not paint. But I do wish my clothing were painted on. It seems ever so much more convenient." She held out her hand, and the puppet girl steadied her cross before taking it. "And what is your name?"

"I do not have a name," said the girl. "I have never met my puppeteer and so I have never been named."

"But what do your friends say when they wish to get your attention?"

"I have no friends."

"How awful."

"But I have only been alive for a single day and haven't met anyone else."

"Well, now you have met me and I will be your friend. Now we must *have a name for me to call you. You must have something you call yourself. When you are thinking about what to do next, whether to have a bit of something to eat or a spot of tea with milk or perhaps you would rather play a parlor game with another little puppet who lives down the lane and so you say to yourself, 'Well, so-and-so, I will go to the kitchen and see what Cook's preparing for luncheon before I decide what to do.' What do you say instead of 'so-and-so' when you think to yourself?"*

"What is a luncheon?"

"Oh, this is no good at all. I can see that I shall have to name you."

"How kind of you."

"What are puppets usually called? Punch or Judy, I suppose."

"I do not think I would like to be called Judy. And especially not Punch. Perhaps you might simply call me Marionette Puppet, since that is what I am."

"Then it's settled. It's a pleasure to make your acquaintance, Mary Annette. May I call you Mary for short?"

"If it makes you happy to do so," the girl said.

"It's only that Annette is so close to being my own name, and I wouldn't want to get us confused."

"Do you think you might?"

"No, I don't think so, but it's always best to err on the side of caution, don't you think?"

"I cannot think. I have a wooden head."

"But you only just now said that you were wondering something. It's the very first thing you said to me. And wondering is much the same as thinking."

"Is it really?"

"I believe so. Is your head entirely wooden?"

"Through and through."

Anna leaned forward and peered at the girl's shiny golden hair. "That must be quite helpful whenever you fall down and don't get a knot on your head. Knots are ever so painful."

"I am sure I wouldn't know about that," said the little wooden girl, "but I do worry about cracking it."

"Well, if you can't think, then you shouldn't worry, either. You're only getting the worst of it that way."

The girl stood still and didn't reply. Anna hated to have to carry the entire conversation herself, but she supposed she ought to set a proper example in manners for the puppet. "Are there more like you?"

"Puppets, you mean? If there are, I have not encountered them yet," Mary said.

"Yesterday this was a plain empty field with nothing in it except grass and dirt and old stumps and bugs. Before that it was a huge place filled with trees, and Peter and I played here every day with a little boy who was our best friend. But then men came with saws and wagons and took all the trees away to make other things out of the wood. I suppose you must be made from one of the trees that was here before. All of the wood must have become homesick and come back again to the place it was born."

Mary looked all round her at the furniture and tools and flooring. "But I wasn't born. I was made. Who made me?"

Anna shrugged. "I don't know." She looked up at the sky. The moon had risen above the coatracks, and stars were visible in the deep blue overhead. "I do miss Peter," she said. "I'm trying to find him, but I'm afraid he's lost."

"I will help you," Mary said.

"Oh, will you?"

"Yes. You are my first friend." Anna imagined she could see her smile, but her painted face did not move. "And perhaps we will find the puppeteer along the way."

"The puppeteer?"

"The one who made me. I need someone to hold this." Mary hoisted the joined beams of her cross onto her shoulder.

"I'm sure we shall find them both," Anna said. She slipped her hand under Mary's elbow, and they walked together into the darkness of the wood, Mary dragging the tail end of her cross, which left a long, ragged mark in the dirt behind them.

—RUPERT WINTHROP, FROM
The Wandering Wood (1893)

27

Sir Edward Bradford had been up before the sun and had dressed quietly in the dark, careful not to wake Elizabeth. She hadn't been sleeping well lately. He swiped imaginary dust from the surface of his mahogany desk. It had been difficult to get the desk moved from Great Scotland Yard, but Sir Edward could not imagine his office without it. Still, it was much too large for the cramped room, and his visitors' knees were smashed up against the other side of the desk. Claire Day and Inspector Jimmy Tiffany were clearly uncomfortable, but were doing their best to appear at ease.

"Are we waiting for Mr Hammersmith?"

As if on cue the door opened, slamming into the back of Claire's chair, and Hammersmith poked his head into the office. "They told me I was expected." He had purple smudges under his eyes and Sir Edward wondered whether the lad had slept.

"Come in, Nevil," Sir Edward said. He waved his hand as Hammersmith navigated the end of the desk. "Watch the corner there."

Hammersmith bowed slightly in Claire's direction and shook

Tiffany's hand before sitting and placing a slim file folder on the desk in front of him.

"Good, we're all here," Sir Edward said. He raked his fingers through his white beard. The empty left sleeve of his jacket was pinned to his shoulder, and the head of the tiger that had taken his arm was mounted on the wall above him, a constant reminder to others that the commissioner was still quite capable despite his loss.

"Claire has good news," Hammersmith said. He was fidgeting in his seat with barely controlled excitement.

"I don't mean to be rude," Tiffany said, "but your news should wait a minute or two." He smiled at Claire. "We have some good news of our own. Commissioner, you should tell them."

"Yes, of course," Sir Edward said. He indicated the telephone on his desk. "Yesterday I received a call. It was . . . um, it was Walter Day on the other end of the line. Walter called me."

"Are you sure?" Claire stood up and leaned over the desk as if she might hear him better. "Are you positive it was Walter?"

"I believe it was. He didn't say his name, but I recognized his voice."

"What did he say?"

"He asked for help."

"Did he tell you where he was? Was he calling from the department store?"

Hammersmith cut in. "Why did he need help?"

"He didn't tell me," Sir Edward said. "He rang off almost immediately. But the point is, he's alive."

"I knew that he was." Claire felt behind her for her chair and lowered herself into it. "I always knew."

"Why did you ask about a department store?"

"That's our news, sir," Hammersmith said. "Claire saw him."

"You saw him?" Tiffany's eyes widened. "He was at a shop somewhere?"

"Yesterday," Claire said. "He was at Plumm's. On an upper level, talking to someone."

"Who? Who was he talking to?"

"Where is Plumm's?"

"One at a time, please," Claire said. "Plumm's is the new place on Moorgate. I went there to research my new book and he was there. I was certain it was him, but I only saw him for the briefest of moments. I'm afraid I . . ." She trailed off, embarrassed.

"Is there a way to . . ." Hammersmith motioned at the telephone. Inspector Tiffany nodded. He reached out and tapped the phone's receiver.

"I've already talked to Sarah, the girl at the exchange. Twice. She doesn't remember where the call originated. A dead end, I'm afraid."

"I receive one telephone call in a month and that girl can't remember anything about it," Sir Edward said. He sighed and shook his head.

"Would you mind if I talked to her?"

"Nevil, I already said I—" Tiffany broke off and waved a hand at Hammersmith. "Do what you want."

"I don't doubt you," Hammersmith said. "I only meant—"

"It's our first real clue in a year," Sir Edward said. He smiled at Hammersmith. "You want to follow it. I understand, and so does Inspector Tiffany. Isn't that right, James?"

Tiffany nodded, but his jaw was clenched.

"You may speak to Sarah," Sir Edward said. "But it's not necessarily a good use of your time."

"We have to do something," Claire said. "You have to keep looking. Go to Plumm's. Walter's alive."

"Of course, Mrs Day. Nobody's proposed that we stop looking. If anything, this prompts us to redouble our efforts. I'm putting the entirety of the Murder Squad on this case today. Most of the men knew Walter well and will recognize him on sight. I apologize to you, Mrs Day. We've let the search dwindle over these past few months, and that's regrettable."

"Sir," Tiffany said, "with all due respect, and you know how much I've wanted to recover Inspector Day, but we have so many other cases, we're already worked to the bone."

"I'm afraid that will always be the case, Inspector."

"I didn't mean to imply that I was unwilling or that I haven't already spent long hours searching."

"Of course not. Nobody here thought you were unwilling to help." In fact, Sir Edward was sure everyone else in the room disliked Tiffany and questioned his willingness to do anything other than the letter of his job, but he was a good policeman. "But with the certainty that Mr Day is still very much alive, now is the time to strike, to bring to bear all of our expertise, all of our manpower, all of our determination to recover our missing comrade, don't you think?"

"Of course, sir."

"Good. That's settled."

"How can I help? What can I do?"

"You, Mr Hammersmith, in addition to having been a very good policeman yourself, were Mr Day's closest ally here. You've stayed with the case all this time and have the most knowledge of it. My men are at your disposal."

Tiffany jumped to his feet. His chair tipped backward, but didn't fall. The space was too narrow, and the top of the chair wedged against the wall and pushed against Tiffany's knees so that he had to bend forward and lean against the desk, undermining his dramatic gesture. He pointed at Hammersmith.

"He's not . . . He's not Scotland Yard. He's not . . . I'm sorry, Hammersmith, but you're not a policeman now. I don't even know what you are or what you do with yourself. You have a shopfront somewhere. You don't command . . . Well, sir, he can't hold a command."

Sir Edward smiled and paused long enough for Tiffany to sit back down and compose himself.

"He can hold any command I give him, Mr Tiffany. Unless he would prefer not to. I know it's unusual, so I'll leave it to you, Nevil. All I want is to see Mr Day back here, safe and sound. Whatever gets us that result."

Hammersmith stood, carefully, and paced around the scant two-foot-square area of the office that wasn't filled with desks, chairs, and people. He looked like a dog chasing its tail. "If it's all the same to you, sir," he said, "I'd rather Tiffany have the command."

"Very well. But I'd like you to share your files and any findings with him, if you're willing."

"Of course, sir." He placed a hand atop the file folder on the commissioner's desk. "I've summarized my findings of the past year. I'm afraid it's not much."

"Every little bit, my boy. And, Tiffany, let's make a plan to divide the city up so we can start the search as soon as possible. We'll start with this department store at the center. I don't want Day slipping through our fingers again."

Tiffany nodded and stood, more carefully this time. He motioned to Hammersmith, and the two men left the office. Sir Edward asked Claire to stay behind for a moment.

"I owe you an apology, Claire. We should have looked harder. Damnit, we practically gave up on Walter. Pardon the language."

"I know you did your best. As Mr Tiffany said, my husband wasn't your only concern."

"No, he wasn't. But he was one of our own."

"Was?"

Sir Edward shook his head. "No, you're right. You're right. He *is* one of us. And we'll find him now." He leaned forward and spoke more quietly so that Claire could barely hear him. "We will find him. I promise you that."

Claire opened her mouth, then closed it and smiled at the commissioner. She turned and left the office and shut the door behind her.

28

Mr Parker woke up late and cursed himself for a fool. He couldn't afford to be careless. Ever. He turned his head and saw nothing, then sat slowly up and looked all round the room. Mrs Parker was gone.

His sense of unease was tempered by his pleasure at discovering he was alive to experience another day. He placed his bare feet on the floor, careful to avoid the wire that ran between the legs of the bed. He disengaged his snares and padded barefoot across the room to the door. The alarm there had been disengaged and the key was missing.

He breathed a deep sigh of relief and busied himself with the morning routine. He washed his face and removed the wooden form that kept his mustache in its proper shape overnight, then brushed his hair and his beard until they glowed. He worked a little Macassar oil into his mustache and beard and sculpted them into sharp points that stuck out from his face at right angles. His fingers were a bit greasy, and he rubbed them dry on his eyebrows, taming the stray hairs there. He examined his handiwork in the polished metal mirror on the vanity and smiled. He had always been a handsome devil. It was no wonder Mrs Parker had fallen for him.

By the time she returned to their rooms, he was fully dressed and all the traps had been disabled. They were free to move about the room without injuring themselves. As long as he remained alert, Mrs Parker posed no danger to him. But they both knew that there would be a day when he let down his guard or forgot to set his snares and that would be his last day. Until then, they had resolved to enjoy each other's company and make the best of their situation.

"I brought you something," Mrs Parker said. She checked once more for wires and blades before she sat on the edge of his bed and held out a plain paper sack for him.

"What is it?" He kept the bag at arm's length while opening the top, but to his extreme relief there were no human body parts inside.

"Biscuits," she said. "I was passing a cart and remembered which kind you liked."

"How kind of you." He sniffed one and took a bite. It was not in Mrs Parker's nature to poison him. "Have you breakfasted?"

"I ate without you. I'm sorry."

"No, no, that's quite all right." He suppressed a shudder.

"You were sleeping so soundly, and I found the key to my shackles. You shouldn't leave it where I can reach, you know. Anyhow, I let myself out and decided to explore a bit while I had the time to myself."

"I thought I'd left the key well out of reach," he said.

She gave him a knowing look and waggled one eyebrow. He smiled. She was able to stretch and contort herself to the most unlikely extremes. She was a marvel, truly.

"I did have to dislocate my left arm, but it's back in place now," she said. "This city has so many interesting things to see."

"How long were you out?"

"Oh, three or perhaps four hours. I wasn't able to sleep well."

"Sorry to hear it." If she had been out by herself for three or four hours, there would be at least one item in the newspapers. But he knew that nobody had identified or followed her. She wouldn't have betrayed the location of their rooms by returning if there had been the slightest chance. She read his expression and smiled again.

"We'll pick up a copy of the *Times*," she said.

"Will I be able to infer what you've been up to?"

"If you read closely."

"Not front-page stuff, I hope."

"You wound me. Nothing so spectacular. We haven't finished our work in London. You know I don't soil the nest before the job's done."

"I apologize."

"I do hope Mr Ripper makes his move today. I'm growing anxious."

"If nothing happens today, we'll find another way," Mr Parker said.

"Oh, good." She sat back and stared out the window. "The sun's finally out. I do hate how dreary this city can be."

They had divided the duties that defined their unusual occupation, and Mr Parker was the strategist. Mrs Parker was rubbish at planning, but she carried out other aspects of the work with great gusto. She was also the prettiest woman Mr Parker had ever seen. He loved her with every fiber of his being, and the only thing he feared more than her presence was the possibility that she might someday leave him.

He polished off his last biscuit and checked the mirror again. Upon removing a crumb from his mustache, he crossed to the door and opened it wide. He picked up his case (heavy with saws, mallets, scalpels, three revolvers, a stout length of rope, and a pair of manacles) and gestured for Mrs Parker to lead the way out.

"Come," he said. "Let's find our pigeon again."

Mrs Parker leapt from the bed like a cat and stopped in the doorway for a kiss before bounding out the door. Mr Parker watched her walk away, his eyes wide and his nostrils flared. He still considered himself the luckiest man in the world.

29

W ell," Tiffany said, "come along if you're coming."

He led the way to a cluttered desk in the far corner of the Murder Squad's room. It was, in its way, isolated, pushed up against the wall as far from the other men's desks as it could be. Piles of paper existed in a sort of precarious détente, threatening at any moment to slide off each other to the floor. Tiffany pulled out a chair and gestured for Hammersmith to sit. Before Hammersmith could demur, Tiffany plopped down on the corner of the desk, toppling an avalanche of papers behind him. He tossed the file folder Hammersmith had brought on top of the mess and it somehow stuck. Hammersmith took the offered chair.

Tiffany tapped the file. "Save me time. What's in it?"

"Not a lot, actually," Hammersmith said. "I did the usual sort of follow-up, went over Walter's old house half a dozen times or more without seeing anything amiss. Fiona Kingsley drew up a terrific picture of him and I took it around, showed it to everyone on that street so many times, I thought they might stone me if they saw me coming round again. Took it across the park, too, and showed it on the other side. Nothing came of it. Quite a few people there knew him; most avoided his house. Too many bad things had happened there, and none of the neighbors wanted a killer visiting them in the middle of the night. Only the one of 'em saw Walter that night."

"The old woman."

"Aye. Talked to her two or three times, but she's not all there. A bit mad, I think. She says she saw Walter get in a black carriage. Right after that, she saw the Devil himself stroll away down the street, laughing, she says."

"The Devil." Tiffany rolled his eyes. "Helpful."

"Couldn't give a good description of him. Wavy sort of dark hair, she thinks. Tall, thin. And evil."

"Right. Evil's, what, a physical trait?"

"I have no idea."

Tiffany sighed. "So I know most of this already. Anything new? Anything in the last month or so?"

"Nothing."

"The old woman, did she say if Day had his hat? Did he have his cane? The one with the brass knob at the end?"

"He had them both. At least as far as she can say. But I wouldn't rely on her for much."

"No."

"I've gone over everything again and again. I've talked to every cab driver, every private carriage owner I can find in the vicinity. I'm at my wit's end. No, I was at my wit's end eight months ago. The trail is dead."

"And yet Walter's alive," Tiffany said. "Or so Sir Edward believes."

"I'll talk to the telephone dispatcher."

"I said I've talked to her." Tiffany ran a hand through his hair and stroked his mustache with his fingertips. It looked to Hammersmith like a nervous tic. "You're welcome to do it again, but there's nothing there. I feel like we're being played with."

"Oh," Hammersmith said, "we are. We quite definitely are."

"By the Devil?" Tiffany chuckled. "Well, there's strength in numbers, I suppose. If we're working together now, however much that's actually practical—which it ain't—but if we're putting our heads together maybe something will finally fall out."

"I know you can't be pleased," he said.

Tiffany shook his head and frowned. "I don't care. Not really. It's not like I don't want to find Walter."

"Good. That's good."

"Yes, yes. But I've also got a woman clubbed her husband to death and took the kids off away somewheres. I don't find her, who knows what she'll do with 'em. And that's a case I could use Walter's help with, but of course I don't got him. And I've got three men who took a woman into an alley and done horrible things to her. She's alive, but I want those men, and I want 'em now. Those are just since yesterday, never mind everything else I ain't got to yet." He waved a hand over the reams of reports on the desk behind him. "So I'll give you what I got and I'll do what I can, and so will every other man in this room, but I'll not answer to you, no matter what Sir Edward's got to say on the matter. I can't. I just don't got the time and I can't go back to that poor woman or to that dead man's mother and tell them I was busy with summat else, can I?"

Hammersmith nodded, then shook his head, unsure of how to agree with the inspector. "I understand," he said.

"Then you tell me what you need and I'll do my best."

"I don't . . . I don't really know what I need."

"What? Men? Guns? I've precious few of either. Same with information. You're welcome to our files, but if we'd found anything out, we'd have let you know by now."

"I've got used to acting alone. Walter was always the one—"

"Right. Well, no sense in that now you've got something real to go on. Take Jones. He's a good fellow."

Hammersmith and Tiffany both looked up at the sound of approaching footsteps. A man as big around as he was tall moved between the queues of desks as if he owned them. And in a way he did. Hammersmith stood and shook Sergeant Kett's hand.

"Good to see you again, boy," Kett said. "Inspector Tiffany, I couldn't help but overhear." (Hammersmith hid a smile. The sergeant had been across the room, but had ears like a bat.) "If it's all the same to you, I'd like to offer myself in place of Jones. I might've said some things to young Hammersmith here that were uncalled for, and I'd like to make up for it."

Tiffany shook his head and frowned. "We need you here, Kett."

"Sergeant Fawkes can handle my duties along with his own for a few days if it comes to that."

"I'd still rather send Jones along than lose you here," Tiffany said.

"Day was a good lad. He was one of my boys, and I don't sleep so good at night since he's missing. Been a long time without a good sleep now."

Tiffany leaned forward, away from his desk. His hands were clasped above his knees and his head was down. He resembled a grief-stricken man in prayer, and Hammersmith wondered how long it had been since Tiffany had slept. How long since any of these men had slept.

At last, Tiffany straightened up and slipped off the corner of the desk. He leaned back against it and crossed his arms over his chest. He nodded. "We'll make do with Fawkes for a day or two. But, gentlemen, let's find Walter fast. Find him fast and bring him home and maybe we can all put this nasty business behind us."

Hammersmith stood. "I suppose we'll tread the same ground again. With two of us at it, we might be able to circle farther out, talk to more people."

"Wait." Tiffany tapped the folder again. "You said the Kingsley girl drew a picture of Day for you?"

Fiona Kingsley worked as an illustrator of children's books, but she had grown up assisting her father, Dr Bernard Kingsley, London's premiere forensic examiner. She had accompanied him to crime scenes and sketched them for the police. Lately, she had used witness descriptions to sketch criminals, giving the detectives of the Murder Squad a visual aid in tracking and catching them.

"She's a good artist," Kett said. "I'm sure it was a good likeness."

Tiffany waved at Kett, irritated. "Of course. But did you ask her dad?"

"Ask him what?"

"For help."

"What could he do?"

"He does that thing of his. Puts powder all over and finds fingerprints."

"What good would that do? And you don't even believe in that, anyway."

Tiffany leaned forward and scowled up at Hammersmith. "I believe in anything that solves a case."

"But you said—"

"I say a lot of things. What does it matter what I said? Turn up the doctor and take him along, if he'll go. He's smarter than the rest of us put together. One way or another, he might figure something out."

30

Dr Bernard Kingsley stood at a table in his laboratory and stared down at the body of an infant. The baby girl had been neglected, left too close to the hearth, and her cotton dress had caught fire. It looked to Kingsley as if the child had actually rolled into the flames. Burns covered three quarters of her tiny body, her dress had grafted itself to her charred skin in places, and her arms and legs had shriveled to stumps. Kingsley bent and kissed her forehead before pulling a sheet up over her. There was no need for an autopsy in this case. The cause of death was obvious. And horrible. He hoped her negligent parents had been burned as well.

"Father?"

Kingsley turned around, startled, and smiled at the sight of his youngest daughter, Fiona, who hesitated at the open door. He wiped his hands on a towel, crossed the room, and took her in his arms.

"Father, are you all right?"

Kingsley sighed and stepped back, looked around at the room he spent so much of his time in. Twelve burnished wooden tables stood in a row, each of them slanted just enough so that fluids could run off them into a drain in the center of the floor. Months before, electric lamps had been installed above the tables, and now the room was brighter, more clinical and less intimate than it had been under the old gas globes. Five of the tables were occupied by the dead. In addition to the baby and one of her siblings, there was a man who had choked to death on his dentures and a woman who had died of pneumonia. Only the fifth body posed any mystery regarding cause of death, and Kingsley had been waiting to get to it, dealing with the easier cases first.

"I suppose I'm a bit melancholy today," he said. "I've a bad feeling."

"Well, of course you do," Fiona said. "You've two children on your tables. The dead always affect you this way, children especially so."

"That must be it." He smiled at her. "What brings you round here today?"

"I wanted to visit you."

"Well, I'm glad of it. Come, let's get out of here."

He turned the knob that shut off the electric lights and ushered his daughter out into the passage, shutting the door behind them. There was a small window at eye level, and Kingsley imagined he could see the bodies on his table glowing slightly, as if they'd absorbed some of the light in the room. He wondered if the baby had been afraid of the dark.

They climbed the stairs to the ground floor, and Kingsley let his daughter lead him through a maze of hallways to his office. He stopped short of the door. It was halfway open and light spilled through into the hallway. He could see a shape moving on the other side of the frosted glass. He moved ahead of Fiona and pushed the door open.

Nevil Hammersmith jumped and turned around from the desk, where he'd been writing something on a slip of paper. He grinned and ran a hand through his dark mop of hair before stooping to pick up his hat. To Kingsley's eye, the former constable looked as if he'd lost weight in the months since he'd last seen him, and Kingsley wondered how that was even possible.

"I was just leaving you a note," Hammersmith said. "Thought maybe I'd find you downstairs in your laboratory, but just in case . . ."

"I was indeed down there. Good to see you again, Nevil. It's been too long."

"It has."

Hammersmith seemed ill at ease, averting his eyes, and Kingsley looked around, confused. Fiona seemed similarly uncomfortable. Kingsley frowned.

"To what do I owe this honor?"

"Ah," Hammersmith said. "Well, Tiffany, Inspector Tiffany . . . By the way, good to see you as well, Fiona."

Fiona mumbled something Kingsley couldn't make out. She curt-sied and backed out the door and was gone. The two men listened quietly until her footsteps had faded away down the hallway.

"That's odd," Kingsley said. "Perhaps she left something in the laboratory. I'm sure she'll be right back."

"Yes," Hammersmith said. He seemed relieved. "I'm sure she will. Um, about the . . . Inspector Tiffany thought you might be able to help us out with a little thing."

The doctor moved around and sat behind his desk. He indicated for Hammersmith to take the only other chair, but there was nowhere else to put the books that were stacked there, so Kingsley stood back up and they both leaned against the desk.

"Is it a new case?"

"Rather an old one, I'm afraid," Hammersmith said. "It's Walter Day." Kingsley listened as Hammersmith filled him in on the fresh developments: the phone call, Sir Edward's renewed determination, and the fact that Hammersmith was working with the police again. When Hammersmith had finished talking, Kingsley sat back down and stared at a corner of the ceiling, pursing his lips and moving them in and out, chewing over the information.

Finally he focused his gaze on Hammersmith, who had waited patiently. Kingsley was impressed. Patience was not one of the younger man's best qualities. "I've quite a lot to do here," Kingsley said. "Five people on my tables right now. They deserve my attention."

"Of course," Hammersmith said. He backed toward the open door. "I knew you were busy, but thought it would be foolish to pass up the opportunity to work with you again, however slim the chance."

Kingsley held up a hand to stop Hammersmith. "As I say, I've a lot to do, but none of it is as important as finding Walter. I'm ashamed to say I'd given him up for dead. If he's alive, of course I must do anything I possibly can to help."

"Oh, that's wonderful news. I haven't made much progress over the last few months. Hell, I haven't made any progress at all. I could use another pair of eyes, especially yours."

"What can I do?"

"Well, on that point I'm not entirely sure. Inspector Tiffany is available to us in an advisory capacity, and so is the entire Murder Squad, I suppose. And Sergeant Kett, you know him?"

"We've met."

"He's waiting for us. Well, for me, but I hoped I'd be bringing you along. He's at the house. The house where Walter disappeared."

"His old address."

"Yes," Hammersmith said. "Just so. Kett's going over the place again. Not as if it hasn't been gone over."

"One never knows. Even a hair found along the skirting might be the one clue needed to break through."

"A hair." Hammersmith sighed. "What about finger marks? Fingerprints? Whatever you want to call them, do you think they might be useful?"

"I did think so," Kingsley said. He closed his eyes. "When Walter disappeared, I went to that house and I looked for fingerprints. I looked for hair against the skirting, for blood, for footprints. I found nothing."

"I had no idea you'd even been there."

"Of course I was there. Walter was my . . . is my friend."

"Why didn't you tell me you'd investigated?"

"Why would I have? I didn't find anything that might have helped you."

"Well, I suppose . . ."

"Yes?"

"I suppose it would have been good to know I wasn't alone in the search."

31

Walter Day had been awake for hours, staring at a dusty orange wedge of sunlight that reminded him of an earlier time. He was in the bottom of a large cart that had a steel frame and canvas sides, and his only view was of high roof beams and dust motes and that wedge of sun. He had no energy, and his vision refused to clear, so that when he held his hand up in front of his face he saw three versions of it. The light, however feeble, pierced his brain, the smell overpowered him, and the thought of what must have happened to bring him to this place was unbearably painful.

He had delivered himself once again to Jack, and Jack had easily stripped him of his independence. Nothing Day did made any difference. Jack always won.

The room was quiet and dim, despite that single orange wedge, and eventually Day gripped the metal frame of his ineffectual cage and pulled himself up. It was awkward, and he fell two or three times to the bottom of the loose canvas sling before he was able to throw his weight the right way to tip the cart over. He landed badly, crushing the fingers of his right hand between the frame and the hard-wood floor. He flopped out and stuck his fingers in his mouth and looked all round him to see if anyone had heard and come running. But no one had. He was alone.

Or at least he seemed to be alone. Jack might be hidden some-where, watching him. But Jack might be anywhere at any time, and there was no longer any sense in fearing that. If the man wanted to show himself, he would, and there was nothing Day could do about it.

In the wan half-light, Day could see that he was in some sort of combination workshop and warehouse. He assumed the canvas cart had been used to remove him from the Plumm's office. The space was a large rectangle with a high ceiling, and each of the long walls was lined with benches and tables. There were bins beneath the ta-bles, and the handles of saws and mallets were visible from where Day crouched, his throbbing fingers still in his mouth. Chisels and picks and short serrated knives hung from nails in the walls, and the floor was mottled with dark stains that had been bleached and mopped, and bleached and mopped again. A machine Day didn't recognize was bolted to one end of the nearest bench. At the far wall was a stack of wooden blocks and planks, and a few of the benches held chunks of wood that were still in the process of transformation: into heads and hands and polished boxes complete with glass tops cut from enormous sheets that leaned against the sturdiest table in the corner. There were other canvas carts, perhaps a hundred of them shoved in random clusters round the tables, and a queue of dozens of silent female mannequins stood at attention behind Day, some of them missing hands and arms and heads, items still in prog-ress, still waiting to be revealed within the big blocks of wood.

He wondered what time it was. Despite the sunlight, nobody was at work; the half-finished carvings had been abandoned.

The room was utterly quiet except for Day, who panted and sniffed and shuffled in place. Dust motes swam through the air around him like curious fish. Beneath the scents of sawdust and iron there was a subtle burnt odor caused by the friction of tools against heavy materials. And there was another scent, too. Fetid, sweet, and coppery. Day recognized it immediately. There was a dead body in the room with him. He hoped it was an animal, a squirrel or rabbit that had burrowed in and died there, unnoticed beneath a bench. But he knew better. Jack didn't murder rabbits.

He lowered himself to his hands and knees and crawled over to the wall. He peered down the queue of benches behind the bins. It was too dark to see all the way to the far wall, but there were no shapes that reminded him of a human body. He pulled himself up and sat on the end of a bench, waiting for his fingers to stop aching, waiting for his head to stop aching. He watched the orange wedge advance toward him from the high windows, dispelling the shadows. Eventually, he stood and walked slowly to the canvas carts jumbled in the corner. He rolled them out one at a time, pushing them away behind him, until he came across one that felt heavier than the others. He took a deep breath and looked down into it. It was filled at the top with a mass of loose bald mannequin heads, and he moved them to another empty cart. Under the first layer of heads was a shock of hair. He moved more heads until a woman's face came into view. Her eyes were open and staring, her grey lips drawn back from her teeth in a hideous grin. His knees felt weak, and he braced himself against the cart's frame until he could trust himself to walk, then he rolled the cart over near the benches and left it there. He went back to the corner and began again, moving one cart at a time until he found another heavy one. This one was filled with wooden hands and feet, and he didn't bother to remove them but instead dug down, pawing them aside until he found a hand that gave under pressure from his fingertips. He pulled on it, and the wooden parts fell aside, revealing a second woman. Her torso was split open, and he could feel her ripping apart as he pulled. He stopped and moved her cart to the benches, parking it beside the first one.

He rested then, and took short breaths through his nose, staring down at his knees. When he was sure he wouldn't vomit, he went back and began searching the canvas carts again. There was only a handful of them left, and he entertained a sad, small hope that they would all be empty. And they were. All but the last one, which was fitted perfectly into the corner, where Day was sure Jack had left it. There for him to find at the very end, a special surprise, a parting gift.

There were no mannequin parts covering this body. Perhaps there hadn't been time to cover Ambrose after transporting Day to the workshop. Or perhaps Jack had wanted to make sure Day didn't overlook the boy's body.

Day didn't realize he was crying until he saw moisture on Ambrose's face. A single tear splashing on his cheek and rolling down, absorbed by the canvas side of the cart, as if it were the boy crying. Alive again for an instant.

Day slumped against the wall and sank down. He buried his face in his hands and did not move until long after the orange wedge was swept away under a fresh yellow carpet of daylight.

32

When Hammersmith and Kingsley arrived at 184 Regent's Park Road, they were astonished to see three police wagons and at least a dozen uniformed bobbies moving in and out of the house through the familiar blue door. A small crowd of neighbors had gathered at the periphery, and Hammersmith pushed through them, motioning for Kingsley to follow him. Sergeant Kett must have been watching for them because he immediately came bounding down the steps, still barking orders at the constables behind him.

"One of you men get down here and control this lot." Kett waved the back of his hand at the crowd, as if to push them away. "Move along," he said. Nobody moved. Kett turned toward Hammersmith. "Good, you brought the doctor. Gonna need him in there."

"What's happened?"

"Ugly stuff, I'm afraid." He was almost out of breath, and Hammersmith wondered whether it was from exertion or shock. "Just come on and you'll see."

An angry buzz circulated through the crowd as Hammersmith and Kingsley were led up the steps and into the house.

"Like as if they got a God-given right to see everything for themselves," Kett said.

A constable lifted a length of rope that was strung across the open front door, and the three of them scuttled beneath it into the house.

"I see you're using the kits I supplied," Kingsley said, "to help keep the scene intact."

"Always do these days," Kett said. He patted a pair of rubber gloves that were tucked into his belt. "Ain't seen you much, though. Always that fellow Pinch who comes round."

Kett led the way through the entry and past the staircase. An aggressive cloying odor filled Hammersmith's nostrils. The scent of decaying meat seemed to coat his tongue. He smacked his lips and nearly gagged. Across from the stairs, on their left, was the parlor, and Hammersmith peeked in as they passed the open door. He caught a glimpse of a man lying naked on the floor, his arms and legs spread. There was something wrong with the body, but he instinctively pulled his head back and kept walking, following Kett down a long passage to the kitchen. Behind him, he heard Kingsley gasp. Whatever had happened to the dead man in the parlor, it was enough to make the seasoned doctor uncomfortable.

"Yeah," Kett said. He didn't turn around. "That's bad enough in there, but the real show's in here."

With that, they entered the kitchen. The room was dominated by a heavy burnished metal table. The six chairs around it had all been moved aside, and four of them were pushed up against a sideboard. A second dead man lay facedown on the table. His wrists and ankles were tied to the table legs, and the flesh of his back had been laid open, exposing his spine. The table was bowed beneath him, and a dry yellow puddle of plasma flaked in the breeze from the open back door. The bodies of two more men sat in the remaining chairs against the far wall. Their hands were raised above them and nailed to the wall, and their feet were nailed to the floor. All three men were nude, their clothes folded neatly and stacked on the sideboard. Next to the back door, above the two men in the chairs, four circles had been drawn on the wall in blue chalk. Beneath the circles was a message, also in blue chalk:

EXITUS PROBATUR MR HAMERSMITH

> **THEES ONES NEERLY DID ME, BUT FALED**
> **I LEFT YOU THE KIDNES BUT FOR THE ONE I ATE.**
> **ALL KARSTS WHO WER THERE HAVE PADE NOW BUT 2**
> **THE CROW AN THE WHITE KING.**
> **THE WIL RUE THE DAY THEY DO ME AS THEY DID.**
>
> **KIND REGARDS**
> **YOUR FRIND JACK**

Hammersmith took it all in quickly, then moved past Kett to the door and stepped through into the thin mist of the back garden. An ash tree loomed out of the fog, its branches hanging heavy over the tops of four pale chairs and a tiny round table. A veneer of lilac smothered the dead meat odor that followed Hammersmith out of the house. He sat in one of the chairs without bothering to dry it off and felt the accumulated moisture soak into the seat of his trousers. He didn't move. After a moment, Kett joined him.

"Rough," Kett said.

Hammersmith nodded.

"You've seen it rough before, son."

"I have," Hammersmith said. "But I still don't like it. And there's the message, too. The writing on the wall."

"Someone copying the Ripper's work, you think?"

"No," Hammersmith said. "I think it is the Ripper. And I'm worried he's trying to tell us that he's killed Walter. That he's been torturing Walter for a year and . . . Is he saying that Walter's dead?" A sudden thought made Hammersmith jump up from the chair. "I saw the three men there, but the one in the parlor . . . I didn't see his face. It wasn't . . ."

Kett shook his head. "Not one of them in there's Walter Day. I checked that first thing."

"So this was all here . . ."

"These dead men have been here for a week or two, I'd say. Few days, at least. Up to the doctor to say for sure, though. He's workin' on 'em right now. Set right in on 'em while you came out here."

"I should go back in."

"Do like I do and breathe into the cuff of your sleeve. Filters it out a bit."

"I'll go you one better," Hammersmith said. He pulled his shirt up over his mouth and nose. His sleeves snugged up under his armpits and he couldn't lower his arms all the way, but he could breathe well enough. He followed Kett back into the kitchen.

Kingsley looked up from the table where he was examining the second body. "I thought we'd lost you, lad."

"Needed a moment's all," Hammersmith said. He was breathing hard now, warm air gusting down across his chest.

"Ah," Kett said, "the private sector's been too easy on you." He grinned, then made a face and stuck his nose into the end of his sleeve.

"Let's get some more windows open in here," Kingsley said.

"On it," Kett said. He hurried away, shouting at his men as he went.

Hammersmith kept his distance from the table. "What do you think of this?"

"There's a lot to deal with," Kingsley said. "A lot to try to put into some kind of context. I'm trying to piece together how many men were here. You've been in this house and examined it, and so have I. How long do you think the killer had to do his work here?"

"It's been at least two months since I was in here," Hammersmith said.

"Aye, more than that for me. It makes me wonder if whoever did this was watching us, waiting to make sure the place was empty. Unless it's sheer chance. It's possible someone came upon the abandoned house and seized on an opportunity for mischief."

Hammersmith pointed to the message on the wall. Kingsley looked up at it and nodded.

"Fair point. That's clearly directed at you, even if your name's been spelled incorrectly. The men who did this—I'm assuming they were men. Or maybe one man. Women tend to be less messy when they kill—they knew you visited here on occasion and they wanted to get your attention."

"I think we both know who did this. There was only one killer here."

Kingsley straightened up and stepped back from the table. "You mean . . ."

"Of course it was him. Of course it was Jack."

Kingsley stared at the message for a long moment. He nodded and turned away. "I believe it."

"You do?"

"Of course. The evidence is too great to ignore. The hard part is figuring out how one man was capable of overpowering four others."

"But Sir Edward doesn't believe Jack exists."

"Sir Edward knows he existed, but he doesn't like to think about Jack. He's a military man. The concept of evil is too huge for him to conceive of. He thinks of murder as an exercise in motivation and reward. In his philosophy, people only kill because they want something."

"Jack wants revenge. That's motive, don't you think?"

"It's more than that. There are things in the air and under the dirt and even dwelling within our own bodies, things that will kill us if we aren't constantly diligent. But we can't see them. They're invisible predators."

"Jack the Ripper isn't invisible."

"He may as well be. He operates on society like those germs and bacteria do on our bodies. You can't go after him the way you do every other criminal."

"I can," Hammersmith said. "I really can. You romanticize him, I think. But I'll treat him like any ordinary criminal because he doesn't deserve better than that. I'm going to find him. Because he's a man, not some demon or figment. I'll find him just as soon as I find Walter."

"You may be able to do both things at once." Kingsley stepped away from the table and walked to the kitchen's back wall, where he stared up at the message there. "It's no accident that he's left these men here for us to find, rather than dumping them in some White-chapel alley. He's taunting us. Well, he's taunting you, actually."

"Telling us he has Walter," Hammersmith said.

"Perhaps. Or maybe just telling us he knows something we don't. Each line of this thing is a separate jab."

"The spelling is—"

"The spelling's a ruse, I think. Meant to make it seem like he's not as smart as he actually is. He's used Latin in the first line, so he's more educated than he'd like us to think. And there are other inconsistencies here. A study in misdirection."

"Do you really think he ate someone's kidney?"

Kingsley pointed to the splayed corpse on the table. "That one's missing his left kidney. But there's no indication that anyone ate it. If he cooked anything here, he cleaned up after himself. And if he ate it raw, there are no signs of it, no bits of it dropped on the body, no extra blood left on the outside of the clothing or on the table itself. Nothing on the sideboard. If he consumed any part of this man, he's not a sloppy eater."

"Then where is it?"

"I think he took it with him."

"But he wants us to think he ate it? Why?"

"Perhaps he only means to disgust us, to throw us off our game. He's taken all their tongues as well. That seems to be his calling card."

"All right," Hammersmith said. "In the second line of his poem—"

"You think it's a poem?"

"I'm more versed in literature than poetry. He makes it sound like they surprised him. Or maybe even hurt him. I'd guess by the fourth line he's talking about the Karstphanomen."

"That seems like a safe assumption. Which would indicate that these four men were all a part of that secret society. But it's hard to say whether he's randomly depleting their ranks or is only attacking the men who were directly a part of his incarceration. Does his revenge extend to all of them or only those few that had a hand in torturing him?"

Hammersmith pointed above the message to the row of four circles. "Four zeroes, four victims. This looks angry to me. I think these must be the specific men who tortured him. Or some of them.

There can't be many more of them, can there?" He sniffed and looked away. "Do you think it's a coincidence that Walter's been missing for a year? The same amount of time Jack was held prisoner?"

"It's hard to say what's a coincidence in all this mayhem."

"If he's telling the truth, I'm sure he means to kill again before he's done. It's all he ever does. It's all he's good at. 'The crow and the white king.' What do you suppose they are?"

"I don't know."

"People? His next victims?"

"Or chess pieces," Kingsley said. "He may be talking about the rook. When he says *crow*, I mean. *Rook* is another word for a crow, and a white king is, of course, one of the two objectives in chess."

"So either he's referring to a game—he sees all this as some sort of gambit and we're supposed to figure out his next move, or maybe make the next move ourselves—or these are references to people and this is some sort of riddle. The white king could be the leader of the Karstphanomen. Who do you suppose that would be?"

"It's a secret society for a reason. I recognize two of these three men, though." Kingsley indicated the dead men lined up under the message, but he didn't look directly at them. "One's a very successful solicitor. He's backed a number of enterprises lately."

"Enterprises?"

"Oh, a small string of tea shops, a haberdashery, I hear he's even got some money invested in Plumm's. I don't know them, but I'd wager the other men here are also prominent in their fields. Once we identify them, we might have a better idea of the circles Jack's stalking."

"Whoever their leader is, he'd best be wary."

"For all we know, he may already be dead. For all we know, one of these men is the Ripper's 'white king.'"

"No," Hammersmith said. "I don't think so. Jack's leaving clues. He wants me to search for him, he wants me there when he does it, when he claims his last victim, doesn't he?"

"What makes you think that?"

"Otherwise, why tease me, why write this here in this way so he can be sure it'll get brought to my attention?"

"Why you?"

"I've been after Walter for a year. Jack's not stupid. He's been watching me." Hammersmith pounded his fist against the palm of his other hand. "He might have been right there the whole while I was looking for him. But why act now?"

"Why does he do any of this? You're trying to make sense of pure chaos."

"If I don't catch him, do you think he'll go back to his old ways after he's had his vengeance? Don't you think he'll start up again, killing women?"

"I don't think he'll ever stop," Kingsley said.

"Nor do I," Hammersmith said.

"Don't let him distract you. Find Day. I'll do everything I can to help."

33

Day came blinking out into the morning sun and rested in the shade of the department store while he got his bearings. He was so used to the smothering fog that the city looked new and bright and innocent to him. The workshop was behind Plumm's, and so, once he realized where he was, he jogged up Moorgate and through Great Bell Alley. His leg hurt and he couldn't go as fast as he needed to, but there was a part of him that was afraid of what he'd find when he got to Drapers' Gardens and Esther Paxton's little shop.

If I hadn't spent so much time discovering the bodies in the workshop . . . But no, he stopped that thought before he could finish it. If Jack had paid a visit to Esther, he had done it in the night while Day was at the bottom of a canvas cart. If Esther was dead, she had been dead for quite some time already.

He bypassed the shrubbery where he had spent his first days of freedom and limped down the stone path to the door. The wire was not across the window, Esther's wares were not displayed, and the globe above the door was still lit, even though it was broad daylight.

Esther would not have wasted expensive oil. Day found that he couldn't swallow and he had to lean over and spit. He caught his breath and knocked at the door. There was no answer. He tried the knob and it turned easily. He swung the door open and stepped inside, careful and quiet, conscious of the fact that Jack might be near.

It was dark inside the room. Day listened and thought he heard a small sound somewhere far away at the back of the house. He left the door open and took a step forward. Something crunched under his foot and he drew back. After a moment's hesitation, he went to the window, keeping close to the wall as he moved, and unlatched the shutters, threw them back. The room was immediately awash in bright sunlight, and Day blinked. He turned around.

Esther's rug was heaped against the wall, and all the furniture that had been on it was scattered about. A table with a pretty glass inlay was upside down, the glass crushed and pebbled. Two chairs were on their backs, one missing a leg. A lamp had broken, adding its glass to that of the table, and a puddle of oil had spread to the bounds of its ability, soaking one corner of the rug. Most alarming was a hole in the wall next to the door, an ugly gash, the wallpaper around it torn and tattered.

Day drew a ragged breath and licked his lips. "Esther," he said. Softly, but the sound of his own voice gave him courage and he called again, louder this time. "Esther!"

There was an answering cry, but he couldn't tell if it was her. The sound was high-pitched but muffled, and there were no words, only a senseless animal sound. Day thought of Jack's victim, the man he had called "Kitten," and he shivered.

Day moved quickly now. Someone was alive in the draper's shop, and that gave him hope. He hurried across the room as well as he was able, avoiding the glass and setting a chair upright as he passed.

There was an inner door and he pushed it open, his fist raised in defense. Nothing. Only a short passage that he knew led to a tiny parlor at the back and a staircase that led to the rooms upstairs where he kept his meager belongings: his change of clothing, his jars of tobacco and rolling papers, a small decanter of brandy. He called out again.

"Esther? Esther, are you here?"

He listened and heard the animal sound again coming from the parlor.

Day bounded past the staircase and through the last door into the room at the back. Esther Paxton was propped up against the far wall. Her legs stuck straight out from her body, her skirts hiked too high for modesty and her hair falling in tangled ringlets round her face. It was not bright in the room, but a window was open and Day could see that she had a black eye. It looked to Day as if her nose might be broken, and blood had crusted around her mouth and chin. The front of her dress was dark and wet, and a long smear of blood trailed down the wall toward her body.

But her chest was rising and falling. She was breathing. She was alive.

He went to her and knelt in her blood, which had pooled beneath her. He stood and opened another window to get more light in the room and knelt again, examining the wounds in her stomach. She had been stabbed at least twice, but not deeply, and her dress was already going stiff as her blood dried. He had no way of knowing how long she'd been lying there, and now he cursed himself for taking so long in the department store workshop. He was always a step behind Jack, and the people around him paid the price.

He took off his jacket and balled it up, lifted her head, and laid it back down on the jacket, hoping it might make her more comfortable. "Don't stop breathing, Esther. Just keep breathing. That's all you have to do now."

He left her there and ran back through the shop to the front door and pelted out onto the street. He dashed up Moorgate as fast as he could, ignoring the pain in his leg. The usual gang of boys loitered at the intersection near Finsbury Circus, waiting to help pedestrians. He recognized one of them, a lad who occasionally scouted tobacco for him.

"How fast can you run, Jerome?"

"Pretty fast, sir."

"Get to a telephone. Do you know where the nearest telephone is? Go to it and call University College Hospital. Ask for Dr Bernard Kingsley. Tell him Walter Day needs him to come straightaway. Can you do that?"

"Yes, sir."

"Do you know Paxton's shop off the gardens?"

"I do."

"Tell him to go there. Tell him to send his best people there. Someone's badly injured and may be dying, may be dead already if he doesn't hurry."

"There's nearer doctors to here, sir, if it's a hurry you're in."

"Yes. That's a good lad. After you make the call, find the nearest doctor and get him over there, too. Get two doctors. Get three. Bring whoever you can muster. Go now."

Jerome nodded and went back to his cluster of friends. Day grew anxious as he watched the boys talk, but in an instant three of the boys had peeled off and were running in different directions. Jerome had delegated his errands to some of the others. He hoped it would be Jerome himself making the call to Kingsley. Trusting that the boys could move more swiftly than he could, Day returned to the shop and checked again on Esther. She was still breathing, steady but irregular.

He wondered at the fact that Dr Kingsley's name had come into his head at the moment he needed to remember it. Now that things were unraveling, there was a lot that was coming back to him. Like a fog being lifted.

The light from the window glinted off something metallic beneath Esther's legs, and Day recognized the brass knob at the end of his cane. He pulled the walking stick out from under her and scraped a few drops of dry blood off the shaft with his thumbnail.

Had Esther used his cane to protect herself or had Jack left it to taunt Day?

He moistened his cuff with spit and used it to clean some of the blood from Esther's face. He willed her to open her eyes, and when she didn't he stood and turned the knob of the cane until it clicked. Apparently neither Jack nor Esther had realized it was a sword cane. He drew a two-foot dagger from the stick and tested the blade against his thumb.

Then he left the shop again, confident in the knowledge that the best doctor in London would save Esther's life. He marched back to Moorgate and west to Plumm's. He had determined that, one way or another, his long war with Jack the Ripper was going to end.

34

Timothy Pinch swept into the kitchen and dropped his black bag on the table next to the body. Dr Kingsley looked up and raised an eyebrow, then returned to his work, probing the incisions in the dead man's back.

"Took you long enough," he said.

"Well, you know, Fiona came round, and I thought you'd want me to give her the details." Pinch removed his jacket and folded it lengthwise, draped it over the back of a chair, and smoothed out the wrinkles.

"Why would I want you to tell my daughter about a murder?"

"She's a curious girl." Pinch stopped rolling up his sleeves for a moment in order to peer over Kingsley's shoulder at the corpse.

"That she is," Kingsley said. "And you're a curious fellow."

"What's that?"

"Never mind."

"What are we doing?" Pinch clapped his hands together and rubbed them. "Are they ready for transport? I've got a wagon waiting at the curb."

Kingsley grunted and poked tweezers deep into one of the

wounds. He pulled out a long dark brown hair and straightened up, holding it to the light that streamed in through the back door. Pinch leaned in for a look.

"That hair doesn't belong to this chap here," he said.

"No," Kingsley said. "Nor does it belong to any of the other gentlemen we've got in here." He gestured at the two dead men sitting with their hands nailed to the wall.

"What about the man in the parlor?"

"I don't think so. I haven't got to him yet, but—"

"I looked in on him before I came in here," Pinch said. "He's got yellow hair. Unless the head in there doesn't belong to the body in there."

"Good point. Let's make sure the bones match up in the spine. It's entirely possible he brought another head with him and took that poor fellow's."

"Who would do such a thing?"

Kingsley raised an eyebrow again, but didn't respond.

"So much anger," Pinch said.

"Not necessarily. Have you got a pouch for this?"

Pinch produced a pouch from his waistcoat pocket and Kingsley dropped the hair into it.

"I think it's possible our murderer has finally made a mistake," Kingsley said.

"What, the hair? It's not much."

"No, but it's more than we had."

"What's all that mean?" Pinch pointed at the writing on the wall, and Kingsley gave it a glance.

"Not sure," Kingsley said. "Chess pieces are the obvious inference. Rook and white king. The rest of it's mostly nonsense."

"Doesn't say rook. Says crow. Could mean a doctor."

"How's that?"

"Crow. Another word for doctor, you know? On account of the black robes we all used to wear. Made doctors look like big black birds to some people, I suppose. Of course the reference is a bit outdated at this point, but maybe if the age of the fellow who wrote this—"

"A doctor?"

"Well, I don't know," Pinch said. "No need to look so ashen and all. Thought we were playing a guessing game."

Kingsley took a deep breath and nodded. "Yes, indeed. Hadn't thought of that, is all. A doctor. And if it's a doctor, what would that make the white king?"

"Haven't the foggiest."

"Hmm."

"All right, then," Pinch said. "Best get this fellow out of here, right? You get his legs and I'll take the torso?"

"Not yet," Kingsley said. "I haven't dusted."

"Oh, that." Pinch turned away and looked at the counter and the sideboard. "Do you think it'll do much good?"

"Perhaps."

"Never has."

"It did once. That was before your time, lad, but it's worth putting the effort in."

"If you say so."

"I do say so."

Pinch lowered his head and cleared his throat. "Apologies, sir."

"No harm done. You're young, that's all. And you're intelligent. I was much the same at your age, sorry to say. Anyway, I've already taken the ink on these men's fingertips. It's over there on the counter, if you'd be so kind."

"Of course, Doctor." Pinch straightened his spine, and his eyes darted over the countertop until he saw a slip of parchment. He picked it up and gazed at it, his tongue rolling over the inside of his cheek. After a moment, he went to his bag and rummaged within until he found a magnifying lens. He held the parchment up so that it got full benefit of the light and went over it with his lens. Kingsley watched him, a smile touching the corner of his mouth. "I see," Pinch said.

"The differences."

"Yes, quite pronounced, especially here." Pinch pointed with the end of the lens's handle. "And here."

"You've got your powder?"

"Of course, sir."

"Let's dust every inch of this kitchen, and the parlor, too. If we're lucky, the killer will have left some impression behind him."

"It's amazing, really. If all the fingerprints are different, then what about toe prints? Or earwax? Someday we'll be comparing blood and saliva and urine. Do you suppose one criminal's mucus is different from every other? Or perhaps the pattern of the growth of his hair?"

"Let's not get ahead of ourselves."

"But aren't you at all fascinated by how similar we are, one to another, but how many invisible differences we have?"

"It does make one wonder."

Pinch opened his mouth to reply, but at that moment a boy pelted into the kitchen, followed by a frustrated constable.

"I'm looking for Dr Kingsley," the boy said.

"Apologies, Doctor," the constable said. "The boy got past me at the door."

"It's all right."

"I know how you like a place to be undisturbed and whatnot."

"I said it's all right. Let's hear what the young man has to say."

"You Dr Kingsley then?"

"I am. What's your name?"

"Jerome, sir."

"Jerome, you have a message for me?"

"It's from Walter Day, sir. I rang the hospital like he told me, and they said you was here, so I came straight over, I did."

"Walter Day? Did you say you've got a message from Walter Day?"

"It's what the gentleman said, sir. I never knowed him by that name, but it's what he said."

"Well? What *did* he say?"

"You're to go to the Paxton place, the draper's. It's in the gardens. Someone's hurt, and he needs you quick as you can get there. You coulda got there quicker, too, if I hadn't taken so much time to find you." The boy scowled and kicked the floor.

"Not your fault, lad. But I don't know this place you're speaking of. Can you lead me there?"

"You know I can, sir! Let's go!" And with that, the boy ran from the room.

"Wait!" Kingsley turned and grabbed his bag, shoving his tape measure, magnifying lens, and tweezers back into it in a jumble. He snapped it closed and turned to Pinch. "You can finish up here, Timothy? Get the fingerprints and compare them to those on the parchment?"

"Of course."

"Good. Prepare the bodies for transport. It seems I've been left behind. I'd better see if I can catch up. Good Lord, Walter Day himself. After all this time."

He stuck his hat on his head and, holding it there, ran from the kitchen.

35

There was a knock on the wall next to the open door, and Sergeant Fawkes stuck his head into the office.

"Sir?"

Sir Edward looked up from his book and smiled. "What can I do for you, Sergeant?"

"The door was open."

"Indeed. And you have rescued me from this." He took off his spectacles and waved them at the book. "Slow going, but our Dr Kingsley seems to feel it would be good for me to read it."

"Medical whatnot?"

"Of a sort. Forensic case studies from France, of all places. The good doctor is catholic in his choices."

"I see, sir."

"Was there something you needed, Fawkes?"

"There's a gentleman says he wants to talk to you and won't have no truck with anybody else."

"A police matter or something personal?"

"Says it's a bit of both. His name's Carlyle."

"Leland Carlyle? Well, send him in, then. I'd best put this away."
Sergeant Fawkes disappeared from the doorway and Sir Edward
scanned the desk for a bookmark, then shook his head and closed
the book, unmarked, and hid it from sight in a drawer. He folded
his spectacles against his chest and slipped them into his breast
pocket.

A moment later, Carlyle hove into sight and bustled into the office, all nervous energy and breathless arrogance. He turned and
shut the door and sat across from Sir Edward before the commissioner could invite him to do so.

"Did she tell you I saw him?"

"Ah," Sir Edward said. "You're here about Inspector Day. Yes, it's
exciting news, and we're acting with all haste."

"But you talked to Claire. Did she tell you I actually saw Walter
the other day?"

"She did not tell me that. But it's good news. Between that and
the telephone call, I'd say we're just round the corner from finding
him at last."

"That's exactly what I'm here to talk about. It really is a matter of
time. And that could be a problem, depending on what he's learned
during the past year."

"What are you afraid he's learned?" Sir Edward slumped back in
his chair and rubbed the bridge of his nose.

"The membership."

"The membership?"

"Of the Karstphanomen. He might know who we are."

"You mean who *you* are."

"You can't deny you were once—"

"I am not a member of your cult, Mr Carlyle."

"Cult?"

"I don't care what you call yourselves."

Carlyle looked down and shook his head. "We've been over this time and time again. Let's not repeat ourselves now. This is a matter that requires serious attention or there will be dire consequences."

"How do you think Walter's learned your membership rolls?"

"Jack knows."

"Jack?"

"Jack the Ripper."

"Oh, piffle." Sir Edward fished his spectacles from his pocket and, ignoring Carlyle, found his book again. He thumbed through the pages until he found the spot he wanted and began to read. Carlyle watched him all the while without saying a word. After a moment, Sir Edward looked up and frowned. "You're still here?"

"You're not going to help?"

"Help with what? Good God, man, you've gone completely round the bend. Jack the Ripper has told Walter Day sensitive information about your secret society, and you want me to . . . well, what? Order Walter to keep mum about it? Am I to pretend I believe Jack the Ripper's still gallivanting about London, despite the fact that his murders stopped two years ago and have not recommenced? Jack is gone. You fear a ghost, a boogeyman. I'm frankly tired of hearing about this myth. Even my own men have tried to bring the specter of Jack back, despite an overwhelming lack of evidence. Go away with your ridiculous children's stories. Go away and don't come back."

"He does still exist. He does. He's killing us. Do you know how many are left? A handful, that's all, and we cower behind locked doors at night, jump at every creaking floorboard, every knock at the window by a tree branch. Have you any idea what it's like to live that way?"

"No. At the end of the day I go home to my wife and have a good meal, a glass of port, and then to bed for a solid night's sleep. I do not burden myself with fairy tales and ghost stories. You may indulge yourself if you like, but leave me out of it."

"You won't do anything?"

"I still don't know what you would have me do. Listen, Mr Carlyle, my men are going to bring Walter Day home. God willing, he'll even return to work. He was a good detective once, and I have every hope that he will still be a good detective. Your daughter will have her husband back, you will have your son-in-law, all will be right with the world, and I may very well enjoy a second glass of port that evening, but I will certainly not bother Walter with your brand of silliness. I would advise you to restrain yourself in the matter and not bring it up with Walter. He's had a rough enough go of it, I think, and could probably use a return to normalcy, if that's at all possible."

"I have taken certain measures. I wondered whether I was doing the right thing, but now I see that I was right to do it."

"What have you done?"

"With luck, you'll never know." Carlyle stood and put on his hat. "Good day to you, sir."

"Leave the door open on your way out," Sir Edward said.

Carlyle stomped away, and Sir Edward returned to his book. After reading the same page three times, he leaned back and sighed. "Lord save me from Frenchmen, Karstphanomen, and other assorted asses," he said.

Fawkes stuck his head back into the office. "What's that, sir?"

Sir Edward jumped in his chair. "Did you hear our conversation, Fawkes?"

"No, sir. Thought you said something about Frenchmen."

"Here, Fawkes, read this book and tell me what it says." Sir Edward handed the book over to the reluctant sergeant.

"I'm not much of a reader, sir," Fawkes said. "What's it all about?"

"To be perfectly honest, Sergeant, I haven't a clue."

36

Hammersmith had two clues to work with.

The words *crow* and *king* written on the wall indicated that the killer might be a chess player.

And one of the dead men in the murder house was a backer of Plumm's.

Adding one and one together, Hammersmith reasoned that Plumm's might sell chess sets. He hadn't figured out what to do if they did or what that might have to do with multiple murders. But it was a place to start.

He had lost a year in the hunt for his friend and he couldn't afford to lose any more time. Walter was alive and needed help. Sleep and food had always been secondary concerns for Hammersmith, but now he pushed them further back, out of his mind entirely. Day had come into his life just when his father had left him. Day was close to his own age, but wiser somehow. Greater, he felt, than Hammersmith could ever be. He needed that in his life, needed Day to give him guidance. He would never find a friend like that again. He needed, for Claire's sake and his own, to find Walter Day.

Plumm's wasn't open yet when he arrived, and he stood in the shelter of an awning across the way, staring out at the street. A light mist still clung to the ground and to the walls around him, and yesterday's drab grey cobblestones were today a mottled rainbow of natural tones in the new sunlight. A tall man with thin hair slicked back along his scalp passed without seeing him and unlocked the front door, slipped through, but no light appeared inside the department store once he was in. Hammersmith waited. Eventually another person appeared, then another. Then lights did come on inside. A white-gloved man came out and sniffed the air. The man stepped forward and rolled a gate back from the doors.

As Hammersmith watched, a young woman appeared at the end of the street and walked slowly toward the department store, hugging the wall. Light shimmered through her hair, which was drawn up at the back of her neck. As she drew near, she noticed Hammersmith and crossed the street toward him. He pulled back in the shadows and motioned to her.

"What are you doing here?"

Hatty Pitt rested her hands on her hips and scowled up at him. "I'm doing my job, Mr Hammersmith. What are you doing here?"

"I'm confused," he said.

"That's not really an answer, you know. More a state of mind."

Hammersmith shook his head. "Now wait a minute. You work for me, not the other way round. How did you know I'd be here?"

"I didn't. And it seems to me you've no right to tell me where I can and cannot be when you've been gone and I've been the one—"

Hammersmith held up his hands and put his head down. He sighed. "Hatty. Why are you here? Why have you come to Plumm's this morning?"

"I've been working on my case for a whole day and a half now. I've made real progress."

"Is it to do with Walter Day or the Karstphanomen or the murders of those four men?"

"What four men?"

"So it has nothing to do with any of that?"

"It's that missing person, Hargreave. He was a floor manager here. The supervisor." She hooked her thumb over her shoulder to indicate the store. "He's disappeared."

"Interesting," Hammersmith said.

"Mildly so," Hatty said. "But not terribly. Men disappear all the time. What makes this case especially interesting is that someone wants to pay us. And with our detective missing from his own detective agency for weeks on end, and with charges coming in left, right, and center, a paying client is very interesting indeed."

"I could swear I told you to consult with me on every development."

"I couldn't find you. Time is of the essence in a missing person case, Mr Hammersmith."

Hammersmith was surprised by her forthrightness. He gave her a rueful smile. "Yes," he said. "Yes, of course." She was, he thought, very much like himself: headstrong and too honest for her own good. He admired these qualities in her, but wondered if he irritated others as much as she was irritating him. "Tell me," he said. "Tell me about the case."

There was little to tell, and Hatty caught him up within five minutes. He made her go back over the bit about how she had found a tongue in a rubbish bin and he admonished her about traveling to strange places by herself. Meanwhile, foot traffic around Plumm's had increased and the shutters on all four stories had been opened.

Elaborate displays were barely visible in the windows of the ground story and the floor above it. Gossamer mist moving over glass gave the mannequins behind it an eerie energetic quality.

"So," Hammersmith said, "your client's brother—or rather, *our* client's brother—was employed here."

"Yes. I thought I'd talk to his coworkers."

"Good. And have you talked to his household staff?"

"Not yet," Hatty said. "I'm starting here at his work. He was the floor manager, so he must have interacted with dozens of Plumm's staff every day. It seems to me there might be clues here."

Hammersmith nodded and pursed his lips. "Good."

"Thank you. But you never said why you're here, Mr Hammersmith. Is it something to do with finding Mr Day?"

"Yes. I've only now come from a murder scene. One of the victims was a backer of this store."

"Oh, he might've known my missing person."

"Hmm. Maybe. But he might never have set foot in here. Might be it's just money moving about and no connection at all."

"What does the murdered man have to do with Mr Day?"

"He was found at Walter Day's old address."

"On Regent's Park? But it's been a year since he was there."

"Well, obviously. It's been a year since anybody was there. Anybody besides us and the police."

"So it might not be related to his disappearance."

Hammersmith shook his head. "It's related, all right. What say we go inside and see what there is to see."

HAMMERSMITH HAD ONCE VISITED a bazaar, and he had been inside mammoth train stations, but he had never seen a space so big devoted solely to selling things. Everyone in Plumm's department store was there to buy something or to entice someone else to buy something. Everywhere he looked, Hammersmith saw wooden mannequins and busts made of wax and papier-mâché, he saw flat wooden forms draped with dresses, festooned with necklaces, and pinned with brooches. Counters were set in diagonal clusters, topped with globes of light that accentuated the sparkle of jewelry and the richness of fabric. A wide spiral staircase with a wrought-iron rail led to another floor, where Hammersmith could see an array of women's shoes and boots. Workers struggled across the gallery above, leaning against the rail, carrying huge panes of glass for an upper-story display in progress. An enormous blue globe spun slowly inside the framework of a brightly lit cube that was tipped up on one corner.

"It's beautiful," Hatty said. "It's all beautiful."

"Welcome to Plumm's." A small, officious man with a pencil-thin mustache hurried toward them. "How can I help you?"

"We'd like to speak with Mr Plumm," Hammersmith said. He worked to put some authority in his voice.

"Mr Plumm? Why, I'm afraid he's in a meeting right now. But I'm Mr Swann. Please, I'm sure I can help you with anything you might—"

"Mr Hargreave said we might be able to see Mr Plumm," Hatty said. "It's dreadfully important."

"Mr Hargreave?"

"Joseph," Hatty said. "Joseph Hargreave."

The prim man drew himself up as if there were some invisible thread attached to his head that extended to the high beams above, through them and to the heavens. "Joseph Hargreave is no longer employed by us. And his brother is not welcome here, either. Not at the moment. There has been some irregular behavior, and at Plumm's we pride ourselves on professionalism and decorum. No shopper shall ever be—"

"Then who's managing the floor now, Mr Swann?"

"That would be Mr Oberon," the man said. "But he's quite busy now, supervising the new installation." He pointed up and back, and Hammersmith looked at the railing above him, where a tall man with dark wavy hair had joined the workmen struggling along with their sheets of glass.

"Mr Hargreave has been replaced?" Hammersmith could hear a note of surprise in Hatty's voice, but his attention was fixed on the man above him. "Already?" There was something about that man on the gallery, something familiar in his movements, the tilt of his head, the halo of light from the window overhead. The man—Mr Oberon—looked down, and a slight smile twisted his lips.

"Mr Angerschmid?" Hammersmith tore his gaze away from the dark man on the gallery. Another man, small and round, was hastening toward him from the far side of a cabinet that displayed cufflinks and flasks. "I thought that was you!"

The little man was beaming from ear to ear, waving his hands wildly, and it took Hammersmith a moment to place him. Then he remembered. "Ah," he said, "Mr Goodpenny, isn't it?" An old acquaintance from another case.

"It's been too long, Mr Angerschmid!" Goodpenny was still moving toward him, but as he spoke, his eyes rolled up toward the gallery and the smile began to slide from his face. "But where is— Oh, my!"

And then the immediate surroundings were a deafening jumble as Hammersmith was toppled off his feet by a rushing weight and he hit the ground hard. A ripple of sound passed over him then was gone, and all he could hear was his own pulse pounding in his temples. Cold pinpricks showered him in a wave from head to foot, followed immediately by an overall itching sensation.

Hatty rolled off him. He sat up and looked around. The shoppers and staff of Plumm's were milling about in slow motion. A handful of them were approaching what appeared to be a large skinned fish in the middle of the sales floor. Hammersmith, Hatty, and half of the hostile Mr Swann were on a small island in a spreading red expanse, which was oozing toward the base of the nearest jewelry counter. A pane of display glass, which had looked so heavy and formidable when up above them, was now strewn everywhere, broken into more manageable sizes, a few of the larger chunks stuck in the mannequin busts at odd angles. Mr Goodpenny was on his knees, holding Mr Swann's wrist as if checking for signs of life, but that was a foolish hope, and he might have been better off tending to his own arm, where an apple-size piece of glass had embedded itself. Across the room, Mr Oberon was descending the spiral staircase, a prince of some golden realm that moved at another speed. The air sparkled with glass dust that was slowly settling over everyone and everything below the gallery.

Hatty had saved his life by pushing him out of the way of the falling glass.

Hammersmith could see Oberon gesturing to the sales force to get the milling women and children away from the grisly sight of Mr Swann's bisected body. He could see Hatty shouting at him, asking him if he was hurt. He could feel the vibrations as small bits of glass continued to plunk down around him and on his clothing and in his hair. He could smell urine and blood.

But he couldn't properly hear anything. Everyone was mouthing words and there was a distant incoherent monotone as noises mashed together into a low groan, as if he were deep underwater.

He got to his feet and ran his fingers through his hair, wincing as a thousand bits of glass bit into his hands. Looking around him again, he could see that there was nothing he could do for anyone. The efficient staff had already ushered everyone who was unharmed away somewhere. He suspected they would be receiving free tea and cakes, at the very least. Aside from himself, the only people left on the floor were Mr Oberon, Mr Goodpenny, at least two sizable pieces of Mr Swann, and Hatty. He gestured for Hatty to turn around. She twirled, and he satisfied himself that she was unharmed.

Hatty pursed her lips and stepped forward. She reached up and touched Hammersmith's neck. He drew back, puzzled, but she shook her head and held up her hand, showing him. Her fingers were smeared with blood. He rubbed his palm across his ear and didn't like the amount of fluid he saw when he held his hand out to look at it. He wiped his hand on his trousers and pressed the cuff of his sleeve against the side of his head, hoping pressure would staunch the bleeding.

He pointed at his ears and shook his head. "I CAN'T HEAR!"

She shrugged and nodded and pointed to her own ears. She couldn't hear, either. At least, when he leaned in to take a closer look, her ears weren't bleeding. He was afraid he'd punctured his eardrums and was glad to think that she hadn't.

He found her lack of reaction remarkable and reminded himself that she had seen her husband murdered in a similarly gruesome fashion. He took her elbow and helped her maneuver over the pool of Swann's blood, tiptoeing across some of the larger chunks of glass. He saw that many of the dresses and bolts of fabric on display had been ruined and he briefly wondered how much money the store had lost in that one clumsy, disastrous moment.

Then Mr Oberon arrived and waved Hatty on, guiding her past

the wreckage. He handed her off to a matron, who took charge of the young woman, steering her away from the horror show. Another man had arrived and was tending to Mr Goodpenny's arm. Goodpenny shouted something at Hammersmith from across the room, but Hammersmith shook his head and pointed to his right ear, indicating again that he couldn't hear. Goodpenny smiled and nodded. He'd never been able to hear.

Hammersmith turned and caught the fading expression on Mr Oberon's face. It was immediately replaced by a comforting smile, but for one moment, Hammersmith might have sworn the other man's eyes were full of hatred and anger. He was struck again by how familiar the man seemed, but he couldn't place him. Oberon leaned forward and put his lips near Hammersmith's ear. His breath tickled and he smelled like metal and fish and old rope. Hammersmith heard nothing more than a cavernous rumble. Oberon pulled back and cocked his head, smiling in an expectant sort of way, one eyebrow arched. Hammersmith shrugged at him. Oberon seemed disappointed, but nodded. He took Hammersmith by the arm and led him away from the scene of the accident.

37

The coffeehouse opened before lunch, and Leland Carlyle was there early. He wasn't sure when the staff would show up to begin preparing, but the place was empty when he arrived, so he stationed himself behind a tree across the street from the front door. He was surprised by how boring it was to simply stand and wait for someone else and regretted that he hadn't brought a newspaper or book to look at.

Just after midmorning, a sour-looking old man unlocked the shop and went in. He propped the door open and drew the shutters. He disappeared somewhere inside and a moment later emerged again with a broom and a dustpan and began sweeping the path outside the shop. Within a few minutes, an old woman arrived and entered the shop without stopping or saying a word to the man. Carlyle could see her passing back and forth in front of the windows, donning an apron and laying cloths on the tables. The old man went back inside and carried his broom to the back of the shop, out of sight. Carlyle waited longer and soon saw the girl who had served him the previous day. She walked down the street, in no particular hurry, looking up at the tops of trees and clearly enjoying the feel of the sun on her face. Carlyle could identify with her. After the blizzard and the slush, the rain and the heavy fog, the sun was a welcome visitor. The girl's skirts dragged behind her on the ground, and he wondered how well the old man had swept, whether the girl was carrying cigarette butts and dog shit around in her hems.

He stepped out and hailed her, watching the door of the shop from the corner of his eye in case the old couple came back outside.

"Do you remember me?" The girl looked at him and frowned. "No? I was here yesterday with a couple. You remember?"

"I'm sorry," the girl said. "Did you leave something behind?"

"No, no, nothing like that." Carlyle hesitated. The girl actually didn't remember him. She hadn't listened to his conversation with the Parkers. "I just . . ." He glanced over at the door of the shop. "I had a wonderful time and wanted to know when you would be open today."

Now the girl smiled, and he realized she'd been afraid he would proposition her. He felt a moment of deep embarrassment, but shook it off.

"We'll be open at half past the hour today," she said. "Mum and Dad should have the tables ready by now, though, if you'd like to come in early. I'm sure we could accommodate you."

It was a family business. Suddenly Carlyle saw her as someone's little girl, and he thought of his own daughter and was ashamed of himself. "Oh, no, no," he said. "I wouldn't want to impose. I'll come back later. I've been away from the office too long as it is."

She looked confused, but smiled again at him and nodded. "Any time. We're open seven days a week."

"Here." He took out his coin purse and handed her a quid. "For your good service yesterday." And without waiting for her to respond, Carlyle trotted away down the street as fast as he could go.

"Oh, my," Mr Parker said. "What's he gone and done?"

"He's reminded her of himself, is what," Mrs Parker said. "And now she'll remember him forever. Maybe us, too."

They were loitering round a stall at the far intersection, pretending to look through an assortment of paper fans. They'd had no intention of buying anything and were only using the vendor as a convenient place to conceal themselves, but Mrs Parker had found three fans that she liked, and the proprietor was trying to haggle with Mr Parker just at the moment he felt they ought to break away to discuss their plans. Mr Parker overpaid him and beckoned for Mrs Parker to come away before she found another fan she fancied.

"She's watching him as he goes," Mrs Parker said.

"We did nothing remarkable yesterday. There was no reason to come back."

"He thought he was going to cover his trace, didn't he?"

"Yes, my darling."

"And instead he made himself stand out from the crowd."

"That he did."

"Amateur."

"Well," Mr Parker said. "They're all amateurs, aren't they?"

"It's why they need us," Mrs Parker said.

Mr Parker sighed. "I suppose we'll have to do something about it."

"Oh, let me. Do let me take care of it."

"Discreetly."

"Of course. I'm always discreet, dear heart. Aren't I?"

"Have you forgotten the Belgian ambassador, darling?"

"But that couldn't be helped. He was so enormously fat. And so loud. Like a squealing pig, he was."

"We led the gendarmes on a merry chase that evening."

"It was exciting, wasn't it?"

"But would not have been so exciting had we been caught."

"That might have been dreary," Mrs Parker said. "But you know I would never have allowed us to be caught. Not alive, at any rate."

How well he knew it. "Yes," Mr Parker said. "You take care of this little mess the high judge of the Karstphanomen has created."

Mrs Parker stood on tiptoe and gave him a kiss on the lips. He felt dizzy at her touch. She pressed her new fans against his chest, and when he took them from her she scampered away from him down the street.

The shopgirl looked up expectantly when Mrs Parker approached her, and Mr Parker caught the fan vendor's attention. He engaged the man in a discussion of his wares, and when he looked up both women had disappeared from sight down an alley next to the coffeehouse.

38

Day stopped abruptly when he reached the junction of Prince and Lothbury. People were streaming out of Plumm's, many of them shouting and waving their hands, trying to attract the attention of passersby. Several men were carrying unconscious women, trying to juggle the women and their hats, struggling toward the opposite curb.

Day held his cane down along the side of his leg and moved through the crowd to the front doors, where he was met by a stern man, his white-gloved hand held out.

"There has been a mishap, sir. Please come back on the morrow."

"I need to get inside," Day said.

"No one is to go inside at the moment. Please come back on the morrow." Clearly he had been given a script.

"I'm an inspector with Scotland Yard. I've been sent to deal with the trouble." Day had no idea what the trouble was, but he was certain Jack was at the center of it and was equally certain that he was the only person capable of dealing with Jack.

The man with the white gloves looked him up and down and

stuck his nose in the air. "I have received no notice, sir, if you are indeed who you claim."

"You doubt me?"

"I did not say that, sir."

"You have a telephone on the premises?"

"Of course, sir. This is Plumm's."

"Call the police commissioner, call Sir Edward Bradford at the Yard and tell him that you won't let me in. He'll put you on notice right enough."

The guard coughed and looked down the street, gathering his thoughts and his dignity. "Do you have a badge of some sort?"

"Inspectors don't carry badges. Only constables."

"This is true?" The guard's expression changed. He was alarmed by the idea that there was something he didn't know.

"Of course. Why would I carry a badge? I'm not arresting anyone. I tell the constables who to arrest. They're the ones need the badges." Day had been hiding deep inside himself for so long that there was no trace of emotion on his face, no way for the guard to tell if he was bluffing.

"Ah, of course. This makes perfect sense." The guard stepped aside and waved Day through, but then followed him inside. "It's . . ." The guard stopped with his mouth still open and waved his white gloves at the enormous ground floor space.

Day stopped, too. Peering over the first queue of low display counters, he could see a man lying on the ground. His eyes were open and one arm was thrown over his head, a white glove spotted with red reminding Day of his new companion. A step farther and the man's waist became visible, his intestines spread out over the floor, a pond of congealing effluvium keeping him afloat. Day turned away.

"It's a bit much, isn't it, sir?" The man with the white gloves (pure white, no blood) patted Day on the back. "I suppose even you must be taken aback by a thing like this."

"What's your name?"

"Gregory, sir."

"Gregory, what happened here?"

Gregory glanced down for the first time at Day's cane. "Don't policemen carry guns, sir?"

"Most do. I'm with the special branch." He twisted the handle and drew the blade out far enough that Gregory could see it. "The swordsmen. You've heard of us."

"Oh, yes, sir," Gregory said. "Of course, sir."

"What happened?"

"A most unfortunate accident. A windowpane that was being installed fell from up there." Gregory pointed at the gallery. "There was no time for him to move, sir. Or so I suppose."

"Did you know him?"

"Mr Swann, sir. I will admit he was not well-liked, but I can't believe it was murder. If that's why you've come, I would have to say—"

"Who was up there at the time? Up there on the gallery when it happened?" Day squinted up at the milling people above. It looked as if someone had ushered everyone in the store out through the front doors or up the stairs, away from the blood. The problem with the latter choice was that women and children might glance down and see the whole grisly mess from above. He hoped the staff was keeping everyone distracted and looking the other way. "I assume not all of those people were up there."

"I was there, on the door." Gregory pointed back behind them. "I didn't see. The installation was a favorite of Mr Hargreave. He ordered that glass last week, and it was very expensive. They wouldn't have risked having it jostled."

"Hargreave, you say? Where is he now?"

"Oh, um, he's gone, sir. Got the sack, as it were."

"But somebody's still putting it together. The installation."

"Well, his replacement has that task, I suppose."

"And who is that?"

"Mr Oberon, sir."

Day squinted at him. "You don't like Mr Oberon, do you?"

Gregory pulled away from him and looked down at his shoes. "I didn't say that, did I?"

"And why don't you like Mr Oberon?"

"He's . . . Well, he makes me uncomfortable. I believe he hates me."

"He hates you?"

"He has no reason, I assure you, but he wants to harm me. I see it in his eyes. When he smiles I . . . He's a cruel man, and I've seen my share of cruel men."

"Why would he single you out?"

"Oh, he doesn't like anyone. The girls all see it in him, too. We stay well away from him. I have no idea how he won his position."

Day nodded. "Thank you, Gregory. Your candor is much appreciated by the Yard, and I'll see to it that you get some sort of commendation. You'd better tend the door now. We don't want any women seeing a thing like this."

"Of course, sir. As you say."

"And call more police. Get more men here right away."

Gregory nodded and hurried away. There was a sense of relief about him, as if he'd been lowered from a meat hook and set free.

Day realized too late that bringing more police would only complicate things for him. He needed to find Jack and deal with him before anyone could try to stop him. He took a step forward and saw the other half of the poor dead man. One shoe had come off and the leg of the man's trousers was split open at the seam, leaving his shin naked and unguarded. Day grimaced. Dignity was a fragile thing, and the dead were so often robbed of it.

He looked up again and two figures above caught his eye. They were moving rapidly across the gallery, one of them steering the other by the arm as they maneuvered through the crowds toward a back hallway.

Day felt his face flush and his stomach dropped. He pulled the sword free of the cane's shaft and ran forward. He slipped in Mr Swann's blood and caught himself, nicking himself with the sword in the process, but he ignored the sudden flash of pain in his arm.

"Nevil!"

The two men on the gallery did not stop moving, but one of them looked over the railing and saw Day. He smiled and gave a little wave with his free hand, then Jack and Hammersmith were lost from view behind a wide marble column. Why hadn't Hammersmith turned around?

"Nevil, stop! It's him!"

Day made it to the stairs and bounded up them. His weak leg took his weight and Day knew that he would suffer later for the exertion, but it was still bearing up for now and that was all he cared about. The stairs bounced beneath him, and he could see screws working loose at the juncture where the steps met the railing. All the people on the gallery must have rushed upstairs in a panicked knot.

At the landing he pushed his way through a mass of milling customers and white-gloved staff. It was early in the day and the store hadn't been very busy yet, but there were still at least five dozen people crowded at the top of the steps as if debating whether to try to skirt the body downstairs and leave. A woman was lying propped against one of the columns and another woman was gently shaking her, trying to wake her. A third woman was screaming, her hands trembling at her face. A man was wandering alone in a daze, blood spattered across his jacket. Everyone around the man was giving him a wide berth. Someone had taken a stack of blankets from a display shelf and was passing them out. Day had once been called to the scene of a traffic accident. Two omnibuses had crashed into each other, killing one team of horses and a driver. Although no one traveling inside had been killed, they had all looked like these people: numb and lost and somehow snapped free from the normal orbit of life around them.

Day did not stop to help anyone. He did not ponder the fact that yesterday his own name had been a mystery, but today he remembered that long-ago carriage wreck. He kept his pace, shoving people aside, ignoring the screams and cries around him. He had one objective and he kept himself focused on it.

Through a break between people he saw the top of Jack's head, dark wavy hair, unfashionably long, and he picked up the pace. Someone grabbed at his arm and he turned. A small round man smiled at him and held out a blanket. Day shook his head, but the man adopted a pitying expression and pressed the blanket against his chest.

"Your arm's bleeding, sir," the man said. "Let me look at it." The man's own arm sported a thick bandage.

"I can't," Day said.

"I represent the store, sir, and I can assure you we wouldn't—"

"I don't—"

"You needn't shout, sir. I can . . . Oh, my, I just realized I really can't hear you. You were speaking, weren't you?"

Day pushed past him and ran on. The top of Jack's head was still visible, and he launched himself through an opening between customers.

The world slowed down. He thought he could hear a tune playing in the background, a high-tempo melody that only served to charge him further. As he moved slowly forward he watched Jack turn, a grin on his face, that same wooden, unfeeling grin that charmed people who didn't know him. Jack brought his arm up at the same speed with which Day was moving and pushed up off his toes, and he was laughing as he hit Day full in the chest.

Day staggered backward into an installation. It was a globe bigger than a four-wheeler carriage, and when Day hit it the framework of the box around it buckled. He put his weight on it and kicked Jack in his wounded abdomen. The monster bellowed and fell to one knee. With a great wrenching sound, the globe tore loose from its perch and toppled to the floor. Day was pulled off balance and stumbled backward. Time froze for one fleeting instant as the great sphere quivered, then slowly rolled away, picking up speed, people jumping out of its way as it moved. It slammed into the railing, and the loose screws of the balustrade gave way. Day followed it, windmilling his arms, unable to get his feet back under him. The wrought iron yielded under the pressure, sending a shock wave back along the metal frame to the stairs, which promptly removed themselves from the landing, bending the footing at the bottom. The entire piece of ironwork dragged itself out into the air, followed by the globe and then by Day's fragile body.

The last thing he saw as he plummeted toward the ground floor of Plumm's was a look of alarm on Jack's face. Day had never seen any sincere expression there before, never seen anything that wasn't meant to reflect malice or authority. The killer scrambled forward on his hands and knees, reached out, tried to catch Day as he fell.

But it was too late.

Day closed his eyes and surrendered himself to gravity. It was the first time in more than a year that he had felt at peace.

39

Mr Oberon dropped down and disappeared in the crush of people. There was a great deal of commotion, and Hammersmith was pushed back toward the wall. He couldn't see over the bobbing heads of frantic men around him. He couldn't hear anything except a low pulsing noise, and he felt confused, slightly panicked, missing one of the primary tools he used to navigate the world around him.

Someone grabbed him by the hand and pulled, and Hammersmith looked down to see Hatty Pitt. She was leading him through a break in the mob, and he gladly followed her. Her hand was warm and dry, and the pressure reassured him that he wasn't completely lost; he was tethered to this strong little person and he would not float away just yet.

She dragged him to the lift at the back of the gallery and let go of his hand. He could see her speaking to the operator, who cowered behind the gate. The operator gripped the curved bars and leaned down to hear Hatty better, and Hammersmith surmised that the gallery must be noisy. Hatty gestured, and the operator shook his head, shouted something at her. Hatty shouted back, gesticulating more wildly and pointing back toward where Hammersmith stood. Evidently she wanted to get on the lift and the operator wasn't obliging her. Hammersmith tried to look engaged and aware of what was going on, but he wasn't sure whether Hatty wanted him to appear friendly or authoritative. He settled on an expression he thought might convey some sort of stern kindness. It was the sort of look his father had often given him when he was a boy, and a look he had seen many times on Sir Edward's face.

The operator glanced in his direction and shrugged, pulled the gate open. Hatty grabbed Hammersmith again, hurried him onboard. The gate shut and the operator worked a lever next to a high stool, and Hammersmith felt his stomach lurch as the lift slowly descended toward the sales floor below. He looked out through the gate at the shins of Plumm's customers who were standing on the gallery, then at their feet, and then they were all gone and he was looking at a massive broadside that advertised C&J Clark beaded evening shoes for women. The advertisement featured a woman who seemed to be able to walk on clouds in her new shoes, and she was followed by a gentleman in laced-up black Clark boots and three children all queued like ducklings wearing patent leather Clark shoes. The image doubled and tripled as it slid past and he blinked to get it back in focus. He assumed the broadside's primary job, other than selling shoes, was to cover the joists and ductwork that might otherwise be visible as the lift moved up and down. He wondered if a third benefit of the happy family in the illustration was to make customers feel a bit more at ease as they moved through the air between floors. With the proper shoes they could walk on clouds, never mind the electric lift.

He checked his ear and saw no fresh blood on his fingers, but the back of his hand was smeared with wide brown streaks that he couldn't wipe away. His blood had dyed his skin, and he thought again of his father, whose tanned brown hands had once laced his boots tight and mussed his hair. Hammersmith wondered what his father would have said about lifts and telephones and men who killed each other for sport. He could not remember his father's voice and he thought it was possible that he would never hear anything again. How long before he would no longer remember what anything sounded like, and how did his life always seem to circle back to death and injury?

There was a slight jolt as the lift thumped to the ground, and the operator leapt from his stool and pulled the gates open as a cloud of plaster dust and powdered stone rolled into the tiny chamber. Something registered in Hammersmith's peripheral vision, a shadow somewhere he didn't expect to see shadows. He put out an arm to hold Hatty back as she began to step out. An instant later, a man's body slammed into the floor in front of them and Hatty jumped, surprised.

The lift operator pushed past them and rolled the man over. A splintered bone protruded from the man's arm and the operator reached to touch it, perhaps to try to put the bone back where it belonged in the man's arm, but then pulled his hands back and looked up at Hammersmith, his face pale. Both men were wearing white gloves, the uniform of the Plumm's employee, and Hammersmith realized that the operator knew the injured man. Hammersmith knelt next to the body and felt for a pulse, then nodded to the operator and gave him a smile he hoped was encouraging. If they could get a doctor there soon, the man would live. Until then it was probably a good thing he had been knocked unconscious by the fall. The pain would be intense when he woke up.

Hammersmith looked out across the sales floor where twisted black metal was strewn over the hardwood and embedded in the bright glass counters. The staircase had wrapped itself round several displays, and a phalanx of wooden mannequins lay crushed beneath a marble column. The brilliant blue globe from the installation, bigger than Hammersmith's flat, rolled lazily to and fro over the ironwork and rubble, crushing wooden forms and demolishing crockery. As Hammersmith watched, it bounced over a segment of the iron stairs, bounced again and again and seemed to pick up energy before bursting out through the front of the store in a silent rain of glass. He watched it bump down off the curb and gain a jolt of momentum before it disappeared from sight down the street.

He looked up and nudged Hatty, who followed his gaze to the gallery above, where a woman was being pushed dangerously close to the edge of the drop-off, no railing there to stop her or hold her weight.

"HEY!" Hammersmith knew he was shouting, but he couldn't judge how loud he was. A man looked round at the sound of his voice, reached out, and grabbed the woman before she could fall, pulling her to safety.

Satisfied that everyone above was reasonably safe for the moment, Hammersmith turned and lifted the unconscious man under his arms and pulled him away from the lift. It was still dangerous there, where anything might fall from above. The operator moved a length of railing to make space, and Hatty stacked bolts of fabric to make a temporary gurney. They laid the man there. As Hammersmith straightened back up, the room spun round him and he put out both arms to keep his balance.

Hatty tugged on Hammersmith's sleeve and pointed. He squinted and saw fingers, a sleeve, partially hidden behind an upended counter. Someone else had fallen or had perhaps still been on the ground floor when the railing came down. He climbed toward the prone figure, moving cabinets and rubble, throwing wood and iron to the side, making a path so that Hatty and the operator could follow.

There was a man lying atop a table on a wrecked display of wicker baskets and carriage blankets. The legs of the table had given out and it had collapsed, but the man moved as Hammersmith approached. As Hammersmith drew nearer, the man lifted a sword and waved it in the air, fending him off.

Hammersmith stopped and moved carefully round the fallen man so that he would be visible. He stumbled and grabbed the edge of an overturned cabinet until he felt steady enough to walk again. The man's torso came into view. As Hammersmith moved, he raised his hands and held them up, palms out at shoulder level. "I MEAN YOU NO HARM!"

He had no way of knowing whether the man responded. He had to trust that he wouldn't be run through if he tried to help. He took another step and now he could see the man's face. The man lowered his sword and smiled.

Hammersmith stopped and stood for a long moment without moving, unaware that Hatty was calling to him or that policemen had begun to stream through Plumm's broken front doors. At last he rushed forward and dropped to one knee and scooped the battered form of Walter Day into his arms and held him tight so that he wouldn't disappear again.

After a moment, Hammersmith raised his head and shouted. "IT'S HIM! HE'S HERE! WALTER'S OVER HERE!" He realized he was crushing his friend and he pulled away. Day's lips moved, and Hammersmith squinted, trying to read what he was saying. "WHAT? I CAN'T HEAR!" Day spoke again, emphasizing his words carefully, and this time Hammersmith understood.

"It's good to see you, Nevil." He closed his eyes and the sword dropped from his hand, clattering unheard to the floor.

BOOK THREE

The two carriages sat facing each other from a distance of perhaps twenty yards. The larger of them was hitched to a team of eight stick horses, all of them champing at the bit, dragging their blunt ends back and forth in the dirt. The smaller carriage, a two-seater, had a team of two rocking horses that moved to and fro, cutting parallel gashes in the path under the runners. The drivers sat up top. The Jack-in-the-box had thrown back his lid, and he swayed gently at the end of his spring and hurled insults at the other driver, who did not appear to notice him or react to his words. As for the other driver, Mary Annette's painted-on face was calm, her rosy cheeks were little red circles, and her smile a droll black bow. Her cross had been made to fit into the seat beside her so she did not need to carry it and could instead hold her lance out in front of the carriage in a straight line that pointed at Jack.

"Oh, I do not like this," Anna exclaimed. "I do not like this one bit. Oh, oh."

"It is a hard world," said the Kindly Nutcracker. "And this is the way of it."

"What do you think, Babushka?" asked Anna. "Isn't there anything we might do to save poor Mary Annette?"

The Russian doll shook herself all over and split in half, as she so often did when she was thinking. Her shiny black hair tipped back and she rolled over and her inner self hopped out onto the path. This version of Babushka had hair that was painted yellow, and her lacquered violet dress was decorated all over with flowers and pretty bulbs. "Perhaps if we were to talk to Jack, he might take back what he said and they would be friends after all."

Anna clapped her hands together. "Oh, let's do!" she said. But then a terrible thought entered her mind and she frowned. "Oh, but he never will listen. He is a scoundrel through and through."

Babushka shook herself again, this smaller part of her that had spoken, and the top of her yellow head popped off. She rolled over again, and an even smaller version of her tumbled out at Anna's feet. This tiny, perfect replica of her outer shell was painted blue with angry red streaks slashing through her painted-on costume.

"No," this miniature Babushka declared. "Jack will never listen to anything that is right and good. We shall kill him and be done."

"Oh, no, we mustn't kill anyone," said Anna. "That would make us every bit as evil as Jack is."

While they were debating this point, Jack removed the wooden cigar from his mouth, which was cut into his face so that he appeared constantly to be grinning but with quite a malicious gleam daubed in his eye. He looked every bit the naughty little elf. He spoke very loudly so that everyone could hear. "I am going to run you through with this lance, Mary Annette, and split the wood that you are made of into two pieces, and then I will do the same to any of your friends who would dare to take up your quarrel with me."

Anna gasped, of course, for this was a truly awful thing to say to any-

body, and especially to her dearest new friend in all the wood. She began to wonder if perhaps Jack was too evil to be allowed to live, after all.

"We should burn him," the smallest Babushka said. "No matter if he wins or loses, we should unstick him from his spring and break him into all his pieces and burn them all until he is gone and can cause no more trouble for anyone."

Anna began to nod, but then she caught herself and reminded herself that she was really a very good little girl and that good people did not break other people into parts and burn them, even if they said cruel things to others.

"If he wins," said the Kindly Nutcracker, "I will bite him very hard indeed. On the nose."

"Yes," Anna agreed. "Perhaps he does deserve a good solid bite on the nose. But I do not think we shall burn him."

"But what if he does split Mary Annette into two pieces as he has threatened to do?" asked the largest piece of Babushka. Anna thought it was quite odd that Babushka should be so concerned about it when she was accustomed to being split into pieces herself.

Anna thought very hard for a moment, and then she smiled. "If Jack breaks Mary Annette into two pieces, why then, we shall glue her back together. And if he breaks her into twenty pieces, then we shall glue those back together just the same, and it will be as if she was never broken."

"I do not have any glue," the Kindly Nutcracker said. "Do you?"

"No, I do not," said Anna. "But we are already on a quest to find Peter, and once we do find him, then we will have to embark upon yet another quest to find a pot of glue like the one that my father keeps in his workshop."

"Why, then we will all be able to remain together for a while longer, and you will not go home to your family and leave us behind," said the middle Babushka.

"I will never leave you behind, no matter what happens," said Anna.

"Unless Mary Annette wins the joust," the Kindly Nutcracker said. "If she wins the joust, then Jack will fall off his carriage and break and we will not need any glue at all."

"We will still need glue," said Anna. "If Jack should break into even a thousand pieces, we will find glue and we will put him all back together in a different way so that he will be good and kind to everyone from this day until the last."

"That is a wonderful plan," said the Kindly Nutcracker.

"Yes," said the middle Babushka.

"I do not like that plan," said the smallest Babushka.

But it was too late for Anna to argue with the angry little Babushka, for just then Jack cracked the reins of his carriage and said, "Hah!" and the stick horses jumped forward, and at the same time the two rocking horses slid on their rockers, pulling Mary Annette's carriage forward, and the joust was under way.

—RUPERT WINTHROP, FROM
The Wandering Wood (1893)

40

The great department store that had tried to reinvent the very notion of shopping was no more. The windows had been broken out and displays removed by police in order to allow easier access, so that now Plumm's façade resembled a toothless skull glaring down the street at anyone who approached. The falling balustrade had rent huge gashes in the walls on either side of the ground floor and had pulled at least one support beam away, causing parts of the ceiling to cave in. The opulence and luster had been scraped away, revealing the poor naked bones of the place. Volunteers pitched in, along with the police and fire brigades, to help bring out the dead and injured. Many men worked well into the night, searching for anyone who might be trapped inside, and women bustled to and fro, bringing blankets, food, light, and comfort to both the workers and the victims.

In the wee hours of the morning, a halt was called to the work. The doors were secured and the windows boarded up, leaving a solitary guard inside. When the last volunteer had trudged homeward, the dregs of the city crept out of the shadows and alleyways nearby. The new boards were pried from the broken windows and, ignoring the ineffectual guard, looters busied themselves clearing the store of anything that could be salvaged.

As the sun rose, the street was quiet again. Plumm's was little more than a dark blotch on the terrain, a stripped and empty husk with no dreams or promises left on offer.

41

The library of Guildhall on Aldermanbury was turned into a makeshift ward for the injured that had been carried out of the Plumm's wreckage. But the Print Room was reserved for two very special patients.

Nevil Hammersmith had succumbed to exhaustion and passed out after finding Walter Day. Immediately after waking up, he had taken a post at the foot of Day's gurney and had not moved since. He was watching Timothy Pinch at work, plastering the inspector's broken ribs, when Fiona Kingsley knocked softly on the double doors that connected the room to the library.

"How is he?"

"Sleeping peacefully," Hammersmith said. He stood aside so she could see Day.

"Oh, hullo, Miss Kingsley." Pinch perked up and smoothed his hair, accidentally rubbing plaster into his scalp.

"Mr Pinch. Please go on with what you were doing. I only wanted to check in on Mr Day."

"Oh, I'm getting him fixed up proper, no worries on that front."

"Yes, I'm sure you are. And, Nevil, how are your ears?"

"Your father looked me over just a bit ago. He says I've ruptured my eardrum."

"Oh, my. Oh, Nevil, can't you stay out of trouble?"

Hammersmith ducked his head and grinned. "It doesn't seem so."

"Oh, he'll be fine," Pinch said. "His ear will heal itself, given time."

Fiona nodded, but didn't even look at the young doctor.

"I can hear out my other ear," Hammersmith said. "And the ringing's stopped now. So it's not all bad."

"It's nothing," Pinch said. "Doesn't even require treatment."

"That's good," Fiona said.

"I hope you've notified Mrs Day."

"There was a great deal of confusion," Fiona said. "So many people were injured and my father had me running round like a madwoman organizing the Hall. I meant to send somebody to fetch Claire, but I simply lost track of time and nobody else thought to send for her. When I realized, I had a boy sent right away with the message, but I'm afraid she's going to be cross. I feel awful about it."

"We could tell her we only found him this morning," Hammersmith said.

Fiona smiled and brushed a stray hair out of her face. "You'd do that for me?"

"No, I'm sorry," Hammersmith said. "Much as I'd hate Mrs Day to think we never considered her, I don't think I could lie."

"Of course." Fiona's smile disappeared and she nodded. "Good old Nevil. Well, I suppose I should go wait for her. She'll want to know where we're keeping Mr Day."

"I'll walk you out," Pinch said. "Give me a minute to rinse my hands." The plaster was drying in his hair, sticking it straight up at odd angles.

"Please don't bother," Fiona said. "I'm fine on my own." She glanced at Hammersmith as she said it.

"Perhaps you should finish with Walter," Hammersmith said.

"No, no, this will wait a bit," Pinch said. "He's not in any pain while he's asleep, now is he? Miss Kingsley, do wait for me. I wanted to ask you something."

"Oh, no, Mr Pinch."

"No?"

"I mean to say there's so much going on right now, I don't think I could possibly answer any questions."

"Ah." Pinch looked round the room and ran his fingers through his hair again. "Yes, well, I seem to be running out of linens in here. Be right back." He made a faint squeaking sound, as if someone had stepped on his toes, and hurried out of the room.

"What was that all about? There's plenty of linens in here," Hammersmith said.

"Oh, Nevil," Fiona said. "Why don't *you* ever ask me anything?"

"I just did. I asked you what was wrong with Pinch."

"But you never ask me anything meaningful."

"That's meaningful enough, isn't it?"

"Nevil Hammersmith, it would serve you right if I married Timothy Pinch." Fiona spun on her heel and marched out of the room.

Hammersmith took a deep breath and frowned at the door, wondering if she planned to return and explain herself. When she didn't, he sat back down at the foot of the bed. He didn't understand what he had to do with Fiona and Pinch, but if she wanted to marry the young doctor, Nevil didn't intend to get in the way.

He thought he ought to be happy that she had found someone,

but something about it all sat strangely in his stomach. He wasn't accustomed to thinking about romantic matters; they made him uncomfortable. It occurred to him that he might be lonely and he thought he might ask Fiona about that, if she was so determined that he should ask her things.

He had just made up his mind to follow her and demand an explanation when Walter Day opened his eyes. Hammersmith immediately put all thoughts of Fiona Kingsley out of his head and breathed a sigh of relief.

The things Walter Day talked about usually made some sense.

42

Dr Kingsley saw his daughter rush from the Print Room, her hair flying, her hands covering her face, and he was reminded of the girl she'd once been, running through the grass, her skirts flitting about her ankles. Nostalgia for those simpler times threatened to cloud his mind, but he snorted and brushed it away. The past hadn't really been any easier, and while Fiona was indeed more complex now, at her core she was the same sweet child she had always been.

"Nurse, take over for me here," Kingsley said.

He didn't wait for a response, just trotted after his daughter. She was in the parlor, sitting with her back to the library. He hesitated at the threshold, wondering whether he ought to interfere, wondering how she had turned from that little girl to this beautiful woman on her own. Should someone have asked him if he was ready for that? Just as he was about to turn back, she looked up and gave him a teary smile.

"I'm sorry," she said. She seemed about to say something else, but then shook her head and buried her face once more in her hands.

Kingsley patted his pockets until he found his handkerchief. He checked it for blood before handing it over to her. She didn't look up as she took it.

"I'm such a . . ." But her voice broke and she couldn't finish.

Kingsley pulled a chair over and sat next to her. He reached out and put his hand on the arm of her chair, there if she needed him, but not ready to intrude. He sensed that he ought to stay there, but he didn't know what he was supposed to do, so he settled on being a presence.

Fiona wiped her eyes with his handkerchief and blew her nose. She put a hand on his, and he was glad he'd stayed.

"I'm a fool, father. All this time."

He had some idea of what she meant. "You're not a fool. You're a good person. And so is he. Perhaps it simply wasn't meant to be."

"Then there is no one else. I shall be a spinster."

He couldn't help it. He smiled, and she turned away from him again.

"Oh, I know you think I'm a silly little girl."

"I've never in your life thought you were silly. You have taught me as much as I have taught you. And I'm not at all the person you need when there are matters of the heart to discuss. I have only felt romantic love for one person in my life."

"You never talk like anyone else does, even at a time like this."

"I talk like I talk."

"Of course you do. I'm sorry. I'm just all . . ." She broke off and waved her hands in the air, but one hand fluttered back down to rest on his again.

"You have no idea how proud I am of you," he said. But he saw that she was about to start crying again, so he felt he ought to change the subject. "You know, young Pinch seems to be quite fond of you." He knew right away that it was the wrong thing to say.

She took her hand back.

"Damnit," he said. "I don't know what's so appealing about Hammersmith. He's a decent fellow, but he's so focused on his work that he doesn't even notice anything else."

Fiona took the handkerchief away from her face and looked up at him, her eyes rimmed red and her nose moist, but a smile playing across her lips. "You think Nevil is too focused on his work? You?"

"Ah, yes. I am perhaps not the right person to point out that flaw, am I?"

"Father, I didn't mean . . ." She looked away again.

"No, no, you're right. Maybe that's why the boy's so appealing. It's what you grew up with. You think it's normal."

"I don't know what's normal, and I don't care what's normal."

"He's what you want?"

"I don't want to want him. Or anyone else."

"Fiona, look at me. Have you told him how you feel?"

"Of course not."

"Well, then all of this is for nothing. How can he know if you don't tell him?"

"I've practically thrown myself in his path. I'm sorry, Father, but I have."

"You were a child when he met you."

"I'm not a child now."

Kingsley smiled a sad sort of smile and looked carefully at the laces of his shoes.

"I know you still see me as a child, Father, but I'm truly not. At least three of the girls I went to school with are married already. I'm practically a spinster. I really am a grown woman."

"Then make him see that. If he's worth all this, then do something about it. You can't simply bat your eyes and hope for the best. Go after what you want, Fiona, because life is too short to do otherwise. Before you know it, you'll be old and you'll have no idea where it all went."

"You're not old."

"What makes you think I was talking about myself?"

She laughed and he smiled. He took the handkerchief from her and wiped her eyes and dabbed at her nose.

"Now come on. I need help out there, and as we've established, Mr Pinch is woefully inadequate."

"Oh, Father!"

But she stood and took his arm, and together they walked back to the library. He felt the slightest bit bad for Nevil Hammersmith. The boy apparently had no idea what was going on, and if he wasn't careful he was going to lose the best person he would ever have the opportunity to meet.

43

When Day awoke, the first thing he saw was Nevil Hammersmith sitting dutifully at the foot of the bed like an old Labrador. Hammersmith jumped up and grabbed the inspector's hand. He seemed incapable of speech, and Day smiled.

"How long was I asleep?"

"All night. I was beginning to worry you'd never wake up."

"Where am I? The hospital?"

"Guildhall."

"Oh," Day said. "Posh."

"Indeed," Hammersmith said. "Nothing but the best. Let me get the doctor. He was just here."

"No need. I'm fine."

"Well, he'll want to see you. And not to worry, Claire knows and she's on her way here. We all want to hear everything that's happened with you."

"Oh, is it Kingsley? The doctor, I mean."

"His assistant was plastering your ribs. But of course Kingsley's here. He's tending some of the others who were hurt, but now you're awake I imagine he'll take over your treatment himself."

"Hold off, would you, Nevil? Don't fetch anyone just yet. In fact . . ." Day struggled to sit up. "Keep everyone out. Do those doors lock?"

"I don't . . . Well, let me . . ." Nevil hurried to the double doors that connected the room to the library beyond it, but they opened outward and there was no way to barricade them properly. He shook his head and returned to the side of the bed.

"Where's my cane?"

"On the chair over there," Hammersmith said. "You drew the sword on me, you know."

"But I didn't kill you, which is not only a huge relief, but it means I can trust myself around you. I don't know that I could guarantee the same about anyone else at the moment."

"What's going on? What's wrong?"

"To be honest, I don't know," Day said. "Not entirely. You must think I'm mad."

"Yes, of course I do. A complete nutter."

Day broke into laughter. He couldn't help himself. After all he'd been through, the constant stress and anxiety, it was good to know he could depend on Nevil Hammersmith to be utterly honest. Pain lanced through his torso, and he clutched his stomach.

"You're not supposed to move," Hammersmith said. "Doctor's orders. You're busted up a bit inside from the fall."

"How bad?"

"Fractured ribs."

"Lucky I'm not dead." Day gritted his teeth and took a shallow breath.

"I think what happened when you fell, you hit a table and the table collapsed under you. Could be worse, though. One chap out there . . ." He nodded in the direction of the library. "He's got to have his arm off." He made a sawing motion with his hand.

Day waited until he had caught his breath and waved Hammersmith closer to him so they could speak quietly. "All right," he said, "so maybe I am mad. Who wouldn't be? I barely remember anything of the past year, but it's coming back to me in bits and pieces, and more and more with every passing minute. I remember snatches of conversations I had with that creature, things that he told me."

"Jack, you mean?"

"Yes. Jack."

"So you've been with him this whole time, while everyone's been tearing their hair out searching for you?"

"Not the whole time. But, yes, most of it."

"How have you survived?"

"Because of something I think he wants me to do. It's why you've got to keep everyone away. And, Nevil, it's why you've got to help me get out of here right away."

"I don't understand."

"Jack wants me to kill someone close to me."

44

Leland Carlyle retreated to his club. Not the secret society, not the underground chambers of the Karstphanomen, but rather the gentlemen's club he frequented while in the city. There he could rest and think, free from the concerns of family and business. He had nearly killed someone that morning, had gone to a coffeehouse specifically to murder a young woman, and the fact that he might even entertain such a notion shook him to his core.

He handed over his hat and coat and retired to the public room, where he took a seat by the fire. He sank into a wide leather chair, ordered a Scotch and soda, and closed his eyes, enjoying the feel of quiet privilege that he no longer felt he deserved.

He had always been able to rationalize the activities of the Karstphanomen. Murder was not the order of the day for that group of men. They championed justice. They taught murderers a valuable lesson about the cost of a human life. But today Carlyle had reduced himself to acting like a common killer.

He wondered when he had lost track of the line that separated the civilized man from the predator. And he wondered when he had crossed that line.

More, he had hired mercenaries to act on behalf of the Karstphanomen. But he had done so at the bidding of the members, and so he didn't feel personally responsible for that miscalculation. He realized they had done it from fear, from a sense of self-preservation. But he understood now that the Karstphanomen could not be personally responsible for murder or they were no better than the men they judged. What they had done flew in the face of everything they professed to believe in, everything they had set themselves against.

They had invited judgment upon themselves.

"Sir?"

Carlyle opened his eyes, a smile at the ready, thinking his drink had arrived. But the valet, Potter-Pirbright, was standing at the side of his chair with a look of concern draped over his normally receptive features. He was holding Carlyle's hat and coat.

"What is it?"

"Your guests are causing a minor sensation, if you don't mind my saying. It might be best to ask them to move along. Or perhaps the gentleman has an errand elsewhere."

"I believe you're mistaken," Carlyle said. "I have no guests."

"My apologies, sir."

"No need. A mistake, that's all."

"Indeed." But Potter-Pirbright didn't move from the side of the chair.

"Was there something else?"

"They arrived at your heels, sir, and have not stirred from the front of this establishment since you entered."

"I told you, they're nothing to do with me."

"As you say."

"Then what is it, man?"

"They are disturbing some of the others, sir. In particular, the young lady wearing trousers has caused a bit of a stir with some of the older gentlemen of the club. Those of us in the younger generation are more open-minded, I'm sure." (Potter-Pirbright was eighty years old if he was a day.) "If she would stop leering at everyone who enters, perhaps her presence would be more easily overlooked."

"But I tell you, they're not— Did you say the woman was wearing trousers?"

"Indeed, sir. And fetching trousers they are."

Carlyle knew of only one woman who wore trousers in public. And if she had followed him here, to his club, perhaps she had followed him elsewhere. Carlyle stood, and Potter-Pirbright helped him on with his coat. He took his hat and, without a word to the valet, left the public room and went out by the front door. He paused and looked back at the club, the heavy oak doors and the marble columns of the porte cochere. He knew he would not be welcomed back.

He turned and looked up and down the street, but the Parkers were nowhere to be seen. He raised his hand and hailed a two-wheeler, hopping in as soon as it rolled to a stop. He gave the driver Claire's address and settled back into the seat. He thought longingly of his Scotch and soda, which had surely been prepared already. What would they do with it? He snorted, a sad, abrupt sort of chuckle. The valet would probably drink it, congratulating himself all the while for having disgraced Carlyle. That sort was always looking for an opportunity at the expense of their betters.

If Mr and Mrs Parker had followed him to his club and seen him inside, perhaps they had turned their attention elsewhere. He had, after all, set them an impossible task. He had asked them to find and kill Jack the Ripper. Who would blithely undertake such a thing? Unless they had planned all along to do away with Carlyle himself and keep that portion of their fee they had already collected. It made perfect sense.

If they had followed him to his club, perhaps they had followed him to his daughter's home. Perhaps they thought she knew something or was an accomplice. He knew he wasn't thinking straight, but he thought perhaps that was a good thing. It showed he wasn't like them. He was a caring human being, a man who had stopped himself from committing violence. A good man.

Leland's wife, Eleanor, was surrounded by servants at all times (and no doubt making them miserable), so he wasn't unduly concerned about her.

But he needed to look in on his daughter before he could think any further. It occurred to him that the Parkers had purposefully drawn him out of his club for some reason, but he didn't care. If Claire was all right, then he hadn't completely ruined his life yet. She was the best of him, and they couldn't take her away. He wouldn't let them.

45

Claire Day ran through Guildhall to the library and spotted Fiona Kingsley talking to her father. Sunlight through the high windows illuminated a ghastly scene, with a dozen or more men and women on gurneys and a handful of doctors and nurses flitting about among them, bringing towels and water and instruments to their bedsides.

"Fiona! Dr Kingsley!" Claire bustled up to them, and the doctor set down a bone saw, wiped his hands on a rag tucked into his belt.

"Claire," he said. "Really, you shouldn't be in here. This isn't something you ought to—"

"Where is my husband? Where's Walter?"

"Ah, of course. He's in the other room. But he's sleeping right now."

"I don't care. Which room?"

"Father," Fiona said, "you can't keep her away from him after so long." Fiona's eyes looked red.

"Yes, yes, I see. If you can be quiet and let him sleep, I'll show you in."

"I'll wake him if I damn well want to wake him."

Kingsley's eyebrows flew up, but he sighed and motioned for her to follow him. He led the way to the huge doors of the Print Room, and Claire averted her eyes as she passed a man who was lucky to have passed out. She looked away too late to avoid seeing the bones of his arm protruding from the flesh.

Kingsley pulled open a door and stuck his head in the room, then rushed inside. Claire and Fiona followed him. The room was empty.

"Where is he?"

"I don't know," Kingsley said. He turned around and shouted. "Pinch! Get in here!" To Claire he said, "Young Pinch was treating your husband."

Kingsley didn't wait for his assistant. He went to the doors at the other end of the room and though them, down a short passage to the art gallery. It, too, was empty, but a window at the far end of the room was standing open, a slight breeze blowing the curtains.

"He's gone," Kingsley said.

"And Nevil's gone with him," Fiona said.

Pinch trotted up behind them. "Well, he won't get far with those ribs," he said.

"You don't know my husband," Claire said. "And perhaps I don't, either."

46

Slow down, Nevil, would you?"

Hammersmith stopped and waited for Day to catch up to him. "I'm sorry. I wasn't thinking. Your leg?"

"No . . . Not at all . . . It's only . . ." Day shook his head and held up a finger, asking for a minute. He leaned on his cane, and when he'd caught his breath he started again. "It's hard to breathe with this plaster on."

"We're well away from Guildhall now," Hammersmith said. "But where are we going?"

"I need to check on someone at Drapers' Gardens. Just need to make sure she's all right."

"You mean Esther Paxton."

"How did you know?"

"She's back there in the library with the Plumm's casualties. We've left her behind."

Day turned and put a hand on his chest. "She was there?"

Hammersmith nodded.

"Is she well?"

"Not bad. The doctor moved her there so he could keep an eye on her injuries while he tended the others, but none of us knows who she is. I mean to say, who is she to you?"

"Until yesterday I thought she might represent a new life for me."

"A new life? Is that where you've been the last year? Taking up with some woman while the rest of us were worried sick about you?"

"It's not . . . Here, let's get off the beaten track so we can talk." Day hobbled down Mason's Alley and ducked into the doorway of a restaurant. Hammersmith followed, and they stood out of sight of the main thoroughfare.

"Well?"

"Nevil, it's not what you think. I was held prisoner for months. By the time he let me go, I thought maybe everyone had moved on without me."

"You fool."

"Yes, well, I am that. But Nevil, I couldn't go back to my life as I knew it. And at first I didn't even know my life. I didn't remember who I was. It's come back to me gradually, and more yesterday than ever before. But I can't trust myself near anyone but you. And it's because I didn't try to kill you already, don't you see? Esther wasn't a part of my old life, and so I could be with her. At least, I thought I could. Only it didn't work that way. He wouldn't let me be."

"None of that makes even the slightest bit of sense, you know."

"Oh, I know."

"Why don't you try telling me again."

"Let's keep walking," Day said. "But slowly. I'll talk along the way."

They walked east toward Drapers' Gardens while Day filled Hammersmith in on everything that had happened to him in the past few weeks. When they reached the gardens, Day pointed out the shrubbery where he had slept during his first few days of freedom. A minute or two later, they arrived at Esther Paxton's shop and Day dug out his key. He opened the door and Hammersmith followed him in. The furniture had been righted since Day had last seen the place and the broken glass swept up.

"The neighbors must have pitched in," he said.

"Neighbors?"

"This was practically demolished."

"It still doesn't look like much."

"I have a room upstairs. She was very good to me. Here, sit down—watch there's no glass there—and I'll tell you the rest. Tea?"

"Please. Unless you plan to poison me."

"Why would I do that?"

"I have no idea. You're acting odd. Talking about killing people."

"If I were planning to kill you, I certainly wouldn't use poison. In the past you've proved immune to the stuff."

"Immune or not, I don't much care for it."

"Fine. I won't poison you. Give me a minute."

Day climbed the stairs and Hammersmith went to the window. He watched people passing by, children running to join their friends, women paying social calls on one another or heading out for the day's shopping trip. The beat constable hove into view down the street, and Hammersmith glanced at the stairs before slipping out the front door. He left the door open and raised his hand, hailing the constable, who strolled over to him.

"Help you?"

"I'm hoping you can do something for me. Is there a telephone nearby?"

"Got my call box next street over."

"Is there any chance you'd be willing to ring Guildhall?"

"'Fraid it's meant for official police business, sir. If you're looking for a telephone for yourself, I can direct you to—"

"No time. I need a doctor here right away."

The constable perked up and turned his gaze on the open front door of Paxton's Drapery. "Someone hurt? Not that same woman got roughed up yesterday?"

"No, no, nothing like that." Hammersmith stopped and scowled at the constable for a moment, trying to figure out how to explain that his friend had become a raving madman, without seeming to be disrespectful of Day or raising any alarms. At last he reached into his pocket and pulled out a half crown, which he held up so that the constable could see it. "Just this once, maybe you could break the rules?"

The constable nodded slowly, then reached out and took the money. "Guildhall, you say?"

"Yes." Hammersmith breathed a sigh of relief that he'd run into a reasonably corrupt policeman. "The doctor's name is Kingsley. Give him this address and tell him to drop everything and get right over here. It's about Day."

"Today?"

"No. Inspector Day."

"Inspector Day? Has he been found?"

"Oh, um, well, yes, actually he has. But he needs help."

The constable handed the half crown back to Hammersmith. "You keep this, then. Day was always good to me. Keep your eye on him and I'll fetch that doctor."

With that, the constable turned and hurried away. Hammersmith put his half crown back in his pocket and went back inside, quietly shutting the door. He crossed to the sofa and sat, and in another minute Day reappeared, holding two teacups by their handles in one hand.

"Here we are," he said. "Were you outside just now?"

"Took the air a bit."

"Hmm. It is stuffy. Here, I don't seem to have any milk."

"It's all right. Just fine as is."

"Good. I put an extra dollop of poison in yours, though, so don't take the wrong cup."

"Right." Hammersmith managed a wan smile and took the offered cup. He stared at it dubiously, then blew across the steaming surface and took a sip. "Funny," he said. "I hardly taste it."

47

Hatty was feeling a great deal of pressure. Now that Inspector Day had been found, she took it for granted that Mr Hammersmith would finally assume the proper duties of a detective and would begin to investigate other cases. Which was all well and good, but Hatty was afraid it would mean the end of her freedom. Would Hammersmith allow her to keep investigating cases on her own? More likely, she would be relegated to a clerk's position at the agency, and she didn't think she could bear that.

She had helped move Mr Day and some of the other victims of the Plumm's collapse to the hall and had seen to their comfort as well as she was able, but as soon as she'd had the opportunity she'd slipped away. Even if she never got a chance to investigate another case, she wanted to finish the one she'd started, she wanted to find Joseph Hargreave and prove, if only to herself, that she was capable of the work.

Success begat success. Perhaps Mr Hammersmith would see how good she was and allow her to help in some manner more substantial than just taking notes and filing paperwork. He was a good man, Mr Hammersmith, and she clung to the hope that he might be a progressive employer. But she couldn't prove herself unless she solved the case. She had to move quickly.

The three obvious places for Hargreave to be hiding were his cottage, his place of employment, and his flat in the city. She had ticked those off in the past few days, but there was one more place to check before she hit a dead end. Plumm's kept small apartments behind the store for certain employees, in order to keep their commute short and keep them on the job longer each day. One had been reserved for the floor manager's use. It seemed to her that it would be hard to hide for very long in a flat behind a department store, but she was desperate and therefore willing to turn over any rock available to her.

The street in front of Plumm's was quiet, people passing by and stopping to stare at the magnificent wreckage. But nobody was going in or coming out. The injured had been moved, and the staff had been dismissed. The police had secured the main doors, but windows had been broken out at the front and sides of the building, and no attempt had been made to board them up again. There was nothing left worth stealing. Tomorrow workers would come and begin tearing everything out, hauling away the rubble. Hatty wondered if they would rebuild or give up and sell the lot. Would anybody still be willing to shop there, knowing what had happened?

She skirted the main building and went around to Coleman Street, where there was a door set into a recess. She knocked on it, and when there was no answer, she knocked harder so that her knuckles tingled. She heard no sound from within. She looked all round, then tried the knob. To her surprise, the door was unlocked, and she opened it and went inside.

She was facing a long passage with doors on either side and a staircase that led up the right-hand wall. All was quiet. The staff had been temporarily relocated. She walked to the first door and opened it without knocking. The small room was furnished with a table, a chair, a bed, and a lamp. All of it looked cheap to Hatty; none of it looked like the sorts of things that were actually sold by Plumm's. The table held a small collection of toiletries and cosmetics, and there was a cardboard wardrobe standing in the corner next to the bed. Inside hung three identical white blouses and three identical black skirts. She left that room and went to the next, where she found similar furnishings and similar clothing hanging in another cardboard wardrobe. Hatty decided that the female staff of the store must be housed on the ground floor, and she went back to the staircase and climbed up.

There was a locked door at the landing of the first floor up, so she kept going. When she reached the next floor, she paused and listened, glad that her loss of hearing had been temporary. She wondered what she would do if she found Joseph Hargreave and he was dead. She had seen dead bodies before, but she didn't care to see another one if she could help it.

The door at the far end of the hallway swung slowly open, an invitation, and her breath caught in her throat.

"Hello? Is someone there?"

Hatty heard nothing but the return echo of her own voice, and so she crept forward until she was just outside the room. There was no light inside and no one emerged into the passage.

"Mr Hargreave?"

"Please come in." The voice was soft and low with a pleasant rumbling quality. "Forgive me for not standing. I'm a bit indisposed."

"Mr Hargreave, is that you?"

"No, indeed," the man inside the room said. "But come in. I'd like to talk with you. You may leave the door open behind you if that puts you at ease."

"No need. If you aren't Mr Hargreave, I'll be on my way."

She turned to go, but the voice called out to her again.

"Which one are you? I'm afraid I get you all mixed up, one with the others."

"What do you mean?" Hatty did not turn toward the door, but nor did she continue down the hallway. She stood, tense and ready to run, with her back to the dark room.

"I know you're not Eugenia Merrilow. She's quite distinct in my mind. You're either Fiona Kingsley or Hatty Pitt. You two are rather similar to each other, if you don't mind my saying, and I haven't bothered to pinpoint which of you is which."

Now Hatty turned and faced the man she couldn't see. He was somewhere far back in the room, and she felt confident she had enough of a head start if he came after her. "How do you know us?"

"Oh, our friend Nevil Hammersmith likes to surround himself with pretty little females of the species, doesn't he?"

"I don't know."

"Why do you think that is?"

"I don't know."

"You don't know much. You might at least venture a guess. I'm going to do just that and guess that you are Hatty Pitt. Ah, by the change in your posture I see that I'm right. Very good to meet you, Hatty Pitt. Please, don't be so rude. Come here where I can see you better. You're silhouetted in the light and I can only see your form."

"I think I'm fine where I am."

"Shall I sweeten the pot for you, then?" Hatty heard the creaking wood of a chair as someone shifted his weight and then a muffled cry of pain. "Did you hear that, Hatty Pitt? That was Joseph Hargreave. Just the man you wanted to see."

"Mr Hargreave?"

"Oh, he can't answer you. Cat's got his tongue. Or something's got it, but he certainly doesn't."

Hatty felt a creeping warmth along her scalp and her throat. She knew where Mr Hargreave's tongue was.

"Did you know Joseph Hargreave and his brother were members of a secret society that tortures people like me?"

"Of course not."

"It's true. I can tell you, this is a man who needed his tongue out, and more besides."

"That's horrid."

"Hatty Pitt, you and I have something in common, did you know that?"

"What have you done to Mr Hargreave?"

"I asked you a question. You can't answer with a totally unrelated question of your own. That's not playing by the rules of proper conversation, now is it?"

She raised her voice, calling out to the other man in the room. "I'm going to bring the police, Mr Hargreave. Please just wait a few minutes and I'll be right back."

"Tut, tut, Hatty Pitt. If you leave here before we finish our conversation, I will kill Mr Hargreave outright long before you return with the constabulary."

"What do you want from me?"

"An answer, to start. Do you know what we have in common?"

"No."

"We have both saved Nevil Hammersmith's life at different times. Isn't that interesting? I stopped his bleeding to death once when there was no one else to do it."

"Why would you do that? You seem ghastly."

"Hurtful of you to say. I did it because I had no reason not to. I didn't wish Nevil Hammersmith any harm at the time. Of course I changed my mind some time later and tried to drop a great gob of glass on him, but you saved him from that. According to Oriental custom, we now share an obligation to Nevil Hammersmith's well-being."

"You're Mr Oberon, aren't you?"

"It's what I've been calling myself."

"You took Mr Hargreave's place."

"Hatty Pitt, I have spent the past weeks pretending to be someone I am not while occupying this shithole of a flat and that stupid wee cottage by the sea with only this dolt for company. He's a terrible conversationalist, owing in part to the fact of his missing tongue. But he wasn't of much use even before he lost that. If it isn't too much to ask, I'd like to have a civil chat with a nice young lady."

"'Come into my parlor, said the spider to the fly.'"

"Did you call me a spider, Hatty Pitt? Are you afraid of spiders? No need to be. Spiders rid the world of filthy vermin. Do you think you're filthy vermin? Is that why you're afraid to converse with me? And would you place Mr Hargreave in mortal danger simply because you're afraid? You seem like a brave girl to me. You wouldn't do that to Mr Hargreave."

"You'd kill us both anyway as soon as you got your hands on me."

"Hmm. You know, you're probably right."

Hatty gasped and took a step backward, but something in her refused to let her leave. The man inside the room was clearly some sort of monster. But she did not want to be cowed by anyone, not man or woman or the Devil himself. "I'm not afraid of you."

"Well, perhaps you should be, after all. I sometimes have the best of intentions, but then my nature gets the better of me anyway. I'll tell you what: I promise not to touch you once you are inside this room. To be quite honest, I could use some assistance. But if you back away any farther, I shall rush at you no matter what the cost to myself, and then I will touch you a great many times and in ways I do not think you will appreciate."

"You may threaten me all you like, but there are people who know where I am. I told Eugenia where I was going."

"Are you lying to me, Hatty Pitt?"

"No. No, I'm not lying to you."

"I believe you. So you see, you're doubly safe. You have Eugenia Merrilow's knowledge of your whereabouts and you have my word that I will not touch you."

"Your word isn't worth anything to me."

"Oh, but it should be worth something at least," Mr Oberon said. "I almost never break my word."

"You won't hurt me?"

"I said I wouldn't touch you and I won't."

"And you won't hurt Mr Hargreave, either?"

"Oh, I've said no such thing. I've harmed your Mr Hargreave on a near constant basis these past weeks, both here in his flat and at his cottage. It was the only thing to keep me occupied, really. I've been so very bored."

"You won't harm him any more than you already have, then?"

"Oh, I'd hate to promise you a thing like that."

"You must or our conversation has ended."

Mr Oberon laughed and she heard the clapping of hands. "Delightful. So very brave. Yes, Hatty Pitt. Come and sit with me and I promise I shall leave Mr Hargreave alone for the time being."

Hatty considered for a moment, then breathed deeply and stepped across the threshold into the room.

"Wonderful," Mr Oberon said. "Now please, call me Jack."

48

He thinks he's mad," Hammersmith said.

"He might very well be mad," Dr Kingsley said. "Who knows what he's been through this past year? Has he told you much?"

"Very little. When we were talking he focused more on the past month than the past year. I don't think he remembers a lot of what happened to him."

"Strange. Amnesia is quite rare. I wonder if he's suffered some sort of head trauma."

"There's one way to find out."

"Yes, of course," Dr Kingsley said. "Let's have a look at him."

Hammersmith opened the door of the draper's shop and followed Kingsley inside. It seemed darker than it had mere moments before, and he realized Day had rehung the curtains in the windows.

"Walter?"

"Back here." Day's voice traveled down the passage from the back rooms. "Out in a moment."

Kingsley set his bag on a table and sat on the sofa, straightened the creases of his trousers. Hammersmith had never seen the doctor act nervous before.

Day entered the room, holding a curtain rod. "I managed to bend this back into—" He stopped when he saw Kingsley and dropped the rod, shrank back against the wall. "Nevil, no! What have you done?"

"He's here to help," Hammersmith said.

Kingsley stood and opened his arms to Day. "Walter, I wish you no harm."

"I don't mind whatever you wish for me. It's what I might do to you, don't you see?" Day disappeared, his footsteps pelting away to the back of the house again.

Kingsley shot Hammersmith a confused glance and went to the doorway. "Walter?"

"Go away, Doctor! I can't guarantee what I'll do if you stay here."

"Walter, you won't hurt me."

"I don't know that."

Hammersmith still wasn't sure how loud he was talking or whether he ought to yell. He cupped his hands around his mouth and shouted in a way he hoped wasn't too forceful or unfriendly. "I won't let you hurt him, Walter. Don't you trust me?"

"Of course!"

"If you try to harm Dr Kingsley, I'll stop you."

"What if you can't?"

"Walter," Dr Kingsley said. "I don't believe you'll hurt me. Don't you trust my judgment? Don't you trust Nevil's judgment?"

They were quiet then and waited. Eventually Day shuffled back into view.

"If I make one move to hurt the doctor, Nevil, you've got to do whatever it takes to stop me."

"That won't happen," Kingsley said. "You won't hurt me any more than you would hurt Nevil, would you?"

"I may not be in control of my actions."

"It doesn't matter, Walter. Let me explain something. Come here and sit."

Day obeyed, perching uncomfortably at the edge of the sofa as if he might flee. He looked terrified, and Hammersmith pitied him, imagining his friend sleeping in a ditch to avoid endangering his friends and family. It was hard to imagine what a year in the clutches of Jack the Ripper might do to a person's mind.

Kingsley settled into a chair across from Day and smiled. "Mr Hammersmith says you think you've been mesmerized?"

"Yes," Day said. "That's what it was. He did that to me. Jack did that."

"It's a popular parlor trick. But the popular conception of it is surrounded by a lot of mumbo jumbo, and most people don't really understand how it works. I don't think you're going to harm anyone, Walter, no matter what you've been told by that lunatic."

"He's ordered me to kill someone, I know that much. As soon as I see that person, I'll lash out. He's done something to my brain to ensure that I've become his weapon against his enemies. Against my friends."

Kingsley smiled. "I see. And you thought I might be Jack the Ripper's enemy."

"The crow," Hammersmith said. "Or the white king."

"I don't know who it is," Day said. "I don't remember that part. He hid it from me. I only know that it's someone close to me, which is why he's done this, why he's used me. I think maybe he can't get close to the person himself, but I can. Or perhaps it's simply his perverse sense of humor to make me do it. To ruin me. I couldn't live with myself."

"He certainly is perverse," Kingsley said. "I'm just not sure he's as smart as you seem to think he is."

Hammersmith cleared his throat. "Can you fix this, Doctor?"

"Fix it? Certainly, if I knew the commands Jack used to do this. Without that knowledge, it might take some time."

"Which is why," Day said, "I've got to stay away from everyone I love."

"Well, it would seem Dr Kingsley and I are both safe from you," Hammersmith said. "What if we introduced you to each person you know, one at a time, and we'll stop you if you try to kill them?"

"Don't be ridiculous," Kingsley said.

"I was being serious," Hammersmith said. "What's wrong with that plan?"

Kingsley sighed. "I'm not prepared to become Mr Day's personal attendant. Walter, you're not a madman. As far as I can see right now, talking to you here, you're as normal as you ever were. Somewhat indecisive, as you have always been, but a sincere and caring individual. Now, if Jack's done something, if he's mesmerized you as you seem to think, there are very real limitations to that. He can't have suggested to you that you murder someone you care about and then really expect you to go through with it. You simply wouldn't do it."

"I wouldn't?"

"No, Walter, you can't be made to do something under hypnosis that you wouldn't have done otherwise. It doesn't work that way. In other words, if you have a strong compunction against harming me or Nevil or anyone else, why then, you'll stop yourself, even without the intervention of Mr Hammersmith or myself. No matter how much you've been told to kill someone, you'll balk at the task."

"Is that true?"

"Well, I'm no expert in mesmerism, but from everything I've read, yes, you are perfectly safe from killing your friends and family. I can promise you that. You're not likely to kill anyone else, either. In fact, given your facility for understanding other people, I'm surprised you would think such things about yourself."

"I was afraid."

"Of course you were. You've been under this person's influence long enough, he might have got you to think anything. I can put you back under hypnosis fairly easily and I might be able to poke around in your head and see what's been done, but it's not necessary at the moment and I hate to do it without knowing more. And I'd like you to be a bit more calm before we make the attempt. Meantime, you're quite safe from becoming a murderer, I assure you. It's this memory loss that's got me more concerned."

"Things are starting to come back to me. I think I can remember nearly everything."

"He remembered I'd been poisoned," Hammersmith said.

"Good. Tell me, what did he do to you? Did Jack strike you on the head or otherwise do anything that caused you pain or headaches?"

"I don't remember."

"Would you allow me to examine you?"

"If you like."

"Thank you." Kingsley stood and approached Day, his hands held out at his sides.

"You seem wary, Doctor."

"I am a bit."

"But you said I won't hurt you. You were certain of it."

"What I meant was that Jack cannot have compelled you to hurt me. But you might still be a danger."

Day sat very still, his hands in his lap, while Kingsley moved around to the back of the sofa and bent down to look at the top of Day's head. "I'm going to touch your head."

"All right."

"Don't be alarmed."

"Thank you. I won't be."

"Good." Kingsley probed Day's scalp with the tips of his fingers, moving Day's hair this way and that. "Hammersmith, bring that lamp over here, would you?"

"What is it?"

"Get that light over here. Look at that. Do you see it?"

"I don't know," Hammersmith said.

"Feel it. Scars. Many of them. Mr Day, have you suffered any head injuries before?"

"I was hit in the head with a shovel. But that was years ago."

"Hmm. More than once?"

"Only the one time. It was enough to put me off the experience."

"Indeed." Kingsley sniffed and nodded to Hammersmith. He moved back round and sat across from Day. "Not so bad, was it?"

"No. But you say I've got scars on my head?"

"I'm afraid so. Quite a few. More than might be explained by your encounter with the shovel. This fellow Jack was unkind to you while you were in his care."

"Is that why I don't remember?"

"I don't think it's that simple. Walter, I think you don't remember because you don't *want* to remember. Sometimes, when a person has experienced something profoundly traumatic, he can sort of choose to forget. I've seen it once or twice in my practice and I believe that's what's happened with you."

"I don't want to remember what he did?"

"Exactly. And because you don't want to remember, you're burying those thoughts and memories deep in your brain somewhere."

"Then can you help me remember?"

"I don't know," Kingsley said. "I don't think so. Nor do I think I ought to. Sometimes the psyche protects itself this way. It might actually cause you harm if you were to remember."

"But I need to know what Jack wanted from me or I won't ever feel at ease around anyone again."

Hammersmith had been standing against the wall, watching them. Now he crossed between them and sat next to Kingsley. "Figuring out what a criminal's after? It's only the sort of thing we do all the time, isn't it?" He leaned forward so that he was looking Day directly in the face. "Why did the man kill his wife? What did the burglar want? Jack is a criminal, and we question criminals all the time, both directly and indirectly."

"Right," Walter said. He perked up a bit and edged closer to them, his hands gripping his knees. "Do you think we can?"

"Yes. Absolutely. Doctor, what was the rest of the rhyme on the wall in Walter's house?"

"In my house?"

"Your old house on Regent's Park. Jack left a message there."

"It wasn't a rhyme," Kingsley said. "At least, not like any rhyme I've ever seen. It started with a Latin phrase. *Exitus probatur*. It means—"

"It means 'the ends are justified,'" Day said.

"Something like that," Kingsley said.

"No, that's exactly what they mean when they say it. The Karst-phanomen, those shadowy men that Jack hates so much."

"So that was a warning to them, not to me," Hammersmith said.

"Jack mentioned Mr Hammersmith in his message," Kingsley said.

"I think he's proud that he saved your life," Day said. "He's responsible for you."

"He'll regret that when I find him."

"What else did the message say?"

"A lot of poorly spelled nonsense," Hammersmith said. "The point is that he's still focused on the society, the Karstphanomen. That's who he's after."

"And that's who he's sent me after, too," Day said.

"Has to be. So someone you know is a Karstphanomen."

"I don't know any of them. Not anymore. Inspector March is dead now and I can't think of any others."

"But you do still know another one, you must. It's why he needed you. You can get close to one of them and he can't. But why can't he do it himself? Why send you?"

"Perhaps it's as Mr Day suggested. Jack could kill that man himself if he wanted to, but finds it more amusing to send our friend to do it," Kingsley said.

"To hurt me, even as he hurts someone else."

"Or to break your will even further."

Hammersmith ran his hands through his hair and stood and paced back and forth. "We have to draw him out somehow. We have to end this. If we can figure out who that evil bloody bastard was trying to get at through Walter, maybe we can get him to make a mistake."

"I might have some idea," Kingsley said. "Something Mr Hammersmith said a minute ago."

"How so?"

"That writing on the wall. He said he was after someone he called 'the crow.' It's been pointed out to me that the word *crow* might sometimes be specific jargon meaning a doctor."

"I hadn't heard that before."

"Possibly before your time, Mr Hammersmith. But Jack may be targeting a doctor, and I might know who that is."

"Who?"

"Me," Kingsley said.

49

Fiona followed Claire through the front doors of the Hammersmith Agency. The young woman behind the desk didn't look up.

"What can I do for you?"

"My husband is missing," Claire said.

"Oh, dear, Mrs Day." The woman jumped up and came around, moved the paperwork off a chair, and gestured for her main client to sit. "What brings you here today?"

"Eugenia," Claire said, "this is my friend Fiona Kingsley. Fiona, this is Miss Merrilow."

"Pleased," Fiona said. "We don't need to sit down. We're looking for Mr Hammersmith. Is he here?"

"I haven't seen him at all today," Eugenia said.

"Do you know where he is?"

"I'm afraid I don't. I'm alone here or I'd try him at home."

"Do you think he's there?"

"No." Eugenia leaned back against the front of her desk and bit her lower lip. "Really, he's rarely at home, anyway. He's out somewhere looking for Mr Day, if that helps matters, Mrs Day."

"He's found my husband already," Claire said. "And now he's run off somewhere and so has Mr Day, and I don't know where they've gone."

"He found him? He finally found him?"

"For a minute or two," Claire said. "But now they're both gone."

"Oh, dear," Eugenia said again. "A cup of tea?"

"No, thank you. You've no ideas?"

"Even Hatty hasn't been in and she usually checks in with me."

"Hatty?"

"Yes," Eugenia said. "I'm sorry, what did you say your name was?"

"Fiona."

"Yes, Fiona. Hatty is the other investigator here."

"She's an investigator?" Fiona had no idea why, but she felt a hot pang of jealousy at the base of her neck.

"Well, she fancies herself one." Eugenia pushed herself off the desk and went round to her chair, sat back down. "She usually checks in with me in the morning, but she wasn't here today."

"Do you think she's with Nevil?"

"No, they rarely cross paths."

Fiona felt a wave of relief pass through her. "Well, we've got to track Mr Hammersmith somehow. Do you think Hatty knows where he is?"

"I would have no idea. The last I heard, she was going to investigate the department store. The new one, you know? She's on her own little hunt for someone. It's awfully ambitious."

"Do you mean Plumm's?"

"Yes, that's the one. The gentleman she's looking for works there. Or worked there. Perhaps he's dead. Exciting! At any rate, he worked there, he lived there. And Hatty's got some kind of list of places to look at."

"If she was going there, then we should go there, too," Fiona said.

"It collapsed," Claire said. "Isn't it completely gone? That's where Mr Hammersmith found Walter."

"Wait," Fiona said. "What do you mean he lived there?"

"I can't believe he found Mr Day," Eugenia said. "How long have we been looking? Months!"

"What do you mean he lived there? Lived at Plumm's?"

"Yes, they have apartments at the back," Eugenia said. "Or so Hatty said. Keeps the workers there longer hours." Her eyes flicked to the clock against the wall.

"At the back? Behind the store?"

"Somewhere back there. I don't know. Nobody tells me anything. I'm quite undervalued."

"I'll tell Mr Hammersmith to give you an increase in pay," Claire said. "Thank you."

They were already out the door when Fiona heard Eugenia's voice. "Does this mean you're no longer a client?"

50

I was old enough to know better," Kingsley said. "But I still allowed my emotions to get the better of me. My wife had just died, and I was angry and I had two young daughters."

They were walking down Moorgate toward Plumm's. Day was leaning heavily on his cane, and Hammersmith was leaning forward, trying desperately to hear what Kingsley was saying. Kingsley's voice was a soft foghorn noise drifting across to him from some faraway place. He could make sense of the words, but the conversation was getting ahead of him.

"They approached me," Kingsley said. "Catherine had died of consumption, and Fiona was at an age when she needed a mother. I wasn't of much use to her anymore."

"I'm sure that's not true, Doctor," Day said.

"Fiona's a wonderful person," Hammersmith said.

Kingsley shot him an arch glance. "So you've noticed that, have you?"

While Hammersmith tried to parse the meaning of that, Kingsley continued.

"I don't think you've met my older daughter. She's been away at university. She didn't come home for the funeral, didn't answer my letters. After a while, I stopped trying to reach her. I felt her disappointment so keenly and I thought she blamed me for her mother's death. I blamed myself. And I blamed this damn city with its horse shit in the streets, the germs and the dirt."

He lapsed into silence as they reached the department store and Day led them around to a tall outbuilding with huge double doors that stretched two stories high. He pulled a handle and one of the doors swung open on well-oiled hinges. The three of them stepped through into the dusk of the warehouse. Yellow light poured through windows that were set high under the roof. Hammersmith marveled at the size of it. A game of cricket might comfortably have been played inside. Much of the vast space seemed to be wasted. The chamber was sparsely filled with construction equipment, lumber and building materials, workbenches, wheeled carts, and a congregation of mannequins in one corner. He imagined the life-size wooden people hushing one another, startled by the three men who had entered their hall uninvited.

"They're over here," Day said. He walked to where a number of the carts, perhaps a hundred of them, had been haphazardly collected and he started to roll them away from one another, checking inside each one. He stopped and stood silently. Hammersmith and Kingsley joined him and looked down into the open top of the cart.

"I knew him," Day said. "Not well, but he was a good lad. He wanted to learn to read. He would have grown to be a good man if anyone had given him the chance. He deserved better than this."

The inspector's eyes welled up, and Hammersmith looked away, pretending not to notice.

"This city doesn't nurture its children," Kingsley said.

Hammersmith leaned forward. "What did you say?"

"I tried to make things better here after Catherine died," Kingsley said. "I did. I moved the morgue into the hospital, I set guidelines for cleanliness, and I looked for new ways to do the same old things, ways to improve on our methods. My methods, police methods, hospital methods. I was trained to think of everything in terms of how it was done, the methodology. It's why I gravitated so easily to helping Scotland Yard. But it wasn't enough."

"There are two others here," Day said. "Two women. Strangers to me, but someone will know them."

"We'll bury them properly," Kingsley said.

"The Karstphanomen came to you?"

"They offered me membership," Kingsley said. "Of course, this was after they'd vetted me, taken me to dinners, studied my reactions to their veiled ideas during long conversations and good Scotch. Some of them seemed to be as angry as I was. Some had suffered losses or worked in positions where they saw firsthand how often bad men got away with their crimes. Some of them were hungry for power or were simply the sort of men who enjoy hurting others. I didn't see that at first. I was blinded by loss and pain and idealism. I feel ashamed now."

"How could you know what they were?"

"I should have paid better attention. We both should have. The clues were there, plain to see."

"Who do you mean?"

"Hmm?"

"You said 'we both should have paid attention.' You're one."

"Ah, yes. I really shouldn't tell tales, but you may need to warn Sir Edward about this man's agenda, too, if he doesn't already know. We were both courted. He was new to his current appointment and would have been a prize recruit for them."

"Sir Edward is a Karstphanomen?" Day took a step back and almost stumbled. Hammersmith leapt forward, but Day caught himself by stabbing the ground with his cane. He waved his friend away.

"No," Kingsley said. "No, of course not. In fact, Sir Edward took certain precautions to protect us from the more zealous elements of the club when we refused membership."

"So you didn't join them," Hammersmith said. "Of course you didn't. But in that case why would Jack be after you now?"

"Oh, I don't know for a fact that he is after me. I know very little, really. It's taken me a long while to realize how little I know."

Day seemed to be ignoring them. He was rolling carts back and forth, checking each one for weight before looking inside them. At last, he turned around and nodded. "They're both here. In these two carts."

Kingsley passed his hand over his face, then moved forward and looked down into each of the carts in turn. Hammersmith followed him, but he didn't recognize either of the women.

Kingsley sighed. "Whoever did this was no doctor. Some say Jack the Ripper must be a surgeon. They say he must have a physician's knowledge of the body in order to do what he does. But they've mistaken passion for knowledge. There's a glee on display here, a monstrous pleasure at work, not a surgeon's technique. He's simply learned by doing, and who knows how long he's been at it?"

"You think they're sex workers?"

"No. Look at their hands." Kingsley reached in and lifted one woman's hand. Neither Day nor Hammersmith leaned in to see. They both waited for the doctor to tell them what he had observed. "They were menial workers of a different sort. Their nails are short and their fingertips are calloused. The skin is bleached from contact with chemicals. These women worked as maids or housekeepers of some sort. I don't say their lives were any better than you assumed them to be, Mr Hammersmith. Life is hard."

"Ambrose said they were in an upper room at the store," Day said.

"Perhaps they found something Jack didn't want them to," Hammersmith said. "Or saw something incriminating. If he's gone to ground here with all the pressure from the police and Blackleg's people hounding him, maybe he was protecting his refuge or his identity."

"Or perhaps he could no longer resist the urge to kill," Kingsley said. "Some of these creatures simply need to kill, and woe betide anyone who crosses their line of sight at the wrong moment."

"Was it really so wrong that the Karstphanomen did what they did?"

Kingsley stared at Hammersmith down the length of his nose, then turned his head to the ceiling high above them. He drew a long breath and blew it out through his mouth. "I'm not sure it's up to you or me to determine that sort of thing. But perhaps I've spent too many evenings discussing theology with my daughter."

"Did you ever see him? Did you ever see Jack after he'd been captured?"

"I did see him," Kingsley said. "It was only the one time. It was a glorious occasion for the Karst. They had come across him while he slept. Or so we were told, Sir Edward and I. We were roused from our beds in the middle of the night and ferried by private carriage to a room in Whitechapel, where he lay stretched out across his most recent victim. I gave him a sedative, stabbed the needle so deep in his neck I might've gone through and hit what was left of the girl under him. I was aiming for his spine, hoping to paralyze him, but I wasn't precise enough. He lived, and he is obviously mobile."

"You helped them."

"That one time. I came to my senses after and haven't had any dealings with them since. I have seen one or two of them in passing. They're unavoidable, really. Some of them are very powerfully connected in this city. And in others. But we spent that night, the commissioner and I, discussing what had happened and what was to be done. We lacked the influence to stop them, not without causing ourselves a great deal of grief. Perhaps we should have pushed harder, maybe even arrested them all. But we would have lost our appointments, him with the police, me with the hospital, and we both felt we could still do some good. I would do things differently now. As I say, it was a confusing time for me."

"They have that much power?"

"Yes, Mr Hammersmith, they come from all walks of life. There are members of parliament, there are lords and judges."

Hammersmith thought he saw Kingsley shoot an inquisitive glance at Day, but the inspector didn't notice or react.

"I should say they *were* powerful," Kingsley said. "Our friend Jack has whittled them down to the bone, I think."

"There can't be many of them left."

"I wouldn't think so."

"What about Sir Edward?"

"We have never spoken of it since. I believe he has blotted the entire thing from his mind, much as you have avoided all thought of your own life, Mr Day. Our minds defend themselves by going dim, the way you might close the shutter on a lamp."

"Why did I do that?"

"You thought you were protecting the people you loved. You loved them so much that you gave up your own life in order to save them. It's not common, but I've read about similar things."

"Jack made that happen?"

"You say he mesmerized you, but that's not what your memory loss was about. You forgot because you needed to forget."

Hammersmith put his hand to his ear. "What about Jack?"

"He's wounded," Day said.

"He's dangerous," Kingsley said.

"He's somewhere nearby," Hammersmith said. "Right?"

"He was losing blood," Day said. "I don't think he could have gone far."

"Where? Where was he wounded?"

"Somewhere in his belly."

"That doesn't tell me much," Kingsley said. "How much was it oozing?"

"It seemed like a lot of blood, but I was disoriented. I feel like I've been disoriented for so long."

"Yes, yes, but was there visible pus? Or anything brown coming with the blood? Specifics, son."

"It was seeping steadily, but not fast. There was pus. I didn't see anything brown. No, I did, but it might have been dried blood. I don't know how long he was bleeding."

"How was he moving?"

"With difficulty, but when there was need, he was quick."

"He's mad," Hammersmith said. "The mad move quickly."

The other two looked at him and he smiled at them, but Kingsley turned away and addressed Day again. "Was he sweating?"

"I don't remember," Day said.

"I'd guess he has gone to ground here. Not in this place." He waved his hand at the high ceiling, the walls that faced each other across the vast distance. "But he might be at Plumm's."

"The store is a wreck," Hammersmith said. He hoped he was keeping up well enough with the conversation.

"So there's this warehouse we're in," Kingsley said. "There's the store proper. What else? Is there a place on the premises where someone might hide away?"

"I don't know," Day said. "He has an office. He stole it from someone. Probably someone he killed."

"You think he could be there?"

"He'd be foolish to go there now."

"Except the store's deserted. Who would look for him there?"

"You could be right."

"Let's look," Hammersmith said. "We're prepared, he's not. Let's find him."

"You lads go," Kingsley said. "I'll join you in a few minutes. My priority is doing right by these poor victims." He nodded at the carts and thought of the boy there.

Hammersmith wondered how well Day had known Ambrose, how much that tiny death had hurt him. He wondered if that might be worse than a year of forgetfulness.

"How long will it take the police to get here?"

"Not long," Kingsley said. "Sir Edward will have a lot of questions. We're all going to be observed carefully after this."

"Then we'll hurry. If Jack's still here, Nevil and I will do our best to deal with him quickly, before he has another chance to get away, to kill more innocents." He indicated the bodies in the carts.

"I'll find a telephone," Kingsley said.

"See if you can't get Inspector Tiffany to come out here," Hammersmith said. "And Sergeant Kett. They may not believe the Ripper's about, but they'll come just the same, and we could use their help."

"I'll do my best to persuade them," Kingsley said. "And I'll get a wagon on its way for these bodies. Then I'll find you."

51

Mr and Mrs Parker had drawn Leland Carlyle out from his club and followed him to his daughter's house, to Guildhall, and then to a shabby detective agency. He went in while his driver waited, then came rushing back out, and the cab rolled away once more down the street with the Parkers trailing after.

"It's quite a cortege we make, dearest heart," Mrs Parker said.

"They're going to want results soon," Mr Parker said. "How patient can they possibly be?"

"Who?"

"Whoever they are. That club that's so secret, we're not supposed to know their name."

"The Karstphanomen."

"Them, yes."

"Have they paid us yet?"

"Not entirely."

"We should get them results then," Mrs Parker said.

"It's a problem. I'm afraid we've taken an impossible case. We can't actually find Jack the Ripper, no matter how formidable we may be. That gentleman has slipped through every trap ever set for him and taunted the newspaper and police in the bargain. Our only real hope was to be in place when he acted."

"But he doesn't appear to want to act against Mr Carlyle, darling."

"So far as we know, Jack doesn't even know Mr Carlyle exists."

"What if he doesn't attack Carlyle?"

"Our reputation will suffer."

"And we won't be paid for more work?"

"We will have trouble getting more work."

"Husband?"

"Yes?"

"Who knows that Mr Carlyle has hired us?"

"I don't know," Mr Parker said.

"Do you think he was acting on his own, or do you think others know about us?"

"I shouldn't think very many others do."

"And none of them have met us. None of them can verify that he actually employed us, am I right?"

"I believe you are, light of my life."

"What I mean to say is . . ." The carriage rumbled over a hole in the street, and Mrs Parker grabbed Mr Parker's arm to steady herself. He caught his breath and tried not to look at her. "What I mean to say," Mrs Parker said, "is what if Mr Carlyle were to disappear?"

"We would be in a very bad place. He's our only way of finding Jack."

"No, my cabbage, what if he disappeared and we went home?"

"Oh, you mean . . . ?"

"I mean what if we were the instrument of disappearance, if you insist on making me say so?"

"We would not be paid the full amount agreed upon," Mr Parker said. "We like to be paid."

"We would eventually be paid by someone else for something else. This all seems so pointless, doesn't it?"

Mr Parker nodded. "It's not really the sort of thing we customarily do."

"Not at all."

"In fact, it's rather more work than usual."

"I don't like it to be so much work."

"Of course." He tensed while patting her hand, but she seemed to welcome the gesture. "Let's give it the afternoon. Imagine if we were the ones to bring Jack the Ripper down."

"The afternoon, then," she said. She let go of his arm and moved away from him, and he wondered if he'd said the wrong thing to her. "We'll follow Mr Carlyle for the rest of the afternoon, and if nothing interesting happens, we'll go home."

"Agreed," Mr Parker said. "Not such a big commitment of time after all, is it?"

"But, Father, what if we do meet Jack?"

"There are two of us to his one. I shouldn't think he'd be too much trouble."

"That's not what I meant."

"What then, turtledove?"

"What if I don't want to kill him? What if I admire his work and find him to be . . . Well, what if we like him? As a person."

Mr Parker smiled at her. "Then we shall invite him to tea and Mr Carlyle will still disappear."

But Mr Parker was not at all sure he wanted to have tea with Jack the Ripper. He would be surrounded and outnumbered by dangerous animals in human guise. He realized that his time with Mrs Parker was coming to an end, and he didn't think their parting would be pleasant for him. He wished he were capable of walking away and leaving her, and he cursed himself for a fool because he knew he could not do that.

52

There's a lamp beside the door," Jack said. "Reach over to your right and you'll feel it."

Hatty took a moment, wondering if there really was a lamp or if she might encounter something awful hanging there instead. But, *In for a penny, in for a pound,* she thought, and felt along the wall in the dark. To her great relief there was indeed a lamp. She detected an earthy mix of odors in the room, sweat and musk and something else she couldn't place.

"Matches are on the table there," Jack said. "Be careful, don't burn the place down."

Hatty fumbled the lamp off its hook and shuffled around until she bumped into a table. She patted along the surface and found a wooden box, opened it, and struck a match. When she'd lit the lamp and slid back the shutter, the room flickered into view around her. It was just like the rooms on the floor below: there was the bed, the chair, the table, and the wardrobe. The men and women did not live noticeably different lives. But in many subtle ways, this room was more comfortable than the others, reflecting Joseph Hargreave's better position within the Plumm's hierarchy. The wardrobe was not made of cardboard. The bed was canopied, with thick mattresses that set it higher off the floor than the others she had seen downstairs. There was a figure on the bed, obscured by heavy blankets and pillows. The chair was upholstered in leather, with bright brass studs glowing along the seams.

The man sitting in the chair was surrounded by a mane of dark wavy hair, thick and unfashionably long. He smiled at Hatty, but he didn't rise to greet her. He was slumped over, leaning heavily on his left elbow, and his face looked pale to her. She recognized him from the gallery railing of the store, from the moment before a sheet of glass had sliced one of Plumm's staff in two.

"Mr Oberon," Hatty said. "Are you quite all right?"

"Good of you to inquire, Miss Pitt," he said. "The best answer I can give is that we shall see."

Hatty kept her eye on him and went to the bed, keeping it between them in case Jack suddenly leapt from the chair. She thought she might be able to reach the door again before he could reach her. She wondered how much damage a swinging lamp might do to a man if she aimed it properly and hit his face.

"I promised I wouldn't touch you," he said, as if he could read her mind. "Don't you trust me?"

"No."

"I should stop asking that question. I never get the response I want."

Hatty leaned over the bed and had to look away again. She closed her eyes, then realized she was leaving herself vulnerable. She snapped them open again, but Mr Oberon had not moved.

"What did you do to him?" She was certain she was going to vomit, but didn't want to give him the satisfaction of seeing her do it.

"I did many things to him," Mr Oberon said. "It would take some time for me to describe them all to you, but I will if you like."

"He's dead," Hatty said.

"Don't look so put out about it. I believe in the end he welcomed death."

"He looks like he's been dead for days."

"Oh, no," Jack said. "If he'd been dead for days, I would've moved him. I moved all the others. Can't draw attention with a stink. No, he was alive when I left for work this morning."

"You went to work every day? While you were pretending to be a Plumm's employee?"

"Oh, but I am a Plumm's employee. The old man kept me on when Smithfield and Gordon moved away. Mr Hargreave's disappearance was a boon for me. I was promoted like a shot, if it's not immodest to say."

"You wanted Mr Hargreave's position?"

"I wanted his apartment. Or perhaps I wanted his cottage at the sea."

"That's where you took him."

"Joseph and I had some fun there before we decided to return to the city. His brother was a bit too nosy."

"Why not kill him, too?"

"Who says I didn't? Oh, but I did enjoy Joseph so very much. There are few of these Karstphanomen left, and I like to savor their last moments when I can."

"I heard Mr Hargreave cry out. When I was outside the room just now, he made a noise."

"Oh, that was me. I thought it might get you in here, and I wanted to cry out anyway. It served two functions. I do like to be efficient whenever possible, don't you?"

"Why did you want me here? What will you do now?"

"You are convenient, that's all. No greater design this time. And you look like a kind sort of a person. There's a stack of clean linens in the wardrobe, and a corset in there, too. Hargreave was a vain man, but I think the corset might work to my advantage, keep my guts where they belong. I was rather hoping you would help me dress this." He opened his jacket and showed her a dark wet stain on his shirt.

She glanced at the closed wardrobe and wondered what surprises Mr Oberon had waiting inside it. "You've been wounded," she said.

"There were four of them there, and I only expected two. They got me in the end." He lowered his voice to a fierce whisper and bared his teeth at Hatty. "But I got more of them, didn't I?"

Hatty moved back toward the door. She held the lamp up high in front of her, hoping Jack couldn't see the fear she felt. "Is it fatal, then? The wound?"

"There are things I know that no one else knows, Miss Pitt."

There was a long silence, and Hatty stood still, waiting for him to talk again. If he had answered her question, she couldn't understand the meaning of it. At last he grunted and began to speak again, but his voice was lower and weaker.

"Quite often people decide to die because it's the easier choice than living. I've seen it, Miss Pitt. Time after time, I've watched their eyes as they make that decision, and then I watch the light leave them. And I've never really understood. Wherever they go when the light leaves, is there still blood?"

"I don't think anyone knows the answer to that," Hatty said. "Not for sure."

"So much of what men do is undertaken only to avoid humiliation. That is what makes yours the stronger sex, Hatty Pitt. You are able to bear up under constant humiliation, to turn it slowly to your advantage. We men wither and beg to be killed, while you bide your time."

"So you're the champion of my sex, Mr Oberon?"

"Why not me? Who knows more about women than I? The linens. Fetch them, would you? I'm afraid the wardrobe's a bit far for me to reach at the moment."

"No," Hatty said. "I will not help you. It's time for you to think about making that decision you mentioned. I urge you to make the proper choice."

She backed out the door and down the passage to the stairs, but he did not chase her. She thought she heard him chuckle quietly in the dark, but she couldn't be sure. She dropped the lamp at the landing and turned.

Behind her there was a great *whomp* as oil hit the flammable carpet and exploded outward, but she didn't turn round or slow down. She pelted down the steps and kept running.

Let it burn, she thought. *Let it all burn to the ground.*

BOOK FOUR

A dozen sets of miniature farm animals, all carved from soft pine and stained dark brown, stampeded out of the smoke, and Anna leapt to the side of the path. There were twelve little sheep and twelve little cows and twelve little goats and twelve little horses, along with a hundred or more chickens and geese and ducks, all of them running as fast as they could and making a tremendous noise. One of the little pigs broke one of its legs off and it stumbled. Anna reached out to pick it up and rescue it from being crushed, but the pig grunted and turned on its side and rolled away, disappearing amongst the other creatures.

Anna coughed and wiped her watering eyes. The sky was obscured by billows of smoke and ash, and all round her the furniture and toys and carriages and statuary were ablaze.

"All of this from a single match," Anna said. "Oh, why must matches also be made of wood?"

She was alone again, her friends having run away at the first sight of fire. She did not blame them in the least. They were all quite flammable.

"It is becoming quite hot now," Anna said.

"Then you should leave." Jack appeared out of the smoke, hopping toward Anna on his spring. The tip of his false cigar was alight now and it glowed a bright rosy red. "You are not made of wood as the rest of us are, and so you do not belong."

"But I can't leave until I find Peter," Anna said. "He must be very scared now, as he has never stayed outside during the night alone, except one time when I went in to dinner and forgot he was with me and accidentally bolted the door and left him."

"Peter will burn here, and so will you, Anna," Jack said. He bounced all round her in a circle as the fire drew closer to them.

"And you will burn, too," Anna said. "I do not believe you have thought this through well enough. You are made of wood just as Babushka and poor Mary Annette are, and also the Kindly Nutcracker you so cruelly broke apart."

"I know that I will burn," Jack said. "And that is what I want."

"I don't understand," Anna said.

"The workmen would have come and taken all of the things here away," Jack said. "The wood will never be allowed to be together as we were when we were trees. And so I have decided to burn us all away and leave our ashes here where there was once a vasty forest, and where for a single day and a single night we were able to return."

"But you are the only one who has decided such a thing, and it is not your place to do so," Anna said.

"It is my nature to surprise others, and that is what I am doing," said Jack. "You should not expect me to be anything other than what I am."

"What you are, you nasty little Jack, is a man in a box," said Anna. "And in a box is where you shall go."

And with that, Anna plucked Jack off the ground by the top of his head and pushed him back down into his case, which was painted all over with colorful circus scenes that were now bubbling and melting in the heat from the fire.

"I do not want to go into my box anymore," Jack said. "It is dark in there and lonely."

He struggled mightily and his spring was very strong, but Anna pushed until he was packed away tight, and then she closed the lid and latched it.

"You might have thought of that before you struck that match," said Anna. "That was not a pleasant surprise in the least."

She put the box under her arm, holding it closed so that Jack could not open the latch and pop out, and she marched away from the flames in what she hoped was the right direction. She had very little time now before everything would disappear and her childhood playground would be reduced to ash, as Jack had threatened.

"Oh dear," she said. "I wonder if the fire will spread to my house. That would be bad indeed. I must find Peter so that we can put out the fire with buckets of water. I know he will help."

And with Jack bumping and thumping inside his box, Anna began to run as fast as she could, all the while calling Peter's name.

—Rupert Winthrop, from
The Wandering Wood (1893)

53

E verything's ruined," Hammersmith said.

Day whistled long and loud and looked round them at the deserted department store. "It's been picked clean."

Much of the metalwork had been disassembled and carted away, the electrical wires pulled from the walls, and the plumbing and much of the wood paneling taken, leaving great mounds of plaster and dust and ruined carpeting. A box fell to the floor in the toy department, causing Day and Hammersmith to jump. They turned and watched as a startled fox ran past them and vanished among the shattered remains of cut crystal glassware.

"How'd that get in already?"

"I'm just glad you saw it, too," Day said.

"The office you say Oberon was using . . ."

"Up there." Day pointed at the crumbling gallery at the back of the store. "He can't possibly be using it now. There aren't any stairs."

"I don't see a ladder, either," Hammersmith said.

"Unless he's using that," Day said. He pointed at the lift, which stood open, the iron gates ripped from their hinges sometime in the night.

"I don't know how that thing works and I'm not gonna gamble on it," Hammersmith said.

"Neither me. I doubt there's any electricity left to power it, anyway."

"Don't understand electricity. Never seen any."

"You can't see it, but it's all round us."

"What, inside the walls?"

"Wires and cables."

"Then how do they keep the walls from catching fire? I don't see it letting off any steam or releasing pressure."

"We'll ask Dr Kingsley. I'm sure he knows," Day said. "But this is a dead end. Even if there were a ladder, I doubt I could climb it."

"How's your leg?"

"Not at my best, but not at my worst, either. I'm not as bad off as you remember me. I exercised well this past year and got a good bit more mobility out of it. It's these ribs bothering me at the moment. Can hardly breathe without it feeling like I've been stabbed in the chest. Oh, sorry, Nevil, I forgot."

"What, my chest? I've still got a horrible scar over my heart, but it doesn't bother me anymore. It's a miracle, really."

"You have an uncanny knack for healing. Your ear seems to be functioning now."

Hammersmith put a hand to his ear. "Not so much. I still can't hear from this one, but if I stand on the right side of you, it seems I do all right. The other ear compensates."

"We're a fine pair, aren't we?"

"Hullo!" They turned at the sound of the voice. An old man

clambered over a distant mound of splintered wood and glass and picked his slow way toward them. "Hullo, I say!" He held up one arm, waving a rifle over his head.

"Oh, no," Hammersmith said.

"You know this fellow?"

"I'm afraid so. His name's Goodpenny. He means well."

"I say," Goodpenny said. He had found a clear path that wound round through the remains of toiletries and sundries and now he trotted up to them, breathing hard. "If it isn't young Master Angerschmid. Good to see you, lad." His hair stuck straight up, one lens of his spectacles was broken, and he was bleeding from a minor scratch on one cheek. He smiled and held up a finger, turned his back to them and tucked in his shirt before turning back and pumping Hammersmith's hand vigorously. "Long night here, lads, but I did my best, I did."

"Your best?"

"Looters, my boy. Looters. Got the trusty Martini-Henry from the back room, but no ammunition for it. That's all on the top floor, and I couldn't get at it. Most called my bluff, but I stayed the course and scared off a man or two."

"Mr Goodpenny, that's terribly brave of you."

"Was it?" He looked around them and sighed. "I've lost everything now, Mr Angerschmid. Sold off my stall at the bazaar to buy a piece of this, and now it's gone, isn't it?" He sniffed and pulled himself up, offered them a wan smile. "I've forgotten my manners. Terribly sorry, long night, as I say. My name's Goodpenny." He stuck out his hand and Day shook it.

"Mine's Day. Walter Day. And isn't that a pleasant thing to be able to say after all this time?"

"Well, I'm sure, except that I can't remember ever saying it before," Goodpenny said. "No, I take it back. I've recently met a lovely young woman of that same name. What a startling coincidence. It's a pleasure to meet you, Mr Dew. You're friends with young Angerschmid then?"

"It's Day."

"Indeed, and I'm glad of it after such a long night. Did I mention I haven't slept? Not one wink."

"I mean—"

Hammersmith put a hand out and shook his head at Day. It wouldn't help to correct Goodpenny. He leaned in close and murmured, "Goodpenny can't hear."

"No," Goodpenny said. "Nobody else here. I say, how is your young lady friend? Miss Tinsley. I saw her just a day or two ago. I do hope she was nowhere near when this happened."

"Who's Tinsley?"

"He means Kingsley's daughter Fiona. You'll remember her. He seems to think there's something between us."

"And is there? I've been away long enough, she must have grown up a bit."

"No, she's not interested in the likes of me. Got eyes for her father's assistant, Pinch."

"Don't know him," Day said.

"He was taking care of you this morning, before you woke up. Young fellow, well dressed, large nose."

"I'm sorry, Nevil," Day said. "Good Lord, but that girl fancied you."

"Did she really?"

"She certainly did," Goodpenny said.

Day shook his head. "How could you not know that?"

"She never told me."

"You're supposed to notice that sort of thing without being told," Goodpenny said. "Not everything needs to be said aloud to be understood."

"Well, it's a little late now."

"Win her back," Goodpenny said. "Go after her and declare your love. It's never too late."

"I never said I loved her. She's a little girl."

"My wife was fifteen when I married her," Goodpenny said.

"Different times, sir. Anyway, whoever she might have fancied at one time or another, right now she fancies Pinch. She said so." He shook his head. "Mr Goodpenny, you say you were here all night?"

"No," Goodpenny said. "I was here the entire night through. Never left."

Day and Hammersmith exchanged a glance. "Was there anyone else here you thought might be especially menacing? Tall fellow, dark wavy hair?"

"Everyone was at least mildly menacing, my dear boy."

"You must have met him. Went by the name of Oberon."

"Doberman? A German fellow? Don't recall. Perhaps if you described him more."

"I can't," Hammersmith said. "But Mr Day might be able to. Walter, you must have seen a great deal of him."

"I . . . I can't describe him. I try to think of him, but the image is hazy in my mind, as if there's a constant fog surrounding him."

"No one like that was in here," Goodpenny said. "Only normal folks fallen on hard times, looking for free wares. Come to think of it, I'm glad this wasn't loaded." He hefted the Martini-Henry and all three of them jumped back as it fired. Immediately a sofa that had already been torn nearly in half exploded in a cloud of cotton batting and wooden splinters. Goodpenny gave them a halfhearted smile and bit his lip. "Well, it's not loaded now."

"Bloody hell," Hammersmith said. "Even if I could've heard proper before, I'm sure I can't now."

"At least you didn't shoot anyone," Day said.

"No, I've never shot anyone," Goodpenny said. "Nearly did just now, though. Frightfully sorry, gentlemen."

"No harm done." Hammersmith looked at Day and suddenly couldn't help himself. He burst out laughing. Even Day cracked a smile.

"That would be quite a homecoming," Hammersmith said. "You disappear for a year and then suddenly . . . shot dead before you've even seen your wife. Welcome back, Walter Day!"

Day's smile disappeared. "Nevil, we've got to find Jack and make him undo whatever it is he's done to me before I can go home or see Claire."

"I understand. I'm sorry. We'll find him."

"Well, he's clearly not here. That shot would have brought anyone out. This place is deserted. He's not in his office."

"And he's not in the workshop."

"Which leaves . . . what?"

"There are flats round the back," Goodpenny said. "Some of the staff live there, on and off. I never did. Got my own place. But the rooms were all cleared out after this happened." Goodpenny swiveled his head to take in the mess all round them. "They'd be empty now."

"Be a perfect place to go to ground if he's injured, as you say he is," Hammersmith said. "Beds, fresh clothing."

"Let's go," Day said. "Is there a street entrance? Or a way in through the store?"

"Both," Goodpenny said. "You can go round by the outside or straight across there. There's a passage behind the lift."

"There's an alley," Day said. "But it dead-ends at a storeroom. It's how Ambrose . . . Anyway, we'd have to circle wide."

"He might see us coming from the street."

"I don't fancy the idea of all that collapsing on us." Day nodded at the gallery.

"Then you go by the street and I'll go through there and we'll have him trapped."

"I'll stay here," Goodpenny said. "There's still a possibility I might discover some of my own merchandise under all this. The stationery will be lost, of course, but I had many fine items of silver and teak. An ivory piece or two. They might have survived."

"You be careful, Mr Goodpenny," Hammersmith said. "That thing's not loaded anymore."

"Nobody knows that but us, lad."

Hammersmith nodded and turned to watch Day, who was already picking his way back across the littered sales floor, but Goodpenny grabbed his arm and leaned in close. "If you've got any feelings for that girl, Mr Angerschmid, you've got to do something about it before it's too late. I miss my wife every day now, but I still wouldn't trade our years together for anything, though they surely led to heartbreak at the end."

"It's not—"

"Whatever it is, don't make it so you're lonely, lad. Don't wait until it's too late. A man's not a man unless he's got someone to share his life."

"Um, right. Thank you, Mr Goodpenny. I'll be off."

"Watch yourself. If you run into that foggy gentleman, you ring for the police straight off. Don't try to be a hero. You don't have the constitution for it."

Hammersmith saluted and trotted away, jumping over a ruined credenza. He didn't look back, but he knew Goodpenny was watching him go. The man was kind, but completely addled. Still, he wasn't wrong in his warning about Jack, and Hammersmith suddenly wished he were armed. He bent and picked up a length of iron pipe. He swung it in a low arc and thumped it into the palm of his hand.

Almost as good as a truncheon.

54

Hatty was halfway down the stairs when a long shadow stretched across the floor below her. A man turned the corner and looked up at her, and in the split second it took her to recognize him, Hatty panicked and stumbled.

Hammersmith bounded up the stairs and caught her as she fell. The impact caused him to take a backward step down, but he held on to her. When she looked up, he was frowning at her.

"Hatty? What are you doing here? It's not safe."

"I know it's not safe. Let go of me." She pushed him away and they stood awkwardly mashed together in the narrow stairwell. She felt embarrassed for having tripped and ashamed for snapping at him when he had helped her. She wished he hadn't seen her lose her balance. She was certain he thought she was nothing more than a silly little girl.

"Hatty, there's a dangerous man somewhere around here. You can't be—"

"He's upstairs," she said. She could already hear the crackle of flames behind her. Soon, the fire would be visible and the stairs would become unpassable. "You're talking about Mr Oberon, right?

I don't think that's his real name. He's killed Mr Hargreave, so we're not going to be paid for that case, I don't think."

"I don't care about that. I need you to get far away from here. But where is he up there?"

"There's a room at the end of the passage on the next floor up. He's injured, and I don't think he can move." She grabbed Hammersmith's arm as he stepped around her. "Mr Hammersmith, I set it on fire. He's going to burn up there. Leave him."

"You have no idea what this man is capable of."

"How do you know him? He mentioned you to me."

"We have a history. I'll tell you about it if we survive until tomorrow."

As they spoke, the landing above them had grown gradually darker and smokier. The wallpaper at the corner of the stairwell began to peel away, curling toward them in long strips.

"Go!" Hammersmith pointed the way down and out, then turned away from Hatty and ran up the stairs, two at a time. He disappeared in a billow of dark smoke.

Hatty looked down, then up, then shrugged her shoulders and followed Hammersmith back up toward the room where she knew Mr Oberon was waiting.

SIR EDWARD BRADFORD GRABBED his hat and stopped at the door, looking back at his office and trying to think of anything he might need. He had learned long ago never to rush into anything without first considering what might happen. The price of that lesson had been his left arm, and he had determined that the loss would only strengthen him. He went back to the desk and took his Webley from the top drawer, stuffed it into his belt.

He rushed down the stairs with Fawkes at his heels and he pointed at Inspector Tiffany, who stood at his desk with a sheaf of papers in his hands. Tiffany was in his shirtsleeves and had the rumpled look of someone who had not slept.

"Inspector Tiffany, you're with me," Sir Edward said. "And I want Inspector Blacker, too. Sergeant Kett, you can come. Fawkes, you'll coordinate from here. Kett will relay anything needs doing."

"What's happening, sir?"

"That damn telephone again. And every time it rings, it's always something about Inspector Day."

"What," Tiffany said, "he's been found yet again?"

"Indeed. We're off to that new department store. Plume's."

"Plumm's, you mean," Kett said. "But, sir, there's nothing there. The place is a ruin and everyone's been cleared out. If Mr Day was there, he ain't anymore."

"I have just received word from Dr Kingsley that our man Day is indeed at that store. And I'll be damned if I let him slip away from us again. I'm going out there myself this time, and I'll grab him by the scruff of his neck and drag him back to the land of the living if I have to."

"As you say, sir."

Tiffany dropped the papers on his desk and grabbed his jacket. Blacker saluted and grinned, and they both hurried after Sir Edward, practically running in order to keep up with the determined commissioner.

"It's eerie," Claire said.

"It is very quiet," Fiona said. "Where are all the shoppers?"

People were, in fact, passing by them on the cross streets, but the space in front of the store was being avoided. "It amazes me how something can go from overcrowded to abandoned in the blink of an eye," Claire said. "Do they all think the building will fall on them?"

A man passed by them, watching them from the corner of his eye, but he said nothing. Claire and Fiona stood on the street and watched him until he had crossed over and walked away round the corner. A carriage drew up to the curb opposite them and stayed there, the driver up top making a point of not looking their way.

"Should we tell him the place is shut down at the moment?"

"I think that's obvious."

"Well, what's he waiting for?"

The four-wheeler sat there unmoving, but a curtain was pulled aside at the edge of one window and then closed again.

"Go over there," Claire said. "Ask him if he's waiting for someone."

"I'm not going over there. You go over there."

Claire had just made up her mind to cross and rap on the carriage door when it opened and her father stepped out into the street.

"Claire," he said, "how lovely to run into you here. What a coincidence."

"Father, are you following me?"

"Not at all. I was . . . Your mother sent me to Plumm's. She wants something for the house."

"What does she want?"

"I've got a list here." Carlyle made a show of patting his jacket pockets and even grabbed the brim of his hat as if the list might be tucked in his hatband. "I seem to have misplaced it."

"As you can plainly see, the store isn't open for business today, Father. It's been wrecked."

Carlyle looked up for the first time at the broken windows, the litter in the street, the lack of pedestrian traffic. "What's happened?"

"I'm not entirely sure, but Walter was involved somehow."

"Walter did this?"

"Well, I don't think that's even possible, but he was here. He may be here again. Fiona and I are looking for him."

Fiona raised her hand in an awkward greeting.

Carlyle shook his head as if clearing it and swiped his hand through the air in front of him, dispelling the lies between them. "Look, Claire, I want you to come with me. Your friend, too. There's great danger. I can't explain, but—"

"What are you talking about?"

"I said I can't explain. But there are people about who might wish to harm you. Or harm Walter. I'm not sure anymore what they intend, but we should leave here, get out of the city, maybe back to Devon, and wait until we hear from your husband."

"Why would I leave with you if my husband's in as much danger as you say?"

"Because, for once in your life, you could simply choose to obey your father. I don't think that's too much to ask."

"I'm here to find Walter. Fiona and I both are. Help us and I'll go with you afterward. Then you can explain yourself. Right at this moment, nothing matters to me except that after a year, I'm finally close to being with my husband again. Nothing, nothing else matters."

"Walter." Carlyle's eyes were wide, and he spoke in a whisper.

"Yes, Walter," Claire said.

"No, I mean, look. It's Walter."

Claire turned and saw her husband climbing out through the smashed front window of Plumm's. Walter was gaunt and had the beginnings of a dark beard. His eyes were shadowed, and he was dressed like a pauper, in a torn and tattered suit with no hat. But it was undeniably him, and he was alive and he was only a few feet away from her, clambering over the remains of a window display.

For a moment, Claire couldn't breathe and the world seemed to hold still, but for the struggling form of her husband. She thought she could hear Fiona saying something, perhaps her father continued to speak, but everything receded and became unimportant.

Then she caught her breath. "Walter!"

She ran toward him, her arms out, her skirts dragging behind her on the ground, as he looked up. But she stopped when she saw his eyes. There was no recognition there. He wasn't even looking at her. He stared past her and his eyes flashed with hatred and anger. She heard a click as the handle of his walking stick disengaged. He drew the blade from his cane and pushed past her. She stumbled and gasped and fell to the ground, looking up just in time to see her husband lunge at Leland Carlyle and impale him on his sword.

MR AND MRS PARKER stood in the shadows of an apothecary down the street from Plumm's. Mr Parker's mind had begun to wander when Mrs Parker grabbed his arm and pointed. They watched a man run out of the abandoned store and stab the high judge of the Karstphanomen.

"That's him," Mrs Parker said. "That's our quarry. Jack the Ripper's finally made his move."

"But we're too late. He's killed our client."

"Can't blame him for that. We considered the same thing ourselves. Anyway, Carlyle's not dead yet." With that, Mrs Parker leapt forward and raced down the street with Mr Parker fast at her heels. They separated in front of the store. Mrs Parker chased the attacker, who had dropped his sword, while Mr Parker stopped to check on

Leland Carlyle, who was breathing but was quickly losing blood. Already a crowd had begun to form, as if from nowhere. The street had been virtually empty, and now people sprang up in twos and threes, gathering around the man on the ground.

"Don't hurt him," Carlyle's daughter said, but she wasn't looking at Mr Parker or her father; she was addressing Mrs Parker, who had stopped to pick up the fleeing man's sword and the barrel of his cane. Mrs Parker didn't seem to hear the woman. She ran on, pushing her way through the onlookers and, now doubly armed, chased the man into an alleyway.

Mr Parker got the daughter's attention. "You know him? The one who did this?"

"It's my husband. I don't know what's going on, but he's not himself. He's a policeman. He must have meant well."

Mr Parker shook his head, unable to believe their bad luck. Jack the Ripper was related to their client? *And* he was a policeman? Things were getting entirely too complicated. He put pressure on Carlyle's wound and turned his gaze again to the young woman. "What's his name?"

"Leland Carlyle."

"Here, let me help. My father's a doctor." The other girl squatted next to Carlyle, and Mr Parker took the opportunity to back away, bumping into the people behind him.

He stood and fixed Carlyle's daughter with his best glare. "I asked the name of the other one. Not this one. I know this one. What's the name of the man who stabbed him?"

"Oh. That's Walter Day."

"Walter Day," Mr Parker said. They had been specifically told not to kill Walter Day, but was it possible Carlyle didn't know Day was the Ripper? There was something strange going on, but Mr

Parker couldn't figure it out and he was suddenly afraid they had been played for fools. He needed to find his daughter, his partner, and take her away, leave this country. He turned and ran down the same alleyway he had seen Mrs Parker enter.

BY THE TIME DR KINGSLEY RETURNED, there was a crowd gathered on the street in front of Plumm's. He recognized Claire Day, who stood alone, leaning against the brick façade of the wrecked store, but few of the others. A man jumped up from the ground and ran down an alley beside the store. Others watched him go, but no one else moved.

Kingsley went to Claire and gently touched her hand. "Claire? Claire, can you hear me?"

She looked up at him, but she didn't act like she knew him. He waved a hand in front of her, but her glazed eyes didn't follow the motion. He checked her pulse and smoothed her hair out of her face. He took her arm and walked her back to the wide window ledge outside the store. He brushed the broken glass from it, then took off his jacket and laid it down so she could sit on it. He had smelling salts in his bag, but he wasn't sure they were necessary.

Kingsley pushed his way through the rabble, rolling up his sleeves as he went, hoping he wouldn't see Walter Day or Nevil Hammersmith dead on the ground. Instead he saw his daughter leaning over a stranger. Fiona was pressing a cloth against the man's abdomen, but blood pulsed out through her fingers and soaked the street beneath them. Kingsley knelt beside his daughter and moved her hands out of the way so he could see what he had to deal with.

She looked at him with tears in her eyes. "Can you help him?"

"You did the right thing, Fiona. If the wound had been just an inch away from where it is, the pressure you put on it wouldn't have been enough to save him." He ripped open the man's shirt and peeled the fabric away from the wound, then rooted through his black bag for bandages, alcohol, a needle, and thread.

"Then he won't die?"

"I'm making no promises, but you've given him a chance." Fiona shivered, and Kingsley wished he had his jacket back so he could drape it over her. "The police are on their way and they'll be able to provide transport for him. Who is he?"

"It's Claire's father. Walter stabbed him. Mr Day tried to kill Mrs Day's father right in front of her. Why?"

Kingsley blinked hard and rocked back on his heels. He shook his head. "He didn't kill him. If we can keep this man alive, then Walter Day isn't a murderer." But he knew that time was of the essence and he hoped the wagon he'd ordered was on its way already. The bodies in the workshop could stay where they were an hour longer so the police could get Claire's father to the hospital for proper care.

Kingsley shook his head again and sighed. He had left Walter Day to his own devices, knowing full well the man might be a danger. He hadn't counted on the Ripper's enemy being someone who had made himself Day's enemy as well. He continued stitching, not looking up from his work as he talked. "Fiona, you must think very carefully. Did Mr Day say anything? Anything at all? Did he mention a crow or a white king when he did this?"

"He didn't say a thing. He just did it. It happened so fast. I don't understand."

"It's all ridiculously complicated."

He finished and cut the excess thread away, pressed bandages around the wound, and taped them securely in place. He checked the victim's pulse again and was gratified to find that it was weak but steady. He stood and helped Fiona up, wiped her hands with his handkerchief, and walked her over to where Claire still sat in the open window of the fabulous department store.

"Fiona, you've done a great deal to help already, but I need you to take care of Claire. She's had a shock, and so have you, but you've got to be strong for me a bit longer. You've got to watch over Claire. Can you do that?" Fiona nodded, and Kingsley smiled at her. "That's my good girl. I'm very proud of you."

He glanced behind him at the crowd, which had begun to break up, people wandering away now that the entertainment had ended. Kingsley was disturbed to see that some of them were only children.

"Tell me where Mr Day went," he said. "Did you see?"

Fiona nodded and pointed at the mouth of the alley.

"Fiona, was Mr Hammersmith . . . was Nevil with him?"

"No. I don't know where Nevil is. Oh, do you think he might be in danger? Do you think Mr Day might—"

"No." Kingsley patted her hand and smiled at her. "Don't worry now. It will all work out. I can fix everything."

But his words sounded hollow to him. He hoisted his bag and took a deep breath. It was, he thought, possible to fix everything, to reverse the terrible mistake he'd made in leaving Walter Day in an unstable mental condition, but in order to do that he would have to find Day before the police did.

55

Hammersmith took off his jacket and ripped the left sleeve off. He discarded the rest of the jacket and wrapped the sleeve around his mouth and nose, tied it at the back of his neck. It made his face hot, but he could breathe a little more easily. He crept forward, gripping the length of pipe tight in his fist. The end of the hallway was a wall of flames and smoke, but Hammersmith needed to see Jack's body for himself. He needed to know that the monster was finally and truly dead.

"Mr Hammersmith!"

Hammersmith turned and saw Hatty Pitt at the landing behind him. She was obscured by smoke and was coming slowly toward him. She reached out to steady herself against the wall, but pulled her hand back. The wallpaper was bubbling in the heat.

"Hatty, what are you doing here? Go back downstairs."

"You'll die up here," Hatty said. "You need my help." Her voice was low and hoarse, and Hammersmith realized his own throat burned when he tried to talk.

Hammersmith reached down and picked up his jacket, ripped off the other sleeve, and tied it around Hatty's mouth. He shook his head at her, but he didn't have enough air to try to speak again, unless he absolutely had to. He waved Hatty back and proceeded once again toward the source of the flames. At least he could keep her behind him.

The fire reached the ceiling and began to crawl across it. Hammersmith knew there wasn't much time left, but he couldn't turn back now. He put his arms over his face, steeled himself, and ran forward, jumping through the flames and through the open door into the room. A moment later, Hatty barreled into him from behind and knocked him forward into the bed. His hand brushed against cold flesh. He pushed himself back away from it and adjusted his grip on the iron pipe, his only weapon. He shook his head again at Hatty, reached past her, and closed the door to keep out the smoke, then checked her arms and face for burns.

Somehow the air felt cooler and relatively smoke-free. The fire was out in the hallway, but soon, he knew, it would consume the doorjamb and make its way into the room. They had a few moments at most to look around. Not much time for detective work.

Hatty pulled the sleeve down off her face and pointed at a chair in the corner of the room. "He was there. Sitting right there. Mr Hammersmith, I didn't think he could even move."

"Well, he must have found the strength." Hammersmith nodded at the corpse in the bed. The man lay in a dried pool of blood and his jaw was missing, the flesh torn back halfway down the length of his throat. "Is this Joseph Hargreave?"

"I believe so," Hatty said. "At least, that's what Mr Oberon told me." She shuddered and looked away. "He does resemble his brother. At least . . ." Her voice trailed off. Hammersmith understood. Hatty was strong, but some things were not meant to be seen.

"Stand back," Hammersmith said. He moved round the foot of the bed and approached the wardrobe that stood between the bed and the window. He took two deep breaths, raised his iron pipe, and pulled the door open.

A second body, stiff with rigor, fell out at his feet. Hammersmith gasped and took a step back, then leaned forward and pushed the body over on its side. It was not Mr Oberon.

"That's Richard Hargreave," Hatty said. "The doctor. He was this one's brother." She pointed at the dead man in the bed. "He's killed both brothers. I mean, he made it sound as if he had, but I was holding out some hope."

"Hope isn't much of a defense against Jack," Hammersmith said. The crackling of the fire had grown much louder, and over the top of the closed door he saw a tongue of flame lick the ceiling of their room. "Wait, Hatty, did you say this man was a doctor?"

"Yes, Dr Richard Hargreave. Mr Hammersmith, I'm afraid we're trapped in here."

"The crow. This was the crow in the message he left at Walter's house. Not Dr Kingsley at all. Dr Kingsley is safe from harm. We need only worry about the white king, whoever that is."

Smoke began to seep into the room, causing Hammersmith's eyes to sting. He looked at Hatty and saw that her eyes were watering, too, tears streaming down her face. She coughed into her fist. "Mr Hammersmith, I think we're going to die in here."

"I certainly hope not. We've got a case to finish." He went to the window and pulled back the curtains, his pipe raised and ready to smash the glass out of the frame. But the window was already broken, and a knotted length of linen hung from the sill, fastened around the window's latch. Hammersmith leaned out and peered down into the narrow alleyway behind the store. He couldn't see far enough into the shadows below the window, couldn't see whether the makeshift rope ladder went all the way to the ground, but decided a broken leg was better than burning to death. He banged away at the bits of broken glass still stuck in the frame. Behind him he heard Hatty yelp and turned to see that the fire had entered the room, eating away at the door all round the jamb and peeling back the wallpaper.

Hammersmith ripped the sheet from the bed, exposing the rest of poor Joseph Hargreave, and grabbed Hatty's arm. She tried to pull back, but he gripped her harder and looped the sheet round her waist. She nodded her understanding and sat on the windowsill, rotated so that her legs were kicking free in the air outside, then pushed off without even waiting to see that Hammersmith had braced himself. He could feel the fire at his back as he strained to support Hatty's scant weight. She turned and grabbed the knotted linen rope, and as he watched her lower herself down the outside wall of the building, it belatedly occurred to him that Jack the Ripper might be waiting for them below.

SIR EDWARD'S CARRIAGE pulled up outside Plumm's, and the commissioner jumped out and scanned the street, taking in the diminishing crowd and the injured man at its center. A moment later, a second, larger carriage stopped behind his. Tiffany, Blacker, and Kett piled out, along with three constables, and they ran to catch up to Sir Edward.

"There's a man down," Sir Edward said. "Blacker, see to him. Tiffany, Kett, catch these people before they run off. Get statements from them. You others, cordon this off. Dr Kingsley will want to look the area over."

He spotted Claire Day and Fiona Kingsley sitting against the building. Fiona stood and approached him.

"Miss Kingsley," Sir Edward said. "Your father summoned me here by telephone. He said Mr Day was to be found in the vicinity, but clearly a great deal has happened since then. What can you tell me?"

"Mr Day stabbed Mr Carlyle and ran away down that alley." She pointed. "Several people have already chased after him. Mr Carlyle needs immediate attention."

"Yes, I see."

"There are wagons coming to take away some bodies in a warehouse, but my father said to tell you that Mr Carlyle should be taken first."

"Of course. And we needn't wait for the wagons. They won't be in any hurry to get here if they think it's not an emergency. Dead bodies are sadly all too commonplace, especially round here these past few days." He waved his arm at Inspector Blacker. "Blacker, use my carriage. This man is Inspector Day's father-in-law. Get him to hospital right away, and make sure the doctors understand he's to be a priority."

"I'll tell the driver," Blacker said.

"Go with him. I want it understood that I'm taking responsibility for this man's well-being and will be quite cross if he's not taken care of."

"Yes, sir."

"And, Blacker, none of your jokes. I want the hospital staff to take this seriously."

"I never joke with doctors, sir. They're not known to be humorous people."

"Away with you." Sir Edward turned back to Fiona. "How is Mrs Day holding up?"

"She's had a shock, sir. It's been a difficult year, and this only adds to her hardships."

"I don't believe Walter is responsible for this."

"I saw it, sir, with my own eyes."

"I don't mean that I disbelieve you. I mean there are circumstances neither you nor I can currently understand. Your father explained a bit of it when we spoke on the telephone, but I'm hoping for more details from him."

"He's gone with everyone else, chasing after Mr Day."

"Then that is where I must go as well. Thank you, Miss Kingsley. Look after Mrs Day, and we'll get this sorted. I promise you that."

He watched her go and sighed again. They had so many problems to deal with from outside the Murder Squad. And yet there seemed to be no end of problems within the squad itself, most of them centering on Walter Day. But he was fond of the lad and was determined that he could be a steadying influence in Walter's life.

Provided he could catch up to him.

56

W alter Day, what a pleasant surprise."

Day stopped and squinted at the shadowed end of the alley. His leg ached, which was often the case when he tried to move too fast. He looked about for a weapon, but saw nothing he could use. He wondered what had become of his walking stick. He remembered having it in his hand and didn't recall setting it down anywhere, but it was gone.

"It's all right," Jack said. His voice echoed weakly back and forth between the brick walls, making it impossible to pinpoint his exact location. "I won't bite you. Or stab you, or cut out your liver and eat it. Unless you promise to remain very still. I don't think I'm in any shape for a fight."

"You don't sound good, Jack."

"The pain is rather exquisite. I'm afraid I overextended myself climbing down."

Day glanced up at a hazy square of light, a window overhead. A rope of some sort hung down from the ledge, and a shape hung there in the dark. The smoke moved above and Day thought he could pick out a familiar figure at the window. He took a step forward.

"That's close enough, Walter Day. You look confused. Is something bothering you?"

"You can't see my face any more than I can see yours, Jack. The light's wrong."

"I see more than you do. And I hear more than you do. I hear confusion in your voice. What's happened?"

"I don't know." Day took another step forward. If he kept Jack's attention on him, the Ripper might not look up.

"Oh, my," Jack said. "You did it, didn't you?"

"Did what?"

"You finally did me that favor you promised."

"Favor?" But now fragments of memory exploded in his head. Images of blood and anger, a man on the ground at his feet, bleeding and unconscious. "Jack, what did I do? What did you make me do?"

"An interesting fact about mesmerism, Walter Day. The public believes you can make a man do anything when he's under your spell, but it's not true. You can't force someone to do something he wouldn't do anyway. It's what makes mesmerism such a limited tool for murder."

"I know that now."

"You could only have killed someone you already wanted to kill. That's what makes it delicious."

"I never wanted to kill him."

"But of course you did. I helped you discard your inhibitions for one glorious moment. And in return you've eliminated the last of those dreadful Karstphanomen for me. Or at least of them what held me in that cold, dank prison and did things to me. I did the crow myself, and his body's burning even as we speak. And you've done the white king. Congratulations, and thank you."

Now Day took a step back. "You've sealed my fate."

"I've set you free."

"What else have you set me to do? What other surprises are waiting in my head?"

"Nothing. That was the only thing. Oh, well, I did leave a little suggestion in there that you mustn't ever harm me or stand in my way. That was only to make things easier for me with my comings and goings. I promise, other than that, you're your own man once again."

"I can never go back."

"You can go wherever you please. And now I set you free from me. I don't think we need each other anymore, do you? If you'll stand aside, I think I can make it to the street. From there, the world is my murky oyster stew."

"I'm not letting you go."

"You have no choice. Oh, but Walter, look out behind you. That young lady has stopped listening to us and I think she intends to do you harm."

Day turned just in time to see a strange woman, wearing trousers and brandishing Day's own sword. The blade came slashing down at him, and at that same moment, he heard a shot ring out down the length of the alley.

57

Ah, Miss Tinsley," Goodpenny said. "And Mrs Dew. What a delight to find you here."

Goodpenny climbed down from the display box inside the window and sat on the sill beside Fiona. He laid a rifle across his lap and took a moment to catch his breath, watching as two constables picked up the unmoving body of Leland Carlyle. The policemen crab-walked the unconscious man to Sir Edward's private carriage and laid him across the seat inside, folding him at the knees so he would fit.

"It looks as if exciting things have been happening out here," Goodpenny said. "What have I missed?"

"I don't think I can bear to repeat it all, Mr Goodpenny," Fiona said.

"A bear, you say? How terrifying. I'm quite frightened of bears. They have a nasty habit of eating people."

Fiona sighed, but didn't bother to correct the well-meaning little man. They sat in silence for a long moment, and then Goodpenny uttered a cry of delight and reached inside his jacket. He pulled out a small horn, brown and translucent, ridged like an oyster's shell, with a leather fitting at one end and a leather strap round the middle.

"Look what I found," he said. "It's a horn."

"I can see," Fiona said. "It's very pretty."

"No, no, for hearing. The horn has been fashioned into an ear trumpet, you see? It's an aid in hearing. Look at what I do." He held it up and jammed the leather tip in his ear. "People speak and the sound goes right in here." He pointed to the flared end of the horn. "It goes all the way through and is amplified during its journey to my ear, like so." He swiped his finger down the length of the horn and ended with a flourish at his ear.

"You'll finally be able to hear, Mr Goodpenny."

"Oh, it's not for me. My hearing's still sharp. It's for your young man, Mr Angerschmid. He's hard of hearing now." He removed the device from his ear and presented it to Fiona.

"Thank you, but he's not my young man," she said. She shook her head and laid the trumpet on the sill beside her.

"Give it time. Give it time. I say, that bear's not still about, is it? We should really get you young ladies to a place of safety. I'm afraid this rifle's of no real use since I have no bullets for it."

"The bear has gone. They took it away to the circus."

"Oh, thank goodness."

"But the bear is quite the least of our problems, Mr Goodpenny."

"Bears are enormous problems."

"Yes, I can see that they might be. But Mrs Day's husband has tried to kill her father. That's him in the carriage."

Goodpenny looked up as the driver cracked his reins and the carriage rolled away, revealing Inspector Tiffany, who had been standing on the other side of it talking to an old woman. Tiffany looked up and nodded at them, then bent his head to hear what the woman was saying.

"What a friendly fellow," Goodpenny said. "Tell me, did Mr Dew succeed? Did he kill the man?"

"No. Claire's father is still alive. For the moment, at least."

"Well, then. Many's the man who's tried to murder his father-in-law. I'm not sure it's even a crime these days. I've been tempted my-self, from time to time. It's that bear we ought to worry about. If it escaped the circus once, it's liable to do so again."

"Oh, Mr Goodpenny! You're impossible!"

"Now, now, dear. I don't mean to make light." He turned and smiled at Claire. "Mrs Dew, where are your delightful children?"

Claire looked up and seemed to notice Goodpenny for the first time. "My children?"

"Young Jemima and his brother, and those two darling babies."

"They're with their governess."

"That horrible woman? You mustn't neglect them for long. They'll need you about. And they'll need their father, too. Unless I'm very much mistaken, I've recently made your husband's acquaintance."

"He's gone." Claire's eyes welled up and she buried her face in her hands.

Goodpenny put an arm around her and fished a handkerchief from his waistcoat pocket. "Forgive me, my dear."

"He's been gone forever and now he's going to prison. He won't ever come home again."

"Going to prison? Oh, I shouldn't think so. I've met your hus-band, and he seems like a good man, a capable fellow. A bit lost, perhaps, but that's why he has you, isn't that right? Someone who will always bring him back home."

"You don't know us."

"I know people, Mrs Dew. And just looking at you, I can tell that you're a strong person, and that you and your husband need each other very much. Where there is love, there is always a way."

"You must love your wife."

"I did, my dear." He nodded and smiled, but it was a sad sort of smile. "Yes, I do love her."

Fiona clapped her hands and stood up. "Mr Goodpenny, you've given me an idea. But I wonder if you will help me with a small matter."

"Anything for you, Miss Tinsley. You know that."

"Might I borrow your rifle?"

"Oh, but it's not mine. It belongs to the store, I suppose. But with all the loss Plumm's has sustained, I suppose they won't miss it for a time."

"I don't think they'll be getting it back."

"Yes, as long as they get it back. Here you are."

"You don't want to know why I need it?"

"You need it, dear. That is all I care to know."

"Oh, thank you, Mr Goodpenny!" Fiona bent and kissed him on the cheek.

Goodpenny rubbed his cheek and watched her run across the street, where she handed the rifle to Inspector Tiffany. Tiffany took it from her, and they stood talking for quite some time. Goodpenny chuckled and patted Claire's hand. "She's a good girl," he said. "Whether Mr Angerschmid realizes it or not, our Miss Tinsley is a prize."

"I do wonder what she's doing," Claire said.

Goodpenny picked up the ear trumpet from the sill where Fiona had left it. He lifted it to his ear and leaned forward. "Listen, my dear. Do you smell smoke?"

58

Hammersmith looked back and saw that the bed was on fire, the ceiling above it a roiling inferno. Advance scouts of flame, like ant columns, stretched outward across the floor, edging ever nearer his left foot. His back and his feet were uncomfortably warm, beginning to itch with heat. Hatty still hung below the window, dangling from the knotted linen rope.

"Hurry," he said. He could barely make out her shape against the dark floor of the alley below.

"Mr Hammersmith, there's someone down there." Her voice was hoarse and quiet, and he had to lean farther out to hear her. "I think it's him. I can hear him. Someone else, too."

Hammersmith strained to hear. There was muffled conversation below, the clanking of metal on brick, the scuffle of shoe leather on stone. More than one person, and possibly a fight. He pulled his head back in and examined his options. There were none. The door was completely obscured by fire and smoke, and he knew that the hallway outside the room would be impassable. His eyes burned and he was having difficulty breathing. He leaned out the window again, enjoying the feel of the cool breeze on his face.

"Hatty, you're going to have to go all the way down. I'll be right behind you."

"They're below me. Mr Oberon will catch me."

"When you're close to the ground, push off from the wall and jump as far as you can. Get as far away as you can, Hatty, and run. You'll only have to worry for two minutes, I swear it. I won't let anything happen to you."

He couldn't hear her response. The flames were licking his ear. His trouser leg was suddenly on fire, and Hammersmith dropped his iron pipe. It hit the floor with a low thud, and at the same moment he heard a gunshot from the alley outside. He leapt out the window, clung to the frame above him, and stood silhouetted against the room, using one hand to beat at his smoldering leg. He knew he was an easy target now if Jack was indeed waiting below them with a gun. The fire crackled at his good ear and he shook his head, trying to get the muffled ringing sound to fade long enough that he might hear whatever it was Hatty was trying to say to him. At least she was still there below him. She hadn't been shot. But she was vulnerable, a sitting duck for whomever was shooting, and her arms had to be close to giving out. He doubted she had the strength anymore to climb down. At any moment, she would lose her grip and drop.

"Stay," Hammersmith said. "Just hang on there."

He eased himself down, hoping the makeshift rope would hold them both and that it wouldn't burn before he reached the alley floor. He grabbed the inside of the frame, ignoring the searing pain in his fingers, rested his weight on the ledge, let go with one hand, reached down, and grabbed the rope. Then he let go with the other hand and dropped down so that he was directly above Hatty. Carefully, he maneuvered over her, pushing her with his body so that she was up against the outside wall of the building.

"Don't let go," he said. She nodded, her eyes closed, and he could feel her breath on his cheek. Her hair smelled of smoke and strawberries, and he noticed how long and slender her throat was, how gracefully her head tilted.

He crawled slowly down, hand over hand, alert to where his hands were in relationship to her torso, her waist, her legs. Finally he was past her and the flames were far enough above him that he no longer felt the heat from them. He reached the end of the rope and let go.

"Doctor!"

Kingsley turned and saw Sir Edward running toward him. "Commissioner, be careful. I don't know what kind of weapons these people may have."

Sir Edward drew up alongside Kingsley and stopped, panting lightly. "Everything's come home to roost, hasn't it, Bernard?"

"I'm afraid it has," Kingsley said. "But this isn't the time to fret over it. Walter's somewhere ahead of us there, along with someone who's gone chasing after him. This is no place for a doctor or an old soldier."

"Did you see Walter?"

"I did. He seemed fine to me. At least physically. But I made a mistake. I let him—"

There was a deafening explosion as the domed skylight above Plumm's burst open, raining glass down on the street. The cobblestones under them bucked and shuddered, and the two men fell back just as a chunk of the department store's brick-and-mortar wall plowed into the ground where they had been standing.

"My God," Kingsley said. "Are you all right?"

Sir Edward staggered to the curb and sat down. "The world seems to be spinning," he said. "I just need to—"

"You're bleeding. Let me—"

"No, I think I'm all right. Get going. Get to Walter before this whole place comes down round our ears. I'll be there as quickly as I can."

MR PARKER WAS FLUNG backward against the opposite wall of the alley as a tall, thin man dropped out of the air above him and knocked both Walter Day and Mrs Parker to the ground. Mr Parker looked up and saw that there was another person, a girl, hanging in the air above him. People were falling out of the building. Mr Parker realized he somehow still had the gun in his hand and he raised it, intending to hit his target this time.

Mrs Parker groaned and raised her head. "Darling," she said, "did you shoot at me?"

"I missed," Mr Parker said. "I was aiming—"

"You never miss. I believe you were trying to—"

"I'm with the police! Please put down your weapon." An older gentleman ran toward them, carrying a black medical bag. "Good Lord! There's a girl up there," he said.

The building beside them exploded a second time in a shower of glass and metal and brickwork. Something heavy smashed into Mr Parker's neck and he fell backward again, but concentrated on keeping the gun in his hand. The policeman was unconscious on the ground, but Mrs Parker was still moving, trying to extricate herself from the tangle of bodies and bricks. Mr Parker shook his head and leaned against the alley wall. He couldn't breathe, and everything seemed to be moving in slow motion.

He was surprised to see that the young woman was still dangling out of the window. The window itself was gone, but the rope had held fast, and so had the girl. The doctor dropped his bag and positioned himself under the woman.

"Let go, dear," the doctor said. "I'll catch you."

Mr Parker raised his gun. He felt panicky, as if he might vomit, and the world seemed to swim in and out of focus. He fired a second time, not sure where the gun was pointed. The doctor staggered forward, but stayed on his feet, his arms out, ready to catch the girl. Mr Parker fired again, then turned at the sound of something moving toward him. A big man with dark wavy hair erupted from the shadows, and Mr Parker felt his abdomen burning. As the man took his gun from him, he looked down and saw a large sliver of broken glass protruding from his stomach. The man yanked and a gusher of blood followed the glass out of Mr Parker's body.

HATTY COULDN'T FEEL her arms anymore, but her shoulders quivered with the strain of hanging on to the knotted linens. She heard the man beneath her urging her to let go, but she wasn't sure she could. Her hands were made of stone. She couldn't see or hear Mr Hammersmith below and she wondered if he'd been hurt or even killed.

The two explosions had knocked her about, banged her into the wall and disoriented her. Blood trickled into her eyes from a scalp wound delivered by a flying brick. But somehow she hadn't been knocked off the makeshift rope.

At last she steeled herself and focused on her numb fingers. She forced them to open one at a time and felt lancing pain shoot up her arms as her petrified knuckles unlocked. She immediately plummeted into the arms of the waiting man.

He staggered forward under her weight and they hit the wall hard. He fell to his knees and gently set her down before toppling sideways on the alley floor. She sat up and looked at him, recognizing him at last. He was the doctor from Guildhall who had helped so many injured Plumm's customers.

"Dr Kingsley? Are you all right?"

He rolled over onto his back and smiled up at her. "Give me a moment, will you?"

"Sir, you've been shot. I'll get a doctor. I mean another doctor."

"Too late, I think. You . . . you hurt?"

"I don't know. My hands hurt, but I'm all in one piece, thanks to you."

"You look a bit like my daughter."

"What should I do? I can't tell where the blood's coming from."

"Just talk to me for a minute, would you? It's quite cold down here."

"Help will be coming soon," she said. "Very soon, I'm sure."

Hatty looked round and saw the unconscious body of Mr Hammersmith. There were other people, but she didn't call out to them for help. They were shouting at one another, ignoring Hatty and Dr Kingsley. One of them (she was certain it was Mr Oberon) stabbed another, and the injured man screamed. Hatty screamed, too, and fought the urge to run. Dr Kingsley needed her help.

She still had Mr Hammersmith's jacket sleeve hanging loosely around her throat and she pulled it off over her head. She probed Dr Kingsley's chest with her aching fingers, and he winced.

"Fiona . . ." He coughed and a bubble of blood burst from his open lips, freckling Hatty's face and arms.

"My name is Hatty, sir. If I can find where the blood's coming from, perhaps I can make it stop."

"Be good to each other," Kingsley said. "Nevil's a fine boy, but he needs you."

"You mean Mr Hammersmith?" Dr Kingsley's breathing had become shallow, and with each breath he made a gurgling sound that alarmed Hatty.

"What time is it? I'm late," he said.

"No, sir. No, sir," Hatty said. "Stay awake." She found a hole in his waistcoat and pressed the soot-covered jacket sleeve into it, hoping that would staunch the flow of blood.

Dr Kingsley smiled at her. His lips were a ghastly red, rimmed with blood. "That's it," he said. "You're doing a fine job. Proud of . . . Tell Fiona."

He closed his eyes.

"No!" Mrs Parker pulled herself up and grabbed the sword from the alley floor.

"Tut tut," the man Jack said. "Let's not be hasty."

"You killed him," Mrs Parker said.

"He's not dead yet. Look at him. He won't last much longer, but who knows? I have a similar wound and I've managed to do a great deal despite it. Was he your lover?"

"Yes."

"Well, this must be heartbreaking for you." He pointed Mr Parker's gun at her and pulled the trigger. There was an audible click, but nothing happened. "Oh," Jack said. "Well, that puts me in a rather difficult situation."

Mrs Parker stepped forward, the sword raised high. "Are you really him?"

"Him? Do you mean God? Yes, I suppose I am."

"Kill him," Mr Parker said. His voice was a liquid whisper. "Help me. We can still get away."

"Yes, one of us requires your assistance," Jack said. "I suppose you have a choice. Him or me. I'm really in no position to blame you either way."

The sword slashed down and Mr Parker's eyes grew wide. A thin red line appeared on his throat, then opened, and blood cascaded over his collar. He slumped, lifeless, to the alley floor.

"Oh, what a pleasant surprise," Jack said. "Now, if you wouldn't mind, I'm not at my best, and we should move quickly if we're to get away." He held out his hand, and Mrs Parker hesitated. At last, she lowered the sword and took Jack's hand.

"Lovely," Jack said. "But we can't go that way, my sweet. There will be more people coming."

"Then . . ."

"We'll go back in. Through this door is a storeroom."

"But the store is on fire. It's falling down."

"What is life without risk?"

He put his arm around her, and she helped him walk to the door. He produced a key and, as Hatty Pitt worked to keep Dr Kingsley alive, the two monsters entered the inferno and were gone.

AFTER

———•———

At last they came upon a clearing in the wood, and there, sitting on a footstool in the center of the clearing, was Peter. The Kindly Nutcracker's head shouted, "Halt!" and the Rocking Horse skidded to a stop. Anna jumped out of the carriage and ran to Peter and lifted him high in the air. Peter's little body made of rag and dowels was limp, and one of his legs had broken at the joint so that it swung awkwardly about in the air.

"Why doesn't he say anything?" asked Mary Annette.

"I don't know," said Anna. "He is very limp. I hope he is not taken ill."

"I know why," said the Babushka. She rolled out of the carriage and hopped over to Anna. She shivered and quivered and split in half. Then she shivered again and quivered again and split in half once more, and the angriest Babushka jumped out into the clearing.

"I do not like breaking open," said the angriest Babushka. But then she did break in half, and an even smaller Babushka was revealed. This one wore tiny painted-on spectacles, and her hair was drawn up into a flat glossy bun at the top of her head.

This new Babushka said, "Peter cannot talk to you, Anna, because he was never truly a part of our wood. When we were chopped down to become toys and furnishings and matches, we wanted to come back to see you again. But Peter was not made from the same wood we were. He was already a little doll of rag and wood when you used to play here. And so he remains a doll, but without the spark of life that we have."

"But what made you come alive?" Anna asked. "If it isn't this place that has the magic, then what has done it?"

"You did it, Anna," said the Babushka.

"You missed the wood," said the Kindly Nutcracker's head. "And you wanted us to come home to you."

"You were sad and wanted to play in the wood one more time," said Mary Annette.

"And so we came to see you," said the Kindly Nutcracker's head.

"If I could bring you all to life, then surely I can bring Peter to life as well," said Anna.

"Perhaps you do not want him to be alive," the Babushka said.

"Nonsense," said Anna. She wagged her finger at her doll as if she were scolding a bad little boy. "Peter, I command you to wake up and do a dance for me."

"But he cannot," said Mary Annette. "His leg is broken, don't you see?"

"The Kindly Nutcracker is broken, but he is still able to talk and to steer the carriage," said Anna. "And, Mary, your strings have all been cut, but you are able to walk and talk just like anything."

"Anna, soon you will be an adult and you will not wish to play with dolls anymore," said wise little Babushka. "What will happen to Peter then?"

"Why, I will give him to my own children to play with," Anna declared.

"Perhaps," said the Kindly Nutcracker's head. "Perhaps you should fix Peter's leg and enjoy him as he was meant to be enjoyed, until such time when you no longer wish to play with him. That would be kinder than *making him a living thing that will be sad when you are no longer interested in him."*

Anna lowered her arms and let Peter sit in the dirt while she looked at her new friends. "What will happen to all of you when I am too old to frolic in the wood anymore?" she asked.

"But we all have new homes already," Mary Annette said. "My puppeteer will miss me if I am not there in the morning. He is creating a new story for me to act out."

"I was going to be on the mantel of a family's fireplace at the holiday so that I could break open tough nuts for them to eat." The Kindly Nutcracker's fuzzy white beard bristled in the breeze. "Perhaps they will fix me."

"I am on display at a fabulous department store," all of the Babushka's heads said at once. "Soon, a child will convince his mother to purchase me and I will provide amusement for that child. That will be a fine life for me."

The Rocking Horse rocked back and forth in the grass as if nodding in agreement, and Anna wondered if it already belonged to a child or if it was waiting for someone to come along and discover it.

"But if you are all meant to be somewhere else, then why are you here?" she asked.

"We are here to say our good-byes and to have one last great adventure," said the Kindly Nutcracker's head. "By morning we will be gone again, and it will be as though we were never here."

"Oh, oh, but I will miss you so," said Anna.

"And we will miss you," the smallest and wisest part of the Babushka said. "But everything must change, and we must go to our new homes and have many more adventures of a different sort. And you must do the same."

Anna looked down at Peter, who hung from her hand the way he always had. In the dim light of distant fires, he looked somehow different. But she knew that it wasn't him at all. He had remained the same, while the world all round her had changed.

"When will you go?" she asked.

"We will be gone when you wake in the morning," said the wise Babushka. "This place will be as it was when you went to bed last, nothing but stumps and brown grass and the sad little creek that now runs through a field."

"And I will never see you again?" Anna asked.

"No, but you will remember us," the Kindly Nutcracker's head said. "And we will still have the rest of this night to be together."

"Then there is time for glue," Anna said. "We must go to my house at the edge of the wood, where my father keeps glue in a drawer in his workshop. He also keeps nails there, as well as the sort of nail that winds round itself."

"You are talking about wood screws," the Rocking Horse said.

"Why, Rocking Horse!" Anna exclaimed. "I did not know that you could talk!"

"Neither did I," said the Rocking Horse. And those were the last words he ever spoke.

"It would be kind of you to glue me back together," said the Kindly Nutcracker's head. "I am glad you were able to find all the parts of me that were broken apart by that rascal Jack."

"Is it possible for you to mend my strings?" asked Mary Annette.

"I am sure we can," Anna said. "Now we must hurry before dawn breaks and you all must leave. I will make you all whole again so you will look proper for your new homes."

Anna clambered back up in the carriage after helping the Babushkas in first and putting all her parts back together into a single egg shape. The Kindly Nutcracker's head yelled, "Haw!" and the Rocking Horse plunged forward.

When they had arrived at Anna's home, she ran to her father's shed, where he kept glue in a drawer and nails in a box, and she put the Kindly

Nutcracker all back together, except for one small piece that she could not find. But the hole where that piece belonged was on the bottom of his feet, which were all fashioned from the same chunk of wood that had been painted blue and did not separate. She did not think anyone would notice the missing piece if the nutcracker stayed in his place on the mantel and did his job, which was to crack open nuts. Then she nailed Mary Annette's strings back into place on her cross.

And she glued Jack's box shut to keep him from springing out and surprising people. While her friends watched, she put Jack's box at the bottom of her toy chest so that the other toys could all keep an eye on him and keep him out of trouble.

When she woke in the morning, she ran to the window. The sky was a light blue color smudged with grey, and silhouetted against it were queue after endless queue of stumps where there had once been trees. Her friends were gone, except of course for Peter, and except for Jack, too, because he had been given to her as a gift.

Many years later, when she had children of her own and they had children, too, Anna asked for her old toy chest to be brought down from the attic, and she took Peter out and gave him to her littlest granddaughter so that she might have a new playmate and so that Peter would have a new friend, too.

Her eyes were not good anymore, and so she did not notice that Jack and his box were missing from the chest.

—RUPERT WINTHROP, FROM
The Wandering Wood (1893)

59

In the spring of 1891, Plumm's department store burned to the ground after a top-floor storeroom full of ammunition and lamp oil exploded. Hundreds of thousands of pounds' worth of merchandise was destroyed, and seven bodies, burnt beyond recognition, were later found in the rubble. John Plumm was traveling in France at the time and he stayed there until the London press moved on to other, fresher stories and his creditors had been dealt with.

Plumm's had been touted as the biggest and most extravagant experience to be had in London since the Crystal Palace, and many years passed before another enterprise of its type was attempted.

But in that same season, the city produced two other momentous events, neither of which received the sort of notice that Plumm's did: Inspector Walter Day resumed his life, and Dr Bernard Kingsley, late of University College Hospital, passed away quietly in his sleep.

60

For the first weeks after Dr Kingsley's death, his daughter
visited his grave every day. Sometimes she would see Timothy Pinch there, and twice she saw Hatty Pitt. She did not
speak to either of them. On her fifth visit she found Walter Day at
her father's grave, standing next to a rather pretty young woman
whom she hadn't met. She ignored Walter, but the woman intrigued
her, and so she introduced herself.

"I'm very sorry, Miss Kingsley," the woman said.

"Did you know my father?"

"Not well, I'm afraid. I was injured and he helped me. I should
introduce myself. My name is Esther Paxton."

"Oh," Fiona said. "You were the one . . ." Her voice trailed off and
she made an effort not to look at Walter, who stood awkwardly
nearby holding a bouquet of flowers.

Esther saw the expression on Fiona's face and she flushed. She
looked at the tops of her shoes. "I just came to say good-bye."

"To my father?"

"Yes, and to Mr Day. I never knew Walter's name or that he had a family. I hope you'll believe that."

"Of course."

"I should have known, I should have thought . . . But I was happy just to have someone there with me again. I would never have—"

"No, I know. Nobody thinks less of you. You helped him when he needed help, and everyone is so very grateful to you."

"That's kind of you."

"Perhaps you could visit sometime. I'm sure Claire would be delighted to meet you."

Esther made a small noise and smiled at Fiona. "No. I have my shop to look after, you see. Business is quite good lately, since the fire. My customers are returning."

Day took a step closer to them and fiddled with the flowers in his hand. "I'm so glad to hear that, Esther. I mean, Mrs Paxton."

"Thank you, Walter." She didn't look up at him. "Miss Kingsley, I'm glad to meet you. From what little I knew of him, I'm sure your father was a good man."

"Thank you."

"If you'll excuse me, I have another grave to see this morning. My husband is buried over there." She pointed. "He's in that copse of trees, and it's been too long since I visited him."

She left them there, and they watched her walk away. After some time, Walter laid his flowers on Dr Kingsley's grave and reached out, touched Fiona's arm, then walked away in the opposite direction.

Fiona remained at the grave that entire morning, as was her custom. It was peaceful there, and quiet. Eventually she took out her sketchbook and began to draw a bird that had perched on her father's stone.

61

Nevil Hammersmith packed away his documentation of the Walter Day case and put it all into storage. With the clutter gone, his office seemed bare and forbidding, and so he moved back into his flat and learned to enjoy the company of his new fern.

Walter Day slept in Hammersmith's office, taking advantage of the empty space and the unused bedroll. He made daily trips to Finsbury Circus, teaching the boys there to sort leftover tobacco by color and age, and to roll new cigars. He gave his folding tray, along with his Reasonable Tobacco sign, to Jerome, who seemed to be the most responsible and resourceful of the lads.

They did not talk about their friend Ambrose.

And Day did not return again to Drapers' Gardens.

One evening, in the second week after his return, Claire Day came to visit him at Hammersmith's offices. Fiona Kingsley accompanied her, but Claire left the children at home with their new governess.

Hammersmith, Fiona, and Hatty Pitt waited in the outer office while Claire talked with her husband, and Hammersmith sent Eugenia Merrilow out to fetch tea for them all.

"It's time for you to come home," Claire said.

"You know I can't do that," Walter said.

"So you plan to live here, in poor Nevil's office on the floor?"

"I'll find another place to live."

"Oh? And will you return to that woman?"

Day knew she meant Esther Paxton. "I never . . . Claire, I wasn't myself."

"That's not an answer."

"I cared very much for Esther, but she was only a friend, and never anything more than that. Somehow, I always knew in my heart I was a married man."

"And that's all that kept you from her bed?"

"Of course not," he said. "And, no, to answer your question properly, I have no plans to ever see her again. Nor do I believe she wishes to see me."

There was a long silence before Claire spoke again. "I think I can live with that," she said. "I do trust you, Walter. But . . ."

"But I stabbed your father." Walter smiled. "You know, I've always wanted to stab your father, but I regret doing it in front of you."

Claire looked away and smiled. "It's not that. He'll live. I've spoken to Sir Edward, and he explained that you'd been manipulated somehow, that you didn't know what you were doing. I can't imagine what you must have gone through."

"I'd rather you never know."

"But I hope you will tell me sometime, when things have settled and you feel comfortable."

"If it's not your father, there must be something else troubling you."

"Why didn't you come back?"

"I didn't . . . I didn't remember."

"But, Walter, why didn't you remember me?"

His eyes filled with tears, and he put his arm up so she wouldn't see. He turned away from her and she waited, without going to him or touching him. When he spoke, his voice was like the fog that had lifted from the city. "I did remember. I did, but I lied to myself. I couldn't lead him back to you. I couldn't bring that to our house again. I thought I had to start anew and let you go on to live a better life."

And then she did go to him and put her hand on his arm, and he turned toward her.

"Oh, Walter, I can't live any sort of life without you."

"At some point, once the police conclude their investigation, they're going to take me to prison, Claire."

"So you've continued to stay away."

"I've only tried to shelter you."

"The men in my life are constantly trying to shelter me, to protect me from themselves and from each other, deciding what's best for me at every turn. I'm quite sick and tired of it all. I don't want everything to be hidden away from me. I'm a grown woman and I'm perfectly capable of making my own choices."

"I don't want you or the children to see me behind bars."

"As I say, I've spoken to Sir Edward and I don't believe he has any such plan."

"I'd like to hear that from him."

"Then we'll pay him a visit today. I want our life back. My bed is cold, and the children need their father."

"Are you sure you—"

"As I say, I can make my own decisions, Walter. And it seems I need to make yours for you, too. So it's settled. You're coming home with me, and I won't hear another word about it."

62

When Walter and Claire emerged from Hammersmith's office, they were holding hands.

"Does this mean I get my bedroll back?"

"Yes," Day said. "Thank you, Nevil."

"Don't mention it. I'm just glad things are back to normal at last." He glanced at Fiona and shook his head. "No, not normal. I'm sorry."

"I know what you meant," Fiona said.

"Timothy Pinch mentioned you yesterday," Hammersmith said.

Fiona wrinkled her nose, but before she could respond, the door opened and Sir Edward Bradford strolled into the office. There was a small bandage on his scalp, just above his temple.

"Ah, everyone's here," he said. "Good. Saves me some time."

Hammersmith poured another cup of tea and set it at the corner of the desk where Sir Edward could reach it. "Did you find Mr Oberon's body?"

"It's hard to say," Sir Edward said. "Three of the corpses found there were women, and one was a child, probably a boy."

"His name was Ambrose," Day said. "I never knew his full name. Just Ambrose."

"Ah. Yes, Ambrose then. Of the three men who were dug out of that ruin, it's impossible to say anything about them. Mr Pinch is working to find identifying marks of some sort, but I've seen the bodies and I don't hold out much hope."

"I was only now on my way to see you," Day said. "To turn myself in."

"Turn yourself in for what? Surely Mrs Day has told you I have no interest in arresting you."

"Someone ought to pay for stabbing Leland Carlyle."

"Oh, that. No. That was clearly self-defense. Fiona was kind enough to pick up Carlyle's rifle, a Martini-Henry, from where he'd dropped it in the street. Inspector Tiffany examined the weapon, and it had recently been fired. We're just pleased that the round apparently missed you."

Day looked at Fiona, who made a show of fixing her hair in its chignon. "Self-defense?" he said.

"Indeed. I've pieced together what must have happened, based in part on knowledge I have of Mr Carlyle's recent activities. Mrs Day, you may not wish to hear some of this."

"It's all right. I can bear it."

"Very well. Your father seems to have been engaged in a sort of private war with this Oberon person, and Oberon apparently thought it was clever to use Carlyle's son-in-law as a pawn. So he captured and manipulated Inspector Day. In return, Carlyle hired a soldier of fortune to pursue Oberon, and Plumm's became their battleground. We found the hired killer's body in that alley, and it turns out the fellow was wanted in several other countries. He's suspected of murdering an ambassador. Honestly, we're all lucky Mr Day escaped with his life."

"Then I'm really free to go home again?"

"By all means, do. You've had a long holiday, Walter, and it's high time you went home and got back to work. That boy Simon is going to be a policeman when he grows up and he needs some instruction. Take the rest of the week, relax. I'll see you first thing Monday morning at your desk."

"My desk? I'm back at the Yard?"

"I never sacked you." He frowned and turned his gaze on Nevil. "Now, Mr Hammersmith, I did make the mistake of sacking you. In light of your single-minded work in bringing Mr Day back to us, I've reexamined that decision. I'd like you back Monday morning as well, if you're willing."

"I thought you—"

"I always worried you'd get yourself killed as a policeman. But you haven't stopped putting yourself in the way of danger and you're not dead yet. I might as well make use of your particular talents if I can. And we need someone to mind Mr Day so this sort of thing doesn't happen again. He gets into an extraordinary amount of trouble himself. I think more than when the two of you are together."

Hatty put down her teacup. "What about this place?"

"If you close the Hammersmith Agency, I will have nothing with which to occupy my days," Eugenia said. "I quite like it here."

Hammersmith sighed. "I do, too, but we've lost our biggest client." He nodded at Claire. "I don't think I can afford to keep the doors open now."

"You could," Hatty said, "if you had a sergeant's salary."

Sir Edward stood quietly watching them, stroking his beard. Hammersmith looked from Hatty to him, and Sir Edward shrugged his shoulders.

"I can't do both things," Hammersmith said.

"I'll run this place for you," Hatty said. "You know I can do it. I'll bring in new clients to replace Mrs Day, and the agency will practically pay for itself."

"You can't call it the Hammersmith Agency if Nevil isn't even here," Fiona said.

"Actually, I do have an idea along those lines," Hammersmith said. "Something your friend Mr Goodpenny told me, Fiona. He made me realize I shouldn't be alone all my life. And seeing Mr and Mrs Day back together again only reinforces that."

"Oh," Fiona said. She took a step forward.

"So if she'll have me, I'd like to ask Miss Pitt to be my wife. Then she'll be a Hammersmith, too, and the agency can remain as it is."

"Oh," Hatty said. She looked round at the shocked expressions on her friends' faces. "I had no idea."

"I've been considering it these last few weeks. It seems like a sound notion. Practical."

"Then, yes," Hatty said. "Yes, I will marry you, Mr Hammersmith."

She was about to say something else, but the front door slammed and, through the window, they all watched Fiona Kingsley run away down the street until she was swallowed up by the unceasing traffic.

Hammersmith frowned at Day. "I wonder what's got into her," he said.

Day leaned close and spoke so that no one else would hear. "I'm afraid you have created a situation, Nevil."

EPILOGUE 1

The giant blue globe had rolled down Prince Street, causing innumerable traffic accidents. At the corner of King William Street and West Cannon, it bounced off Monument Station, crushing a dog against the west wall of the building, and rolled south along King William to London Bridge. The globe hit the eastern side of the three-foot-high balustrade, breaking the rail and twelve posts, then caromed away to the other side, where it launched itself high into the air.

It went down with a splash and floated away downriver.

It eventually came to rest at the East India Docks, where it bobbed in the water for weeks, slowly losing its color. Boys from the area made a game of throwing rocks at it, trying to spin it or sink it, but despite the shoddy workmanship used in the construction of the Plumm's building, it's centerpiece installation proved to be surprisingly sturdy and watertight.

John Plumm eventually had it hauled from the water, and a wide hole was cut through it. He furnished the inside as a foyer and attached it to the front of his renovated building, but he no longer had any interest in running a department store.

His new venture, called the Globe, introduced cosmopolitan culture to the neighborhood, but at affordable prices. A rotating mural of foreign lands and people was painted, at great expense, along the spherical inside of the foyer, which whetted the public's appetite for the sorts of unusual cocktails served inside.

The nightclub was a success and remained open for many years, until a second fire on the premises ruined Plumm and prompted him to leave London for good. The globe was detached, the remains of the building torn down, and a small emporium was built in its place.

The first stall to open there was Goodpenny's Fine Stationery and Supplies.

EPILOGUE 2

In the summer of 1891, a man and a woman who claimed to be married moved into a cottage at the end of Prince Albert Street in Brighton. Their name, they said, was Oberon, and the man said he was a cousin of Richard and Joseph Hargreave. He also said the brothers had lent him their home so that he could take the salt air while convalescing from surgery. He moved slowly and rarely left the house, but those neighbors who visited found him charming, even courtly. His wife was not as agreeable, and so, before long, the couple was left alone.

No one had been particularly close to the Hargreaves, and so no one bothered to write to them in London to verify the couple's story. In fact, neither Richard nor Joseph Hargreave was ever seen in Brighton again.

It was during this same period that the number of unsolved murders and unusual deaths began to increase in East Sussex, and the constabulary was kept busy. The couple who were staying in the Hargreaves' cottage stopped receiving visitors, and their windows were hung with black crepe. Neighbors were told that Mrs Oberon's sister had taken ill. Mr Oberon was often observed on the beach and he was always polite but distant. He walked slowly with a cane that had a distinctive brass knob at the handle. It was rumored that Mrs Oberon had left in the night to care for her sister, but she never returned.

In the spring of 1892, Mr Oberon reported the news of his wife's untimely death. She had fallen from a horse in Provence and had been instantly killed. Many residents of the area thought it strange that the crime rate fell back to routine levels after Mrs Oberon's departure. It was unthinkable, however, that anyone would bring the subject up to Mr Oberon, who appeared quite distraught.

Three months later he took a second wife, a young widow with a son. He took his new family away, claiming that there were too many memories for him in Brighton. He left no forwarding address or clue regarding his destination. The cottage on Prince Albert Street was shuttered and abandoned.

A week after that, two detectives arrived from London. One of the detectives was tall and uncommonly handsome, though his clothing was stained and creased. The other man walked with a slight limp. They carried with them a sketch of Mr Oberon and asked about him in all of the local establishments. They spent some time walking up and down the beach, observing crowds at the racetrack and talking to the beat constable on Prince Albert Street. They did not answer anyone's questions about themselves.

There was much speculation after the detectives had gone, but soon life returned to normal. Every once in a while someone would see a silhouette on the beach at twilight and think, *There goes Mr Oberon for his after-dinner smoke,* before remembering that he had moved on.

Many years later, when the cottage was torn down to make room for new terraced housing, the body of a woman was found behind the plaster of a pantry wall. No one living in the area was able to identify the badly decayed corpse, and there were no fingerprints left. She was buried in an unmarked grave, and her clothing, including her torn and tattered trousers, was burned.